Lavos

I0685861

VLG – Book Five

Vampires, Lycans, Gargoyles

By Laurann Dohner

Lavos by Laurann Dohner

Jadee Trollis knows a little something about things that go bump in the night. Thanks to a father obsessed with myths, legends, and the paranormal, Jadee was dragged around the world in his pursuit of everything from ghosts to Sasquatch as a child. She got away from all that craziness in her teens, seeking a normal life as an adult. A trip to Alaska to visit her father quickly turns into a nightmare. Jadee ends up trapped in her father's tricked-out RV, hiding from the dangerous Vampires outside.

Lavos is the hottest man she's ever seen when he comes to her rescue. He growls, has some seriously strange but beautiful eyes, and he's not human. But returning to the lower forty-eight might not be the safety net she's expecting, and the normal life Jadee craves more than anything means never seeing Lavos again. When she finds herself in need of his help, it seems her new normal may be back in Alaska, waiting in her VampLycan's arms.

VLG Series List

Drantos

Kraven

Lorn

Veso

Lavos

Lavos by Laurann Dohner

Copyright © February 2017

Editor: Kelli Collins

Cover Art: Dar Albert

eBook ISBN: 978-1-944526-81-8

All characters and events in this book are fictitious. Any resemblance to actual persons living or dead is coincidental.

Lavos - VLG – Book Five

By Laurann Dohner

Chapter One

Jadee unlocked the RV and stepped inside. "Dad?"

The silence seemed ominous but the lights were on. She entered and did a quick search of the interior. He wasn't there but his bed had been made. She paused in the kitchen area, studying the gun sitting on the surface of the table. He usually kept his weapons locked up. The security shutters were all down, blocking out the sunlight. It was odd. A prick of apprehension stabbed at her.

She turned, going to the open door to peer out at the woods. It was late afternoon and the sun was going down fast. There was no sign of her dad or his car. She closed the door and locked it. There could be bears or other wildlife she didn't want to meet up close and personal.

She walked to the front and sat down in the driver's seat. The bad feeling increased tenfold as she stared at the metal over the windshield and side door windows. Why were they down? She turned on the CB and made sure it was on the channel her father usually used.

"Dad? Come back. It's Jadee."

She waited, hoping he was within range. The mountains were rugged and she doubted the antenna on top of this mobile tank would reach far. He might have gone to pick up supplies, but he'd been expecting her. Something was off.

"Jadee? Is that you, hon?"

The voice didn't belong to her dad. The usual irritation rose as she identified the southern accent. "Mark?"

"Where are you?"

"Dad's RV. Where is he?"

"Lock the doors. Do it now."

"Don't give me orders." She leaned back as bitter memories of her childhood flashed through her mind. She always had that reaction to her father's research partner. "Where's my dad? Is he with you?"

"Listen to me, damn it! Lock the doors—and are the shutters down? Please tell me you didn't open them. You're in danger."

"I locked the door after I came inside."

"Are the shutters still down?"

She stared at the thick metal. "Yes."

"Good. We didn't know your father's code to get inside. We'd hoped you would go there first whenever you arrived, and then reach our camp before the sun went down."

Mark's droning voice grated on her nerves. "Where is my dad?"

"Um…" Mark grew silent.

She tensed. "What's going on?"

"They got your father," he stated softly.

"What are you talking about?" A list of reasons why she hated Mark Tarnet filled her head, beginning with the way he could never just spit something out. He seemed to take pleasure from annoying others. "*Who

7

has my father? Was he arrested? What for this time? Did he trespass on private property again?"

"Do you see his tablet? Open it and let's do this live."

"Tell me what the hell is going on and where my dad is!"

The silence was on purpose. He refused to answer.

She cursed, hanging up the CB and rising from the seat. The tablet was charging on the kitchen counter and she turned it on. Within seconds, an incoming request came for video chat. She clicked it on and glared at her father's research partner.

His appearance stunned her. His hair was wild and his usually rounded face looked slimmer. He sat in what appeared to be a metal room, and she saw two people crouched behind him. Peggy didn't appear as if she'd brushed her hair in a good while and Brent's normally clean-shaven face had days of growth. The siblings both seemed exhausted.

"You look like hell." Jadee lifted the tablet, making sure the plug wasn't pulled, and took a seat at the table in front of the gun. She used it to help prop up the device. "I take it that's the interior of that new trailer my dad told me about? It looks industrial."

"What did your father tell you about why we're here?" Mark leaned in closer.

Jadee wasn't in a mood to play games. "The same crap he always says. He thought he was finally going to have proof about his theories. I only came because he was so worked up. He's already had one heart attack. Someone needed to talk some sense into him. I would have called to ask how to find him faster but my cell couldn't pick up a signal. Speaking of, how come we can get the internet here?"

8

"It's a short-distance signal we set up." Peggy bent lower, peering at the camera over Mark's shoulder. "Are you sure the doors are locked and the shutters are still down? It's important."

"Let me guess. It's getting dark and you're expecting visitors." Jadee became more annoyed. "I'll tell you the same thing I told my dad. Nobody in their right mind would want to live out here—including Vampires. They theoretically would stick to large cities with lots of people since they're supposed to drink human blood. This was a bullshit trip you made. There isn't even a hospital near here. What are you geniuses going to do if my dad gets sick again? Somebody has to look out for him since none of *you* will."

Brent leaned forward, hogging the screen. "I'm so sorry, Jadee. We believe your dad is dead."

The shock felt as if she'd been punched in the gut. Denial was instant. "What do you mean you *think*? What are you talking about, Brent?"

Mark shoved him aside, intently peering at her. "We found damaged night walkers."

Jadee was about to lose her temper—big time. "I don't want to hear this crap! Is he lost in the woods or something? Did you call in search and rescue?"

"It's true," Brent swore. "We were contacted by a reliable source via our website about a sighting of Vampires. He also said some people he knew had disappeared. He was certain the Vampires were taking them."

Jadee resisted rolling her eyes. "Oh, someone from your website said so? It must have been true. How do you know he was reliable?"

Brent hesitated. "Well, he sounded sincere and he had specific details, so we packed up and headed here. We lost contact with him after that

9

though and were worried that something happened to him. We arrived six days ago and set our trap a day later. We caught *four* of them!"

"They're Vampires," Peggy whispered shakily. "Real ones."

"They were more animalistic than we expected," Mark added. "They seemed mentally unstable too but they're allergic to sunlight. It burns them. That's why you've *got* to make sure you're locked in and the shutters are down. It's too late to reach you. It's already getting dark. You're going to have to stay there until morning."

"The Vampires escaped!" Peggy blurted. "Your dad had already called you and you said you were flying here. We weren't sure when you'd arrive and we can't get cell service, so we weren't able to warn you to stay away. We didn't even know they'd escaped until we woke two days ago. They were too strong to handle at night so we were only running tests on them when the sun came up. Th-that's when we discovered your father missing."

"We locked ourselves inside every night, thankfully. Otherwise we'd all be dead." Mark paused. "I'm so sorry, Jadee. They got him."

"His car is gone. He must have driven to get groceries." Jadee wondered if the extreme isolation had made them jump to the worst conclusions possible.

"They pushed it into a ravine," Peggy whimpered. "The first thing they did was trash our cars. And we found tracks where they pushed the big rig that hauls this trailer into the river. They've stranded us!"

"Right." She was fed up. "This guy who contacted you probably has friends and they're seriously messing with you."

"No! It's all true!" Peggy swore. "This isn't a hoax."

"The RV is fine." She glanced around.

"The undercarriage isn't. We checked it during the day once we realized we were trapped. The RV's impossible for them to move. There were signs that they'd crawled under it so we took a peek. Your father had activated the emergency pillars on the motor home. They are six footings that flatten to the ground. It's a precaution for high winds and bad storms. The wheels won't roll. We have the same setup here. It's why they haven't managed to kill us yet."

Jadee was officially fed up. Their paranoid delusions had finally gotten the best of them. Her father ran for supplies often and his hunk-of-junk tow car had probably broken down again. He refused to spend money on it. "The RV has power. Notice the lights on?"

"It's the solar panels. I'm telling you, we looked under it and they ripped out the oil pan on the motor home. It wasn't shielded as well as the hood is with the reinforced steel." Mark shook his head. "We're stranded. They've taken out all our vehicles."

Jadee clenched her jaw, ready to start screaming at the idiots. They were so gullible. "Have you guys been smoking pot? Been adding a little LSD to it again? Is that it? Or have you totally lost your damn minds? Dad probably went to a bigger town because he needed his car repaired. Remember New Mexico? You called to tell me you thought he'd been kidnapped by an army of ghosts. Instead, he was waiting on a new transmission to be installed in some out-of-the-way repair shop."

"Wait until darkness falls," Mark said, suddenly looking exhausted. "They tried to break into our trailer for hours last night."

Peggy leaned in, her face close to the screen. "Do *not* let them in! I know you don't believe us but damn it, we found Vampires, hon. These are *real*! They kill their victims by tearing out their throats and drinking the blood."

"Show her the evidence," Brent urged. "We found a few bodies of the locals. They decapitated them postmortem. We believe it's so they won't turn, if legend is accurate about their bites transmitting the Vampire disease. Maybe we should ask her to rush outside and make a run for it in her rental car. She could come back in the morning to rescue us."

Jadee frowned. "I rented a truck from the airport, not a car. Dad said I'd need one to get to your camp."

"It's too late," Peggy moaned. "It's miles to the main highway. You've seen how fast those things run. They'd catch up to her and attack. Hell, they'd probably be on her before she made it ten feet out the door. Look at the cameras. The sun is too far down. It's already dark enough for them to be awake and moving around in the shade of all the trees."

"They have us cut off," Mark agreed. "She'd never get out of here in time to escape."

A bad feeling settled in the pit of Jadee's stomach but she didn't want to believe what they had to say. In decades of searching, her father and his team had never found anything real. They sure weren't going to locate a nest of Vampires in the middle of the Alaskan woods. "Hey, loco researchers," Jadee interrupted. "I'm done playing this game. Where the hell is my father, really?"

"Maybe they won't go to the motor home since they already took Victor." Mark ignored her to instead stare at Peggy. "It's possible they won't find her rental if we make a lot of noise and keep them occupied. At first light, we can make it out together."

"That means they'll attack us again!" Peggy backed up and bumped against the wall. The terror on her face appeared genuine enough as she frantically looked around. "Can the exterior take it?"

Mark stood, approaching her with his hands outstretched to grip her by the shoulders. "The trailer shell is two inches of solid steel. We're safe. Stay calm. We built it to withstand a Sasquatch attack. They're supposedly bigger and stronger than night walkers. We made it the last two nights, didn't we?"

Jadee rolled her eyes. "Sasquatch?"

Brent dropped into Mark's empty seat. "We were on Bigfoot's trail, and your dad had designed this trailer after hearing about how the creatures were breaking into cabins. He wanted us to be safe. It's a nine-by-twenty-five-foot container with all our monitoring equipment. We even have a toilet and two pull-down bunks for taking naps."

"Oh my God. Does it have windows? Maybe you guys are experiencing carbon monoxide poisoning or something. Open a door and let in fresh air. How long have you been locked in there?" Jadee wondered if that was the reason they'd lost their minds.

A loud thump sounded over the speakers and all three people on the screen looked upward toward the roof of the metal container they were inside. Brent's eyes widened as he gasped, "They're back!"

Peggy began to sob.

Mark hugged her against his chest. "Quiet!"

"Where's the trailer?" Jadee stood. "I'm coming over there to prove that you guys are nuts. Or your so-called source is just some asshole having fun at your expense. You've lost it. You need to open the doors and I'll take you to a nice hospital where they'll treat you for whatever the hell is wrong with you."

"Hook her into the outside monitors," Mark hissed. "Show her what we're seeing."

"Did you hear me?" Jadee's frustration rose. "Tell me where you guys set up in relation to the RV and I'll come to you."

Brent twisted to the side and suddenly her view changed. She could tell by the gray-toned images that they were using the night-vision cameras. The trees were crisp and clearly outlined, and they seemed to be set up in a small clearing without any signs of civilization. The image switched, going to another camera angle.

A man stood on top of what appeared to be a shipping trailer, the kind usually hooked to a big rig. It was a view from the top of the roof looking down the length. Jadee frowned, staring at the back of the person. He wore slacks and a ripped-up dark shirt. His hair was shoulder-length and scraggly. He turned, facing the camera as he jumped once, seeming to test the roof of the trailer. The night camera made him look really pale, and his eyes appeared black as he scanned the top of the roof.

She gasped when a second figure suddenly seemed to drop from the sky next to the first man. The sound was loud when he landed and it happened so fast, she hadn't expected it. It was another man, his hair almost as stark white as his skin. He wore a dark t-shirt and jeans.

Jadee gripped the tablet with both hands and sank back into the seat.

The image changed to a view of the back of the container. It had double doors, just like any other big-rig trailer she'd ever seen, and a woman in a long black dress was trying to pry them apart with her bare

14

hands. Her hair was dark, hanging down to her ass in a ratty mess. The angle was from above, and she looked up, almost as if peering into the lens. Her mouth opened, revealing some gnarly, sharp-looking fangs.

"Holy fuck," Jadee whispered. Shock kept her gaze glued to the screen.

The woman resembled something right out of a horror movie with that scary open mouth. It got worse when she bent, suddenly jumping. Her body passed the camera at least twelve feet above her, her clothes a blur. She was gone from view in a flash.

The camera feed switched back to the top of the trailer, showing all three of them on the roof. They jumped around, the sounds loud and relentless. Their erratic, weird movements reminded Jadee of marionette dolls being jerked upright, only they didn't have strings attached, helping them to leap that high. They fell hard enough that it made her wince every time their feet hit metal. It should have hurt, possible even broken their bones.

The feed changed again, showing Brent's face very close to the camera. "Did you see them? Make a run for it," he hissed. "While they're here."

"Don't! There's only three of them. The fourth one might be close to her." Mark was suddenly there, tearing the tablet out of Brent's hands. "They run fast, damn it! It's too quiet without the wind blowing and they might hear your engine start. Sound carries in these mountains. Stay there until the sun rises. You're the only hope we have!"

"Shut up!" Peggy hissed. "Listen. They stopped."

Mark turned his head, staring at something to the side of the camera. His mouth parted. "They're gone. I don't see them on any of the cameras." He looked at Jadee. "You're locked in, right? You didn't open the shutters?"

"You think they heard us talking to her?" Brent cursed. "Fuck!"

She abandoned the tablet on the table. Pure fear coursed through Jadee and it helped launch her to her feet, moving fast to the side door. She reached it and threw the bolts and bars that helped secure the door in place. She glanced at the windows, making certain all the security shutters were down. They were.

"Jadee!"

She returned to the table and picked up the forgotten tablet. "What?"

Brent's eyes were wide with fear. "Are you locked in with all the shutters down?"

"Yes."

"Keep quiet and turn off the lights. You don't want to draw their attention if they don't know you're there," he whispered.

"She said the shutters are down. They can't see if the lights are on or not," Peggy whispered. "Be quiet."

Jadee didn't move. No way was she going to turn off the lights and sit in the dark to startle at every sound.

She remembered the camping trip on her twelfth birthday, when they'd told her Werewolves were coming, and her father's team had played some recorded wolf howls. She'd damn near peed herself sitting in front of the campfire until they'd laughed, pointing out the speakers.

Then there was the time they'd left fake gold coins around her bed when she'd been eight, telling her leprechauns had visited while she slept.

Saying how luck she'd been not to be carried off by them. She'd believed it until she'd realized the coins were made of chocolate, covered with foil. Other pranks they'd pulled flashed through her mind, too many. It made her think this had to be another joke. They could have put footage together of the so-called Vampires and staged the entire thing.

It had sucked being Victor Trollis's daughter at times, thanks to her father and his team of researchers dragging her all over the world hunting for mythical creatures. It had only stopped after she'd demanded to live with her grandmother, to have some semblance of normalcy.

She got a grip on her hammering heart and glared at the camera. "You guys suck. Put my dad on *now*. Is this payback for not driving to Arizona for his birthday two months ago? Some of us have to work real jobs instead of living off my dad's trust fund, pursuing crazy notions of myths. How did that last trip work out for you guys, anyway? Did you find a Chupacabra? No? Big surprise!"

Something landed on the roof of the RV hard enough to make it rock.

Jadee lifted her gaze, her mouth parting.

"Be quiet," Brent breathed.

Heavy tread stomped from the kitchen area above her to the back, toward her father's bedroom.

She put the tablet down, ignoring it, and grabbed her dad's gun.

The handle of the door she'd used to get inside rattled but the lock held. Something smashed into it, sounding very much like a fist. A deep hiss followed.

"Fuck me," Jadee muttered. She stood, only glancing down to make sure the safety was off on the gun.

17

The stomping ceased for a second. Whoever was up there turned around, walking back. Each footstep was loud enough for her to track easily.

She slid out the gun's clip and checked the ammunition. It was loaded with real bullets, not blanks. She'd been raised around enough guns to know the difference by sight. She slid the clip back in and checked the chamber, seeing a round already loaded. "Dad? Not funny."

Something smashed into the glass behind one of the shutters. The sound assured her it did enough damage to probably web the safety glass. That had to be either a baseball bat or something equally destructive.

Her father wouldn't harm his precious Road Warrior—the title he'd dubbed his RV—for a joke. It had cost him hundreds of thousands of dollars to specially outfit it the way he'd wanted.

"Shut up!" Mark demanded, his voice coming from the forgotten tablet on the table.

She turned, glancing down to see all three of her father's team staring at her, huddled around their camera. She reached over and found the volume, muting them as she stood in the middle of the aisle, body tense.

A loud boom came from the top of the roof. In seconds, it repeated, and in her mind, she could almost imagine one of those things doing the same thing to her father's RV that they'd done to the trailer, those freaky, weird leaps into the air only to slam down moments later. A third and fourth loud boom assured her one of them seemed to be testing the strength of the roof.

Jadee looked at the gun in her hand. The Glock 19 suddenly didn't make her feel safe. She kept hold of it and inched down the short hallway, going directly under the loud thumps from above to reach the hall closet. She yanked it open, shoving coats aside to get to the hidden back panel. The six-digit code had always been her birthday. She opened the safe and reached for the thigh holster. It took about a minute to secure it on and snuggly slip the handgun into the cradle, the weight of it comforting. She felt a little safer gripping the Bushmaster ACR rifle. It only took seconds to slide in a clip.

Her hands trembled as she shoved another clip down the front of her shirt. She kicked the closet door shut, hugging the weapon close.

"I'm loaded for bear," she yelled. "Break in and I'll open fire on you. I don't give a shit what the hell you are. Having holes ripping through your body is going to ruin your fun! I've got enough rounds to turn your ass into Swiss cheese."

A female scream coming from outside made Jadee jerk, shoving her back against the closet. She was afraid she might fire out of pure fear and pressed her finger down along the underside of the weapon. She used her left hand to chamber a round so it was ready to go if the side door gave way.

A second set of footsteps stormed closer from above and suddenly what sounded like a heavy body dropped flat. She winced, swearing she could hear something scratching the roof.

"Do you hear me?" she yelled louder. "I have live ammunition and I *will* shoot you!"

Something slammed against the door but the locks held. There wasn't a window there, and the closed shutters next to it didn't give her a view outside. She braced her legs, worried her knees might collapse under her otherwise. The last thing she wanted to do was fall over from fright.

Another loud thump came from up top, near the back. That made three she could count, since the scratching sounds didn't stop and the person on the other side of the door continued to batter it with what sounded like a heavy object.

"Assholes!" Jadee shouted. "Enough! I'm not screwing around. I have an arsenal at my back and I'm gripping an assault rifle. My dad is a paranoid gun fanatic who made me learn how to fire anything that took bullets or shells from the time I could walk. I won't miss, and I'll keep firing. I can reload faster than you can say 'oh shit'. Take your freaky circus act somewhere else!"

Silence reigned. It was eerie and sudden.

Jadee sucked in a deep breath, blowing it out slowly. It was possible her threats had made them reconsider making her a target. She bit her bottom lip, relaxing her grip on the rifle. The weight of the handgun against her outer thigh seemed suddenly heavy.

"Goddamn," she rasped. Her dad and his geek squad had *actually* found a fucking nest of Vampires. *What are they doing in the middle of Nowhere, Alaska?* It didn't make sense.

"Come out," a man's creepy voice crooned.

Jadee stopped breathing, trapping air inside her lungs. It sounded as if a nail slid across metal above her, from where the voice had originated.

"We want to play," a female voice called out from the other side of the door.

"And make you bleed." Another man laughed above.

20

"And scream!" the female added.

Jadee forced herself to breathe and tightened her grip on the rifle, sliding her finger over the trigger. A chill ran down her spine. They sounded deranged. She was tempted to tell them to break in and find out who did the bleeding, but she remained mute, waiting to see what they'd do next. The RV was a tank on wheels. Her father had designed it to withstand anything he hunted.

She moved fast toward the front cab area, reaching up to the control panel that was mounted on the ceiling right above the driver's seat. She read each button and hovered her finger over the one labeled Panic.

She hesitated. The siren blasting might scare them off. She debated pressing it. Another scenario popped into her head.

Someone might hear it and come. Like the cops.

* * * * *

"What are we doing way out here?" Kar jerked his coat tighter around his body. "It's a Friday night."

"We have to go check on a human family and relay a message to them. Lorn wants us to do it and he's our leader, so here we are. A human called the lodge because she can't reach her family." Lavos nonchalantly shrugged. "Besides, it's not as if you had anything else to do."

"Fuck you."

Lavos grinned. "No thanks. You're not my type."

His friend flipped him off but grinned. "As if you could get that lucky."

"Not even in jest, man. Although, you do have big tits."

21

"I don't have man boobies."

"Yeah, you do. You get any bigger and we're going to have to special order your shirts with built-in bras."

"Shut up," Garson groused from the backseat of the open Jeep. "The Tab sisters are visiting and I could be pounding Ginna if I hadn't been assigned this bullshit task. I don't want to hear anything about sex or tits."

Kar snorted. "The only pounding you'd have been doing is with your fist after you watched Ginna walk off with *me*. Everyone knows she only visits our clan because I'm there. And who knows? Maybe Kinna's given up her preference for men over sixty and would have bedded me too. I bet they're crying right now because I'm out on this stupid drive."

"I want a mate. You just like fucking. I'm a better choice than you, and I would have told Ginna so. She would have come home with me."

Kar snorted and shot Garson an amused grin. "Your place is a mess. You ever take a woman there and they'd be convinced you're looking for a maid instead."

"It's not that bad. I'm just not a neat freak. Why did you pick *us* to go with you, Lavos?" Garson asked. "What about Veso? Couldn't you have called him?"

"He's bonding with his new mate."

"A human one at that." Kar chuckled. "I never saw that coming in a million years. I almost feel sorry for her. He's a grumpy bastard."

"I couldn't believe Lorn was so great about accepting her into our clan," Garson mused. "Does Veso have blackmail on your older brother the way Davis had on Decker?"

Sometimes Lavos's friends annoyed him. "No. Of course not, Garson. We wanted change in the clan."

"That's a big one," Kar sighed. "Human-huge."

"Lorn is very smart," Lavos said. "We talked about it afterward. He figured some of the clan probably hoped Veso would challenge him for leadership once he showed up alive. They believed until then that he was loyal to Decker."

"So Lorn accepted his mate as a thank you for not making him have to fight and kill another one of our clan members? I get that." Kar nodded.

"Wrong. Lorn knew Veso had already made enemies who might come after him. Veso pledged loyalty to him, so my brother did the same. Only a dick like Decker would deny a man his mate."

"So that means we can start testing matings with humans?" Garson sounded excited. "That's going to be awesome! I'm *so* getting me a mate."

"Wrong again. Keep your hands off women in the nearby towns."

"That's not fair," Garson snarled. "I could rock a human chick's world."

"Maybe if you ever learned mind control," Kar muttered. "And told her to pretend she was experiencing an earthquake."

"I heard that." Garson reached between the seats and punched him in the arm. "I'm great in bed."

Lavos gripped the wheel and turned off onto a dirt road, slowing the Jeep. "The house is ahead. Knock off the banter before they overhear your conversation. We're here on official business."

"So who bitched because someone else had better things to do than answer their phone? I'm sure that's all this is." Garson cleared his throat. "They were probably avoiding talking to them."

Lavos slowed more, on alert as he glanced all around, mindful of his surroundings. "It was the man's mother. He didn't call her when he should have. I'm not going into the full story but she's worried. Lorn said to check on them and give them the message. That's what we're doing."

"Why is this our problem?" Garson leaned forward between the seats. "Bullshit, I tell you."

"You're supposed to be an enforcer, not a whiner," Kar replied. "Can you at least act like you take your duty seriously? And the task probably *is* bullshit but we still need to check it out. I'm sure the lines are down because of that storm that blew through and they'll get fixed eventually. It's normal, but people who don't live in this area wouldn't know that."

"I'm hungry," Garson muttered.

"Shut up." Lavos frowned as the darkened house came into view. No lights shone in any windows of the two-story home set back into the woods. A truck was parked by the front door and a sat car next to it. "You should have eaten before we left."

Lavos hit the brakes and stopped behind the truck. He didn't bother to wear a seat belt so he slid out of the driver's seat and quickly approached the front door.

He was three steps up the porch before he came to an abrupt halt.

Kar bumped into his back. "Why'd you stop?"

Lavos sniffed again. "Smell."

His friend inhaled and suddenly moved to his side. "Shit."

"That stinks," Garson whispered. "What the hell died?"

Lavos took a few more steps, his vision adjusting to the darkness. The door was closed but upon closer inspection, he saw the splintered wood near the handle and lock. He kicked out, slamming his boot against the door to send it flying inward. He entered the house first, knowing his friends followed close behind. The stench greatly intensified now that there wasn't a barrier between them and the interior.

The dining room table lay in pieces with glass fragments all around it. Lavos reached out and flipped on the lights. They instantly came on, and more destruction awaited, with the couch in the living room on its back. Dry red stains were smeared all over it.

"Blood," Kar confirmed. "A lot of it."

"Shit," Garson muttered from another room. "It looks like someone was slaughtered in the kitchen. There's enough splatter in here on the walls and ceiling to assure me they didn't survive."

Lavos spun, following the source of the putrid stench of death, tracking it up the stairs. Dark stains on the carpet revealed more blood. He located all three bodies in the master bedroom. He hesitated inside the room, his gaze traveling over the horror of what remained of the family that had lived in the house.

"What the hell did this?" Kar inched around him. "They're in pieces. I don't pick up any traces of gunpowder. This sure wasn't a murder/suicide of someone going on a bender and losing their shit."

"It wasn't an animal," Garson announced. "It would have eaten them where they were killed instead of obviously carrying them upstairs to dump in this room."

"No shit," Kar muttered. "Animals wouldn't have politely closed the front door either after they were gone."

Lavos approached the body closest to him and crouched, studying it. "They've been dead for at least two days, and you're right. This was done with intent." He reached out and dreaded touching the head but had no choice as he pressed his fingers against the back of blood-matted hair. He studied the way they'd been torn apart and cursed. "This wasn't done by an animal or one of ours. I'm thinking Vampire."

Garson walked around the carnage, studying the other two corpses. "How the hell can you tell?"

Lavos sighed. "They'd be even more shredded if a Lycan had done this."

"This wasn't a feeding," Kar spat. "Too much blood was spilled. This was outright cruel and vicious. It had to be a human."

"No." Lavos examined the remains. "See this? The bones were snapped and this person's arm was ripped off. A Lycan would have used his claws. We'd see a lot more shredding of the skin. A human wouldn't have been strong enough to do this without a weapon. I'm not seeing any sharp instrument marks on the exposed bones."

"GarLycan? Gargoyle?" Kar inched closer.

Lavos shook his head. "They would have disposed of the bodies. They're anal about that. Whatever did this was stronger than a human but not a shifter. There's no animal hair in this mess. Look at the hand over there." He pointed. "They grabbed some long hair from whoever killed them. It looks human, and it's black. Notice these people have light brown to blonde hair? It came from whoever attacked them."

"Fucking crazy Vamps," Garson cursed. "Why are they screwing with us so much recently? Who wants to make the call?"

Lavos rose up. "There's no cell signal this far out and I didn't bring a satellite phone. I wasn't expecting to find this kind of trouble."

Kar grimly stared at Lavos. "Are you thinking what I am? They must have intentionally taken out a pole somewhere so these people couldn't call for help. How many Vamps do you think did this? A nest of bloodsuckers or just one sick bastard?"

"I'm guessing it wasn't a full nest. They wouldn't have allowed that much blood to go to waste. The stink of death is too strong to detect how many were here," Lavos stated. "We'd better check the neighbors."

"Shit. You think there could be more victims?" Kar didn't wait for an answer. "What are we going to do with these three to hide their murder? The state troopers can't find this shit. Burn the house down?"

"It's too close to the woods. We'd risk it spreading despite all that rain that came down in this area a week ago," Lavos decided. He shot a look at Garson. "Tag, you're it."

"Fuck no." The other man shook his head. "No way."

"I'm sure they have a shovel in the shed," Kar snickered. "You said you wanted to pound something. Try earth while you bury them deep, and make sure it's far enough away from the house that they aren't found."

"What about all the blood?"

Lavos felt a headache coming on. "We'll handle that later, once we call for reinforcements. Maybe Davis can set a few bombs along the foundation and bring it down without causing a fire. He might be able to make it look like a propane accident. Nobody is going to want to waste the resources to rummage through the rubble if there's no smell of death. They like to bring in cadaver dogs for that shit. No bodies means no digging. Get rid of every piece of those poor victims. Wrap them up in the destroyed carpets and bury them far from here. We're going to go check out the nearby houses."

"You guys suck ass!" Garson stomped toward the door.

Kar grinned, following Lavos. "That's what you get for bitching so much in the Jeep."

"Shut up," Lavos warned. "Or *you* can do the digging."

Kar frowned but didn't make another comment.

Lavos hurried down the stairs and walked outside. He bypassed the Jeep and his gaze roamed the landscape. "That way." He pointed.

"You picked up the scent of the prick who did this?"

"Nope. I see a faint light coming from that hill over there."

"Why not drive?"

"It's faster to run, and quieter." Lavos took a deep breath. "Race you." He rushed forward before his friend could respond.

Ten minutes later they walked out of the second cabin. Lavos fought his rage. "Two people lived there, and they didn't leave willingly."

"No shit. It looks like someone put up a fight. Why did they take these ones away when they left the bodies of the other family? Do you think these are victims of that nest that attacked us? Those soldiers had to come from somewhere."

Lavos shook his head. "Those bodies in the other house aren't more than maybe a couple days old. We'd taken that nest out before then."

"Shit. More Vampires in the area?"

Lavos glanced up at the night sky. "I'm hoping they didn't turn them. What if they're starting a new nest? That first family could have been slaughtered by a newbie group if they put up too much of a fight. You know how nuts they are right after they change."

"Fuck." Kar lifted a hand and ran it through his hair. "Why would they do that?"

"Decker already sent some of these assholes to cause trouble. I'm sure he's heard from someone that Lorn took the clan and we extinguished Borrow's nest. Payback. To be a prick. Should I go on?"

"Nope. Do you want me to take the Jeep and drive until I get a cell signal to call in reinforcements? We could be dealing with a blanket effect in this area if they've decided to take it over. How many residents do you think live within the Kegslee town limits?"

"Maybe twenty-five tops. That's a lot of Vampires to support in a nest, and it still doesn't account for why the master allowed the waste of that family of three. You saw all the blood spilled. Every drop would be precious, unless they're killing the wildlife to feed from."

"This is all kinds of fucked up. But this town is close enough to launch an attack against us."

Lavos blew out a breath. "Exactly. Stick close. Let's go check out more homes. We need to discover what we're dealing with before we ask more of our people to come here to clean up this mess. I don't want them walking into a trap."

"What about us?" Kar frowned. "I don't want to end up facing down a few dozen Vamps."

"You were bitching about no excitement on a Friday evening. Feeling bored *now*?"

"Sometimes I hate you."

Lavos grinned. "You don't mean that."

"How can you smile? We might end up tangling with a nest of suckheads. It's just the two of us," Kar reminded him. "Three, if we go back and grab Garson."

Lavos lifted his hand, concentrating until claws slid out of his fingertips. The deadly tips were a menacing sight. "Decapitate the fuckers. We can handle some Vamps."

"You're crazy."

"I'm pissed," Lavos admitted. "Lorn's got enough shit to deal with right now. He doesn't need this on top of it all. Stay close and alert."

"Fuck." Kar allowed his own claws to slide out. "I liked these clothes. I got dressed up for the Tab twins because I figured we wouldn't be gone long. Blood is a bitch to wash out."

"This is more important."

They went north, jogging through the woods. Lavos came to a sudden halt and cocked his head. "Do you hear that?"

"It sounds like someone's car alarm."

"The battery would have died if it had been going for more than a few hours. That means the scene will be fresh. Let's go." Lavos zeroed in on the direction of the sound.

Chapter Two

Jadee couldn't take the siren for long and shut it down. It was starting to give her a headache, and she wanted to be able to hear what was going on outside. That thought reminded her that her father had cameras mounted to the exterior of the RV.

She placed the rifle on the dining room table but kept it close. She found the remote for the television near the driving compartment and flipped channels to locate the feeds. The first one revealed the passenger side of the RV.

The woman by the door wasn't there anymore. A little satisfaction struck. She flipped to another channel, getting a view of the front. Jadee didn't see anything on the driver's side or on the rear camera. She lifted her chin, peering at the roof. It was all quiet up there.

"They don't like loud noise," she deduced. "I might survive this after all." She spun, talking to the tablet. The three people locked inside the trailer were still in view. Mark's mouth moved soundlessly, a reminder that she'd muted the device. She turned it back up.

"Jadee? What happened? Are you okay?"

"Yes. I hit the panic alarm and they stopped attacking. I don't see them on my cameras."

Peggy clutched at her brother Brent. "They're coming after *us* again!"

Mark turned in his chair. "Shut up." He faced forward. "They're sensitive to noises. That was smart of you."

"Didn't you try that last night? I'm hoping someone heard it and help arrives."

"There's no one within range to hear us." He paused, probably for effect. Mark loved dramatics. "All the residents are dead. We found blood in every home we checked when we arrived."

"Everyone?" The news stunned Jadee. "As in, the entire town?"

"We can't be sure, since we only went to a few homes," Peggy whispered. "But we didn't see anyone while we were driving around, before they took out the vehicles."

"We checked the home of our website tipper first," Brent explained. "His front door was kicked in but he wasn't there. It's not a big town and they only have one diner. It was empty." Brent kept Peggy in his arms, trying to ease her visible shaking. "Probably sixteen homes in all in this area. We couldn't find any survivors in the few homes we searched the first day. Then we set the trap, hoping to catch whatever had made people disappear."

Jadee was outraged. *"What in the hell were you thinking?* Normal people call the police when they find blood! You should have gotten out of here the second you realized something was actually wrong!"

"We caught four Vampires!" Mark boasted indignantly.

"And *lost them*, you stupid bastard! Why didn't you get help before they escaped?"

"We couldn't have someone else taking credit for our work! We planned to study them and document everything before we reached out to a few of our colleagues."

"So no one else knows you guys are out here and what you were involved with?"

"Just you, Jadee." Brent frowned. "Your father wanted you to be a part of this."

"Oh, I am." She wanted to kill someone, preferably Mark, since she disliked him the most. "Now my father's missing and I'm trapped just like you are." She breathed deep, trying to calm down and think. "Okay...how did you catch them the first time?" She was hoping they might be able to do it again.

"We used the motor home," Peggy whispered. "The bedroom is caged in, so we put a recording devise inside the storage section under the bed to mimic a heartbeat and breathing, left worn clothes and fresh blood for them to scent. It lured all four inside the room. They thought someone was hiding there."

Jadee had to admit that sounded smart. "And then what?"

"We had cameras to see inside the RV and a remote-controlled trigger to seal the door," Mark added. "Once they were locked in, we waited until the sun rose, and were able to go in to get them. They do sleep during the day."

"It was just a matter of shooting them with high doses of paralytic drugs to be sure they would stay down before we opened the door. We put them in body bags and carried them to the cages we brought. We dumped them out of the bags into the cages so we had access to draw blood and do tests on them," Brent added. "We'd put up a tent to protect them from the sun."

"They shouldn't have been able to escape those cages." Peggy paused. "But they somehow did. We only managed to contain them for a day."

"Fantastic." Nope. No luck calming down. She was still furious. "Now we're in *this* mess."

"They might not see your rental and leave it alone." Peggy's expression became hopeful. "You could drive us out of here in the morning."

Jadee resisted calling them idiots again. Her rental was about fifty feet from the motor home. Only a blind person would miss it.

A loud noise struck the top of the RV roof and Jadee almost dropped the tablet. Her gaze instantly fixed on the television to see outside.

The camera feed died, the screen going black.

"Shit."

"What is it?" Mark demanded from the tablet.

She placed it on the table and grabbed the remote, flipping to another channel on the television feed. It was out too, and heavy footprints crossed the length of the roof.

"Jadee?" Brent hissed her name.

She bent over and braced her hands on the table so they could see her. "It knows where the cameras are. It's tearing them out or covering them."

"That's not good. How would they know they were even there?" Mark scowled.

"Probably because they can see them from the top of the roof." Jadee rolled her eyes.

Mark shook his head. "Your dad had them hidden to look like part of the framing at the top. There's no red eye or anything to give them away."

A jingling noise—like metal on metal—came from the door, and Jadee instantly straightened, spinning around. She grabbed the rifle, cradling it against her chest with one arm. Her stomach clenched. The bars were down to keep the door secured, but she wasn't certain how strong they were if the locks themselves were disengaged. "Tell me you don't keep spare keys to the RV inside any of the tow cars."

"We don't," Mark responded.

"Does anyone else besides my dad have keys to his RV?"

"No. Just him."

The sick feeling intensified as she concentrated on that slight jingling sound...

"You must have used the electronic keypad to get into your dad's motor home," Peggy said. "The second your dad activated the shutters, bolts slid into place on the two driving-area doors, so they can't be opened with a key anyway. Only the side door can be."

That was unexpected but good news. "When did he have that changed?"

"We were investigating Bigfoot reports and some witnesses said the creatures could tear off vehicle doors to steal food. Your dad had the motor home and the trailer modified so that couldn't happen. Regular locks weren't enough." Mark paused. "He also had our roofs reinforced, since Bigfoots are supposed to weigh up to a thousand pounds and are reported to have sharp claws."

Jadee felt only a small relief. She still had hope that her father was alive and awaiting car repairs somewhere away from the campsite. But if someone had his keys...it would mean he hadn't made it out of the area after all.

A new threat popped into her head. "Are there weapons in the tow cars?" She cocked her head, staring the shutters covering the front windshield. "Something strong enough to go through safety glass and metal?"

"No," Mark sighed. "No weapons. They're all in your father's safe."

Jadee bit her lip, thinking. "What about a tire iron? Could that work? Every car has one of those and a jack."

"It wouldn't cause enough damage to breach the exteriors of the motor home or this trailer," Mark swore. "They were built to withstand a lot of damage."

A chill flashed down Jadee's spine at the sudden beep by the door.

Her gaze flew to the electrical pad—and it flashed green.

One of the locks inside the door slid, creating a soft scraping noise. Something outside tugged on the door hard but the extra bolts and bars across it held.

She yanked the tablet from its charging cord and clung to it. "Oh shit."

Jadee hesitantly stepped toward the door to get a better look. The light turned red and the main bolt clicked back into place.

A quiet beeping sound repeated and the pad flashed green a second time. The bolt slid again inside the door, unlocking it. The handle moved slowly as she stared at it in horror. Whoever was on the other side tugged hard but the extra dead bolts and bars kept them from getting inside.

36

She stumbled back until her ass hit something solid. The pad turned red and the interior bolt slid into place again.

Her hand shook hard as she lifted the tablet to peer at the screen. "Who has the code to my dad's RV besides me?"

"Why?" Mark sounded wary.

"Because someone is punching in the right numbers and trying to get in," she whispered. "The emergency bolts are holding and I pulled both of the bars down across the top and bottom of it."

"Only your dad," Peggy gasped. "Open it up! He's outside!"

"Don't do it!" Mark shouted. "He could be one of them!"

"It's Victor!" Brent argued. "He's alive. Open the fucking door before they find him!"

"What if they already did? He could be a Vampire," Mark warned.

That's what Jadee was afraid of. She muted the volume of the tablet and dropped it on the dining table. She took a small step forward and gripped the weapon in her arms, aiming it at the door. She balanced it and reached out with one hand to push down the intercom button. "Dad?"

"Let me in, Jadee."

The sound of his familiar voice almost buckled her knees.

Her first instinct was to unlock the door and pull him inside to safety before the Vampires attacked him. Reason made her hesitate. That panic alarm might have chased away the ones attacking the exterior—but it also could have drawn more of them, like a dinner bell being rung.

No way would he be outside that door unless he was one of them.

She might not have been on his research team, but Jadee wasn't clueless about the things he believed in.

"Where have you been, Dad? Who took out the cameras so I can't see you?"

"Never mind about that. Unlock the door and let me in, honey."

"*Where* have you been?"

"With friends."

He sounded calm, not stressed at all. He knew Vampires were out there, had been studying them. It screamed all kinds of wrong to her, and made her wonder who these "friends" were.

A hot tear slid down her cheek but she didn't bother to wipe it away, not willing to release the rifle.

"What did they do to you, Dad?"

"I'm okay. Unlock the door. It's going to be fine."

Oh God. She fought the urge to scream and cry at the same time. Part of her felt tempted to release the intercom and curl into a fetal position. He hadn't denied that someone had done something to him. *Nothing is okay. Nothing.*

"Jadee," he soothed. "Open the door, honey. We need to talk."

Her knees finally gave way and she collapsed onto the carpet. She reached up and blindly turned on the intercom fully so she didn't have to hold the button down. The rifle ended up across her lap. She leaned sideways a little, pressing her face against the smooth wood of the counter next to the door.

"Do it," he demanded. "Let me in."

"Are you going to kill me, Dad?" It was hard getting the words out.

"Of course not."

She squeezed her eyes closed. Her dad was still in there, even if he had been changed into a Vampire. He knew the code to his RV and who she was. All the movies she'd watched regarding Vampires flashed through her mind. She really hoped they were the friendly types who were basically the same once they were turned...

But then there were the horror versions, who lured people into letting them inside to rip out their throats.

According to her father's team, they'd already found the bodies of some residents. She couldn't forget about that.

"Jadee? I'd never hurt you, honey. Let me inside. It's cold out here."

"Vampires aren't supposed to get cold," she responded, holding her breath to see how he'd respond.

"You don't believe in Vampires. You're being ridiculous. I was with friends. Open the door."

The lock beeped and the interior bolt slid. The door she leaned against moved slightly but held. It was enough to get her to open her eyes and stare up at the pad. It went from green to red, the bolt sliding home again.

Anger suddenly surged and she turned her face into her shoulder, wiping it against her shirt to be rid of the tears. She'd always feared his lifestyle would get him killed. Just not like this.

Whatever he was, whoever he'd become, he was still her dad. She had to at least give him a chance.

"I'm not dressed," she lied. "Give me a few minutes, Dad."

"I've seen it all before. Open the door."

"Two minutes." She forced her body to move, standing and turning off the intercom. The cold metal of the rifle helped her stay calm. She went to the front cab where the security panel was, removing the key that controlled the shutters. She hoped he didn't have a spare as she pocketed it. The gun safe in the closet remained open and she went to it next.

Her movements were jerky as she collected the weapons from their nesting places in pockets attached to the wall of the safe. She rested the rifle along the closet wall and strapped on a waist holster. The twin Smith & Wesson 380s were shoved into it after she flipped off the safeties and pushed in a cartridge for each one. Her hands didn't tremble when she lifted the rifle and closed the closet, not bothering to secure the concealed panel. There was nothing left inside to take.

She approached the side door, taking calm, steady breaths.

Her father grew impatient and slapped the door. The pad beeped as he punched in the code again to unlock the bolt. It scraped open but the interior locks continued to hold. She paused by the door, fighting fear and the uncertainty of her actions.

This is so fucking stupid, she tried to reason with herself. She reached out before she could change her mind and turned the intercom back on. "Dad? Stand back, and once I unlock the door, count to ten before you come in. Do you understand me? You don't want to scare me, do you?"

"Of course not, honey."

She wanted to believe him. One way or another, she needed to do this. She had to know if he was still her father or a fiend.

40

Her grip on the assault rifle tightened as she hefted the first bar out of place. The second one she had to bend a little to reach. The interior bolts were easier to yank to the side, and she backed away quickly when the last one was pulled.

"Come on in." She didn't dare glance away from the door as she inched down the hallway, closer to the bedroom. She could always escape into it if need be.

The beep was a menacing sound...the bolt slide terrifying.

This time the door opened, fresh air pouring into the interior as it was thrown back wide.

Jadee lifted the assault rifle, gripping it with both hands, pointing it at the darkness beyond the door. She located the trigger with her finger, resting it there.

The white-haired man who slowly entered looked so familiar, but she noted the differences immediately as he stopped in the aisle, turning her way. His skin still looked weathered from the sun but his complexion had become unusually pale, with dark veins showing. His normally sparkling blue eyes appeared duller. What used to be the whites of his eyes were bloodshot and appeared wrong. *Evil*.

A soft moan sounded and Jadee realized it had come from her.

His gaze lowered, studying the rifle she held. "It's okay. You can put that down."

"Close and lock the door, Dad."

He didn't move to do it. "You're safe. You don't have to point that gun at me."

"Close and lock the door," she repeated.

41

He slowly lifted his hands out to his sides. She glanced at them, saw a lot of dirt and what appeared to be some dark red stains. It was possibly blood.

"Easy, honey." He took a step forward.

"Don't," she ground out. "I'll shoot you. Stay right there and lock that fucking door."

He didn't blink at all. The eerie way he stared at her was freaking her out. She glanced at his chest and saw that it moved, as if he breathed. It could have been force of habit, or perhaps Vampires did need oxygen. She focused on his face again.

"I want you to meet my friends. They aren't what we expected."

"What happened to the people who lived in the nearby town? I heard they'd all disappeared by the time your team arrived. Where are they?" She backed up more, reaching the doorway to the bedroom.

"You don't need to go in there and activate the safety door, Jadee."

She wasn't so sure.

"Don't be afraid. We were wrong about them." He took another step forward.

Jadee aimed the gun at his heart. "Don't come any closer."

His smile chilled her to the bone. "Bullets won't kill me."

Fear nearly overrode her anger. "I bet they'd hurt." She adjusted her aim, targeting his head. "And I'm pretty sure some of them tearing through your brain would slow you down."

"Why did you let me in if you planned to shoot me, honey? I raised you to never point a gun unless you were willing to pull the trigger."

"I needed to know if you were still you. You're not." It broke her heart. "My dad would have locked that door so no one else could get at me. He would have gone to the cab area and stayed as far back from me as possible to make sure I felt safe. I'm so sorry, Dad. I came as soon as I could get a flight...but I got here too late."

"You're not too late. You're right on time. We're not going to kill you, honey."

His repeated use of that endearment was becoming disturbing but the use of "we" was worse.

"I told Mitch all about you, and he needs someone at his side. I even showed him your picture from my wallet. He thinks you're beautiful."

Jadee tensed. "Who's Mitch?"

"He turned me and gave me eternal life. He's going to bestow that gift upon you too. We'll be a family again."

She had a name for the bastard who had taken her father. "Where were you when the other ones attacked the roof and the door?"

"I thought you hadn't arrived yet so I was waiting along the road with Mitch to welcome you. Then I heard the alarm. Mitch wants to meet you."

"Where is he? I'd like to meet him too."

"He's outside, allowing me to calm you down. This doesn't have to hurt, honey. Put the guns down and we'll walk outside. He'll be gentle, and he promised to take good care of you. You need that. I always worry about you being alone."

"How sweet." She swallowed down the bile that rose. "Why don't you have him step in here and introduce himself? It's bright in here so I can see better."

Her father turned his head, seeming to stare at something right outside the open doorway. Movement drew her attention but she was careful not to allow it to distract her from her dad. He was a threat, and she couldn't forget that.

The tall, thin man who climbed inside looked horrific. He had black, scruffy hair, a narrow, long white face, and his black clothes were Gothic. It might have been the way they were made, but the arms and legs of his pants and shirt had rips in them, revealing slices of his white, skinny limbs. Dirt also covered his hands. Dead leaves were stuck to his clothing in a few places, as if he'd been digging or rolling in the dirt. She didn't even want to imagine why he'd do that.

The top of his head nearly brushed the ceiling of the RV, putting him at about six foot four. In life, he'd probably been odd looking with his lanky body, but he was horrific as a Vampire. Bloodshot eyes met hers and his thin lips curved upward. The dark veins on his face became more pronounced.

"Hello. I'm Mitch. It's nice to meet you, Jadee. I've heard so much about you."

She saw the sharp tips of his fangs when he spoke. They scared the shit out of her. The smell coming from him reached her nose and she inhaled through her mouth. It reminded her of the time she'd found a dead mouse under her mobile home in Washington, where she lived. It was faint, but the smell of death clung to him.

"The feeling isn't mutual, Mitch. You took my dad from me."

He tilted his head, his cheek almost resting against the top of his shoulder, and it make him look even more inhuman. "He's right here."

"Did my dad ever tell you that I had a rough life, being pulled around with him on his hunts? Kids made fun of me all the time. It was a bitch always being the new student at school. We never lived in one place for long. I was bullied until I learned how to fight back at a young age. It kind of gave me anger issues."

His head straightened. "You won't be alone ever again."

"That's the thing. I kind of like it now. I learned to never depend on anyone besides myself. Remember that anger issue I mentioned? I'm pissed, Mitch. You might be the big bad, but guess what? I loved my dad, and he was all I had left after my grandma died. I want to test a theory. Dad was big on those."

Jadee opened fire without any other warning, the sound earsplitting in the confined space.

The first bullet struck Mitch in the forehead. He jerked back from the impact. She got three more into his chest before he fell. She turned the weapon on what used to be her father. His mouth hung open. He looked stunned as she shot him in the head.

She backed up and blindly reached out, hitting the round red button on the wall. The gate slammed across the door as she fell backward, forgetting about the bed being in the way. It took her seconds to sit up and scramble toward the side of the bed frame, backing up into a corner far out of reach of the gate.

She was aghast when she saw Mitch coming down the hallway.

The healing holes in his chest were visible and a dark red substance poured out of them before they sealed.

She opened fire again, targeting his heart. He roared out in pain or anger, twisting away and presenting her with his back.

The gun emptied and she popped out the clip, grabbing another one to slam home. She fired again.

Mitch used the bathroom for cover, darting into it. What used to be her dad came down the narrow hallway next.

"Stop it, Jadee!" he yelled.

They weren't dying, seeming to heal in seconds. She struck Victor mid-mass a few times, sure she hit his heart at least once. He stumbled and crumpled to the floor. She held her breath, praying he wouldn't get up.

"You're making me angry," Mitch hissed from around the corner, out of her line of sight.

She sucked in a lungful of air. "You don't know what pissed is, fuckhead! Why don't you step out of the bathroom and stop cowering in there? I'll show you angry."

She glanced down. Victor still hadn't moved. She pushed back the grief and guilt over having to kill her dad. He had already been gone before she'd arrived.

I put him out of his misery. She clung to that idea. It helped her keep her shit together. *Crying comes later. Right now, kill the other bastard.*

Victor's arm twitched. Then she watched him attempt to sit up. She was glad she couldn't see his face. It made what she had to do easier.

"Oh God." She pointed the gun, aiming for his spinal cord, and fired into the back of his neck. He jerked once and became still.

"You're only delaying the inevitable," Mitch yelled. "I'll make you pay if you don't stop right now. I'm offering to make you my wife."

46

"Were you nuts before you became a Vampire? Now you're stupid *and* crazy if you think I'd agree to that. You're a walking horror show. Did I mention ugly too? You're disgusting and you smell like a dead rat."

"You bitch!" he shouted. "I'm going to make you hurt when I get my hands on you—you'll beg me to die. But that's not going to happen. I'll keep you around to watch you suffer."

Jadee wished her father had kept more clips inside his safe for the ACR. She removed one of the guns from her waist. She needed to be more careful with her rounds. Summer in this part of Alaska meant a lot of daylight, but it was still hours away. She had to survive that long. They couldn't get into the room but that didn't mean they couldn't kill her if they had a weapon. The safe was empty but they might have access to other guns. She was in a cage, with no place to escape gunfire directed her way.

Mitch suddenly stepped out of the bathroom and grabbed the bars across the door. She pointing the gun at him while they glared at each other.

"You're going to bleed, bitch."

"How's the head?" She made a point of staring at where he'd taken a bullet to the forehead, seeing only blood but no gaping hole. "I'd ask if you have brain damage but you'd have to have one first, right? It doesn't seem like you do."

He growled and his mouth opened, showing those sharp fangs. "This isn't going to keep me out." He looked down and started to shake the bars. They held, but slight popping noises sounded from the walls around them.

She had a sinking feeling that with enough abuse, he'd bust inside.

She opened fire, aiming for his heart. It might work if she totally annihilated the sucker, so she blasted holes into him.

He slumped, dropped to his knees, but didn't fall over completely.

Minutes passed. His chin finally lifted and he growled again.

"I recover, bitch. Bullets won't stop me." He got to his feet.

"They slow you down though. I also notice you're not healing as fast as you did before." She shot him in the head again and he jerked back, crashing to his knees once more. He didn't fall over but he did bump Victor.

Victor moved, turning his head. He stared at Mitch, then at her.

"Dad?" She felt hope he still might listen. "Try to remember your old life and how much you loved me."

"You shouldn't have pissed Mitch off, honey. He's going to have to make you pay for that now."

Jadee backed up and bumped the wall. This was a nightmare. She never should have opened the door to let Victor inside but she had to know what he'd become.

I know now. I'm so fucked.

"I'm your daughter." She made one last attempt. "Don't you want to protect me? Fight him and get him out of the RV. Lock the door and keep him away long enough for me to seal it again."

Victor's limbs were jerky as he rose to his feet. The wounds she'd inflicted weren't bleeding anymore, the only proof of his injuries were bloody stains and holes in his clothes. He did seem sluggish though, as if being shot all those times had drained him of some energy.

"I'm doing what's best for you. That's being with Mitch. We'll be together forever."

"Who the hell *are* you?" She lifted the gun. "Don't talk to me. You break my heart. My dad is dead. You're a mockery of everything he stood for."

He hissed and sharp fangs slid down from a row of what had been mostly straight teeth. "Don't talk to me that way!"

"Go to hell."

She shot him in the heart and watched him fall back. He was only down for a short time before he struggled to sit up. Mitch began to rouse too.

She'd tested a theory and it hadn't panned out. Shooting them in the heart and brain put them down but it wasn't for long, and they seemed to heal from injuries, regardless of how severe.

Her gaze swept the room for a different weapon. There was another theory she wanted to test. The cabinets and the bed frame were made from wood.

She placed the handgun down and lifted the ACR. It was out of ammo but it would work great to smash shit with. She used the butt of the weapon and slammed it against the footboard, breaking off a jagged chunk.

She gripped it and turned. The only problem was she'd have to get close enough to stab one of them—and that meant they'd be close enough to grab her.

"Fucking great," she muttered. She glared at Victor. "Couldn't you have equipped your armory with water guns filled with holy water? Some crossbows? I'd like those options right now way better."

He hissed at her.

49

Chapter Three

Lavos tracked the female while Kar had gone after the male. They'd run into the Vampires on the way into the canyon where the car alarm had originated from. The sound had stopped shortly after it had begun or they might have missed the slight noises the couple had made traipsing through the woods.

The Vamp had long, tangled black hair and smelled as if she hadn't bathed in a week. He was glad it was easy to follow her by stench alone, since her dark dress and all the trees made it difficult for him to keep her in sight. The raspy noises she made when she ran helped, too.

He'd finally gained enough on her when Lavos found himself on top of a crest, with the Vamp below in a ravine. He dove, his bigger body slamming into hers. She screamed, and he focused on grabbing her wrists before she could scratch him as she tried to claw his face. Her fangs flashed in the moonlight a second before she attempted to bite. He threw his head forward, slamming it into her forehead.

She cried out in pain and Lavos felt guilt. Hurting a woman wasn't something he had ever done before, bloodsucking enemy or not. He cursed under his breath and shifted his weight, flipping her over onto her stomach as he released her arms. He fisted her hair at the back of her head instead, while he shoved his other hand against the middle of her back and pressed down with his weight. He lifted his chest, effectively pinning her down.

"Stop fighting," he demanded.

She struggled and made hissing noises. He thought of his brother and the woman he loved. Kira had been turned into a Vampire against her will.

They were the enemy, but he was glad Lorn had spared her life. The bloodsucker under him might have a similar story.

"Stop," he growled, allowing his voice to show his temper.

She stilled under him and tried to twist her head. He eased his hold on her hair just enough to permit her to look at him. He studied her face, the veins showing along her forehead and cheeks. They were black, faint lines marring pale skin. What should have been the whites of her eyes showed a deep red of busted blood vessels.

"Fuck." Anger stirred but he fought it back. It wasn't her fault, what she was.

She spat dirt. "Let me go."

"Not a chance."

"What are you?"

"Not like you."

"You're not human."

He shook his head. "Nope. I'm something worse."

"Let me go!"

"Answer my questions."

She struggled again but ceased when she realized she couldn't break free. "What do you want to know?"

"How many of you are there?"

Her gaze flickered away, seeming to frantically search for help. Lavos inhaled deeply, regretted it since she reeked, before shaking his head. "None of your kind are near. I'd smell them."

"My kind?" She fixed her attention on him.

He hesitated before leaning down to get closer. He allowed his eyes to glow.

Her features softened and she stared at him in awe. "That's beautiful. They're so blue."

"Thank you. *Your* eyes tell me exactly what you are."

"I'm a Vampire. What are *you*?"

He inwardly winced. Someone had been telling big lies. "That's not important."

She frowned.

"Think of me as a peacekeeper—and you've been very bad by breaking laws. Do you understand? Killing humans is a crime. Did you know that?"

"We have to feed on them to survive. We have to kill them so they don't change into one of us."

Alarms went off inside Lavos. "Is that what your master told you? What's his name?"

"Mitch."

He'd never heard of the master but that wasn't a surprise.

The sound of gunfire jerked his head up, and he knew he'd run out of time. He focused on the woman, allowing his eyes to glow brighter. "I'm sorry. This is going to hurt."

He stared deeply into her eyes and she whimpered. To force his will on someone like her was painful for the one it was done to. "How many of you are there?"

"Five," she whispered.

"How many are older Vampires?"

"Only Mitch."

"Describe him to me."

"He's tall with black hair and wears black clothes." Her nose started to bleed.

"Don't fight me. You'll cause your brain to hemorrhage. Do you understand?"

A thin trickle of blood ran out of her ear next and he was tempted to stop, but he had no choice. She was dead anyway. He couldn't allow her to live. "Did he kill everyone in the area?"

"There's a few people we couldn't get to."

He let go of her mind and eased some of the weight off her back by lowering until his elbow was braced on the ground. "You're not a Vampire, sweetheart. Someone turned you but they didn't do it all the way. You're what they call a soldier. You heal faster than a normal Vampire but it has consequences. You would have had about six weeks before you couldn't even remember your name. Your master could have turned you all the way but chose not to. They're cold bastards by nature. You'd have felt sheer agony eventually, craving blood all the time. It's the curse he infected you with. It eats you alive, and no amount of blood can cure what's wrong."

Her eyes widened. "That's not true. Mitch said we're Vampires. We'll live forever!"

"He lied. But I'm going to make him pay for what he did to you. I give you my word on that. I'm going to spare you from suffering." Lavos felt pity as he watched bloody tears fill her eyes.

"You're lying!"

"I'm not. Vampires look human for the most part. Have you seen your eyes? The blood in them is a giveaway. You're damaged. I can't put it any other way. Sometimes Vampires make soldiers to increase their numbers to win a war, and then dispose of them when they're no longer needed. It's also how I can force my will on you. You were made mentally weak enough for a Vampire to control. Your Mitch never meant to keep you around. I can't let you go. You'll become a danger to everything living, and could expose secrets to the humans."

"I *am* a Vampire!" she insisted.

He heard more gunfire. The people she'd mentioned must be a group of campers, probably hunters, and they clearly needed help. He wanted someone to survive this—and his best bet of finding Mitch would be where the blood was.

"Close your eyes. Think of something good. I'm so sorry."

She struggled and he lifted up, pinning her again. The quickest way to kill her would be brutal but it would also be painless. He extended his claws and rolled over fast, taking her with him by keeping ahold of her hair. He slashed her neck as they twisted, removing her head.

Lavos stood, resting the head next to her body.

"I'm going to shred you for making me do that, Mitch. Your throat is mine."

He couldn't stand to look at what was left of the first woman he'd ever had to kill. Mitch had lied to her about her future. Lavos had been brutally honest, and by killing her, he had done her a kindness...but it didn't feel satisfying.

One glance up assured him what remained of the woman wouldn't be shaded from the sun once it rose in the sky. He spun, running at full speed toward the sound of random gunfire.

He became aware of someone else running and caught a glimpse of Kar. They drew closer, glancing at each other. Kar looked killing mad, telling Lavos all he needed to know. Blood stained his shirt and hands. He'd dealt with the male bloodsucker.

They stopped when they caught sight of the motor home. It was down a hill from where they stood. The side door hung open, light spilling out from the interior. A truck was parked nearby.

A gun blast came from the interior.

"Mine said there were five of them. He was a fucking soldier," Kar panted.

"Mine said the same; she was one too."

"Carl was a local resident turned twelve days ago by Mitch. I got a description. I also asked about that family we found torn apart. It seems Mitch knew them and held a grudge against the youngest member. That's why they were slaughtered. It wasn't for food, but revenge."

"Were there any remains of this Carl?"

"Yeah. I dragged what was left of him to a clearing."

Lavos growled. "Let's go." He took a step downhill.

Kar gripped his arm. "What about whoever is firing that gun? I'm guessing it's a human who's seen too much, or maybe the Vamps are torturing them with bullets."

"We won't know until we get down there."

"Fuck." Kar let him go. "You know if we have survivors we're going to have to use mind control to make them forget. I'm not good with that."

"You have at least a little experience. Garson doesn't. That's why you're here and he isn't. I can probably handle any survivors but I might need help."

Lavos jerked out of his friend's hold and rushed down the hill at full speed, only slowing when he got to the side of the motor home. He hid to one side of the open door, Kar on the other. He held his breath to keep from betraying his presence to listen to what was going on inside. There were only a few windows on the motor home and all of them remained dark, something covering them.

"Goddamn it!" a man complained. "How in the hell do we get past that door?"

"We can't. She stole the key, so I can't even put the shutters up to try to reach her through the windows. I had that gate built to withstand a yeti," another man answered.

Lavos glanced across the open space to gape at Kar. There was a speaker on the side of the door and it was active, broadcasting what was being said inside.

"A yeti?" Kar mouthed, looking equally as confused.

"Huff and puff, asshole. You can't get in—" The woman's voice was cut off by a single gunshot.

"Stop that!" It was the first man who'd yelled. "That was my hand, you bitch!"

"Then don't reach inside to push the button. It's not a release, moron. It's the trigger to close the gate. I told you that I'm going to shoot anything you put between the bars."

"How many bullets do you think she has left?" The first man sounded furious.

"I would guess maybe a dozen or less. We came here to do a study, not kill," the second man answered. "I keep some weapons for protection from regular wildlife."

"I'm going to kill her," the one with the deeper voice threatened. "I'm going to rip out her fucking throat and watch her choke on her own blood before I drain her dry."

"That's my daughter. You promised not to hurt her!"

"That was before she decided to keep tearing holes into me! I've lost a lot of blood."

"Boo hoo," the woman yelled. "Go away if you don't like being shot. You should change your name to whiner." She paused. "Or wiener. Both apply, you dick."

Lavos grinned. Whoever the woman was, he had to admire her spunk. Kar shook his head, lifting his hands as if to say "what the hell?"

One of the Vamps inside roared out in rage and glass shattered against something. The woman screamed.

Lavos'd had enough, less wary of the danger and more worried about her wellbeing.

"Stop it!" the second man shouted. "You could kill her!"

Lavos entered the motor home by jumping up inside.

The sound of voices had come from the left. One quick glance to the right, toward the cab, revealed no additional danger—but the sight of a tall, scrawny, black-haired Vampire struggling with a short, wrinkled, white-haired one *did* surprise him.

They were wrestling between the kitchenette area and a built-in table with bench seats. The taller Vamp backhanded the shorter one, sending him sprawling onto his back on the table. The glass pitcher in Skinny Vamp's hand was chucked down the short hallway, smashing into something with a metallic sound.

Both seemed unaware of Lavos, or the fact that Kar had also entered behind him.

"How do you like that, you bitch?" The taller one shouted.

"Fuck you, dickhead," the woman yelled back. "You got me the first time but now I have the comforter up so you won't cut me again."

"What the fuck?" Kar muttered.

The tall Vampire spun around and Lavos lunged, grabbing him by the neck. The white-haired Vamp struggled to right himself on the table but Kar was on him before he could manage, slamming him flat.

"Soldier," Kar confirmed. "What about that one?"

Fear was easy to read on the scrawny face as Lavos pinned the tall male against the wall, crushing his throat to keep him still. He stared into his bloodshot eyes. "Soldier too." His eyes glowed and he punched into the soldier's mind, not feeling an ounce of pity for the one who'd threatened to rip out a woman's throat and watch her choke on her own blood. "Where is Mitch?" He eased his hold so the thing could talk.

"I'm Mitch," the man quickly confessed.

Lavos lifted him off his feet, slamming his head into the ceiling. "I'm talking about the one who turned you."

His nose started to bleed. "I don't know."

"Ask that one," Lavos urged Kar.

"Where's Mitch, the one who turned you?"

"Right there," the white-haired man whispered.

Lavos turned his head, looking at his friend.

Kar shrugged. "I'm confused."

Lavos glared at the soldier in his grip, easing him down a bit but staring hard into his eyes, forcing his will on the bastard. "Did you turn others?"

"Yes."

"Son of a bitch," Kar muttered. "I didn't know they could do that."

"Me either." Lavos took a deep breath. "How many did you turn, Mitch?"

"Four."

"I'm starting to get a damn headache," Lavos admitted. "Who turned *you*?"

"He never told me his name. He was injured on the road and I stopped to help him. He grabbed me and bit into my neck. Then he had me drive to a house in this area. He took my blood and forced me to drink some of his. I passed out, but when I woke a couple hours later, I watched him drink from the two people in the house, and he made me feed from them too. I was tired afterward and went to sleep. When I woke again, he was gone. I knew he was a Vampire, and he turned me into one. That's what we do. We turn others who are worthy of being Vampires."

59

"Where did you pick this guy up from?"

"Near Pick. I go out there with some friends to get high."

"This is fucking great," Kar cursed. "Some Vamp created a moron he left behind to take out a small town. I want to find this bastard."

Lavos tried to think. "Shit."

"What?"

"We missed a Vamp in that raid."

"You mean when we went after the asshats who took Veso?"

"Yeah. An injured Vamp who wanted a ride to the nearest town? Think about it."

"Damn."

Lavos dropped the tall soldier then slammed him hard against the wall, damaging it in the process of knocking him out. He reached into his back pocket and removed a set of reinforced specialty handcuffs. He dropped the bastard on the floor and none too gently flipped him over, securing his wrists behind his back.

"We're going to need a detailed description to track the Vamp. I wonder if he paid any other towns a visit?"

"Fuck. We could have a shitload of soldiers making other ones. It's a nightmare. What about this one?" Kar kept the other Vamp secured on the table.

"Kill it outside."

A slight noise drew Lavos's attention and he peered down the hallway. The sight of the woman staring back at him—from behind bars—came as a shock. It looked as if the room was somehow caged.

Her brunette hair was long, untamed waves, her light blue eyes wide. He lowered his gaze to take in the black shirt revealing some appealing cleavage. His attention wandered to a narrow waist that flared out at hips wrapped in snug jeans.

The handgun she pointed at him at that height kept his focus, plus the fact that she had two more guns holstered to her body.

"Who are you?"

He recognized her voice. She'd been the one giving the two soldiers verbal hell. He flicked his gaze back to her eyes. "Lavos. I'm law enforcement. Are you okay?"

Her blue eyes narrowed and her luscious lips curved downward. "Try again, handsome. This time keep it real. You tossed that dickhead around like he was a marionette doll after the dozens of bullets I put in him couldn't keep him down."

She thought he was attractive. Lavos smiled. That was the first bright spot of his evening. He stepped over the unconscious soldier—but paused fast when she lifted the gun, aiming it at what he estimated would be his heart.

"Stay back." She turned her gaze on Kar. "That used to be my dad you have on that table. I'm not sure what the hell to call him now, because he's not the man I knew. I'd appreciate it if you could hold off on dragging him outside to kill him just yet. I'd like to know who you two really are first."

She'd witnessed too much and had become guarded. Lavos didn't blame her. Intelligence shone in those pretty eyes of hers and he hated to do it, but he needed to find any remaining soldiers before they attacked other innocents.

He allowed his eyes to glow as he stared at her, waiting for her to look back at him. She did, and he saw her shock when she instantly noticed the change in his eyes.

"It's going to be fine. You can trust us. We aren't here to hurt you. Put down the gun and stay where you are. It's safe. Lay down on that bed in there and take a nap until you hear my voice again. I want you to have peaceful dreams about your favorite childhood memory."

Chapter Four

Jadee had missed seeing them enter but she'd heard it all. She'd dropped the comforter that had shielded her from flying glass shards cutting her skin when Mitch had begun his rampage of showering her with anything breakable he could fling at the bars.

The biker and his pal wearing the trendy club threads had handled the Vampires as easily as if they were rag dolls. They were both in shape, with those muscles and thick bodies. Both of them looked like contenders for fighting. Often.

The biker wore black leather pants with a matching muscle shirt stretched over a buff body. Dark stains on his chest were probably blood, and he had some on his hands. His blond hair almost hit his shoulders and it had some curl to it. He had gorgeous hair. She doubted they were Vampires, with the deep tans they both boasted. His good looks were model worthy, but he had enough masculinity not to be a poster child for any of the magazines she detested. He had to be about six foot two and probably two hundred and forty pounds of solid muscle.

His eyes were stunning, with their bright blue color, but with the way they glowed as he spoke, Jadee was assured he was something not natural. No human could do that.

Those eyes were gorgeous enough to almost make her stop listening to what he said, but the words penetrated.

"I'm not tired, and why don't you start telling me what you are?"

His lips parted and she studied his mouth. No fangs showed, a good sign in her book. He had nice teeth, white, and it looked as if his parents had sprung for braces. His mouth was the only part of his face that became unattractive when he clamped his lips together into a tight line, showing off a faint dimple in his chin.

Her gaze rose to once again appreciate how odd yet striking his incredible eyes were. She'd bet they'd literally glow in the dark.

"Shit," his friend whispered.

"Shut up," the biker snapped, never taking his gaze off her.

She raised her other arm and pushed back her hair from one side of her face where it had fallen forward. His nostrils flared and those eyes of his seemed to grow brighter. They reminded her of a blue neon sign over the bar at her job.

"So, what are you, Bright Eyes?" She was ready to leap back if he came at her. "I'm racking my brain here but coming up blank. Those kickass boots you're sporting are at least a size fourteen but you aren't hairy enough to be a Bigfoot, and you're too tan to be allergic to the sun. That's a bad joke. Sorry. I'm trying to remain calm."

"My name is Lavos." He watched her closely. "You're bleeding."

She ignored the blood siding down the side of her face near the ear her hair had been stuck to. "Tell me something I don't know—like what you and your friend are. Not human, with those sparkler eyes and that super strength. Aliens maybe? Please don't be that. I laugh at those people who say they've spotted little green people. Of course, you're not little or green, but you see where I'm going with this. No ass probes either. Not my thing."

Club Threads got her to glance his way when he chuckled. He smiled and she was glad to see his eyes looked normal. She stared at the biker again.

"I'm glad that your friend thinks this is funny, but I don't. I'm having a real bad night, Lavos." She used the gun to tap the bars. "I'm claustrophobic on top of it all, and armed. Not a good combo. Plus, there's the whole horrendous thing with my dad. Start telling the truth or I'm going to see how many bullets it takes to put you down."

"We're not aliens," he stated.

"Good."

"We're really law enforcement, but not one you'd know about. I tried to embed suggestions into your mind but you have a very strong will."

"Is that why your eyes are doing that mega-bright thing? Stop it."

She was relieved when his eye color returned to a nice-looking blue that didn't freak her out.

"You're better off not asking questions," his pal said. "The more you know, the more dangerous it is for you. We have laws to follow."

"I said shut up," Lavos growled. It was a very animalistic sound, reminding her of a guard dog.

It was a hint that Jadee jumped on. "Werewolves?"

Both men looked at her in an alarming way that had her taking a step back. "Okay. I like dogs. Wolves are good. I can handle that way better than aliens." She focused on Lavos. "Please tell me that if you kill the master Vampire, it will return my father to normal...or is that movie bullshit?"

He was either brave or stupid, she wasn't sure which with her gun still pointed at him, but he took a step closer. His shoulders were broad enough that both sides of them nearly brushed against the hallway walls.

"I'm sorry, but there's nothing we can do for him except stop him before he tries to kill again."

His statement dashed her hopes. "You don't know for certain if he's killed anyone."

"It's irrelevant. Everyone in this region is dead except you and perhaps a few others, if they were lucky enough to find sanctuary. This bunch did it. It needs to end before they travel to another town and kill *those* residents. There's no way to cure or bring him back from this."

That news devastated Jadee, but she believed him. "There are at least three more that I've seen, plus my dad and the one you have on the floor." She stepped back and sat heavily on the bed, placing the handgun on the mattress next to her. "Do it." She lowered her head, staring at her lap. "Please don't make the one who used to be my father suffer. He was a good man. He wouldn't want to live at the cost of innocent lives being taken."

"Jadee!" Victor sounded outraged. "Don't do this, honey!"

She winced and wrapped her arms around her waist. Pain squeezed at her heart but she didn't beg the two strangers to release what used to be Victor Trollis.

"Take him outside," Lavos ordered. "You heard her. Make it fast and don't allow him to suffer. I'll be out in a few minutes. Wait there."

"Okay," his friend replied.

Jadee closed her eyes, hating to hear the sounds as her father was removed from the RV.

"He wasn't a Vampire."

That soft, masculine voice had her peering up at Lavos. He'd come closer, right to the edge of the bars to grip one of them with his hand. His other one was hidden behind his back. She should have been afraid but she

66

didn't jerk away, pretty certain he couldn't reach her. She had nowhere to hide if he possessed a gun. She said nothing, waiting for him to speak.

"He was a soldier."

"He said he was a Vampire."

"Vampires can create these kind of halflings they call soldiers. Do you want to know more?"

She hesitated, stood, but kept back from him. "Not really."

He frowned. "Why not?"

"I heard your friend. Knowledge is dangerous, right?"

He moved slowly, withdrawing his hand from behind his back. She held her breath, expecting him to point a gun at her, but instead he fisted a plaque her father had kept hanging in the hallway. "Explain this to me."

She knew the words inscribed on it, since she'd been the one who'd bought it. "What do you want to know?"

He glanced down at the writing, then back at her. "Best Bump-in-the-Night Hunter? What does that mean?"

"I was ten at the time, and didn't know how to say paranormal-slash-legend tracker." She shrugged. "That's what my dad did. He and his research team searched for things like you and that asshole who changed him into a monster."

She didn't miss the way Lavos seemed to slightly pale. He returned her gift to her father to its hook on the wall. He kept his back turned away while he took a deep breath. It made her once again notice his broad shoulders. He slowly faced her. The grim look on his features didn't bode well for her.

"That's why you were in the area? Hunting for Vampires? Were you looking for anything else?"

"You mean Werewolves? No. I'm not a part of my father's team." She paused, realizing her dad had to be gone by now. "He called me a couple weeks ago and begged me to come visit. I had to arrange time off from my job and caught a flight this morning. I got a rental and drove here. I made it right before the sun went down, and he showed up a little bit ago the way he is now. Was. Whatever. The dad I knew was dead by the time I got here." She shifted her stance and got a look at Mitch. "The dickhead behind you is moving. Don't those things ever stay down?"

Lavos spun, took a few steps, and made Jadee wince when he brutally brought his boot down on Mitch's head. She swore she heard bones break but no sympathy welled. Lavos returned to the gate as if he hadn't just bashed in someone's head.

"He's not moving now."

She had to give him points for having a sense of humor, twisted as it was. "You didn't answer my question. How do you kill one of those things?"

"Remove the head and it dies forever. What were they investigating?"

She debated answering but he'd saved her ass. At least for the time being. "From what I understand, someone reported seeing Vampires. They came to check it out but they lost contact with their source on the way here. The team captured four of these things but then they somehow managed to escape. I'm not clear on all the details. That moron on the floor got ahold of my dad after that. The rest of my dad's team is locked inside a trailer they use as a headquarters for these little hunts. They're alive—or were recently, when I spoke to them via a tablet." She hesitated. "It's on the table behind you in the kitchen area."

He walked back down the hallway and lifted something. She couldn't see around his body but he turned, holding the electronic device so she got a good view. It was smashed, the screen shattered. Her father had probably broken it when he'd been thrown onto the table.

Lavos dropped it and returned to the gate. It was unsettling to watch his expression harden and his eyes start to glow again. But the sight was equally fascinating.

"You can remove your weapons and lay them all down."

"Not a chance, and your eyes aren't working on me."

The corners of his mouth curved upward for a second. "It was worth a try."

"Are you going to kill me?"

The seconds of silence had her guts twisting. He finally shook his head. "I see no reason to if you help me."

"I'm not opening that gate across the door. No way, no how."

"It would be difficult for you to help me otherwise. Have you seen the fifth soldier? We located a man and woman in the woods, then what used to be your father, and Mitch behind me. That's only four. You said there were five. One is missing."

"I got a good look at three of them when they were attacking the research team in their trailer. I saw the feeds from their cameras. Then those same three came over here to try to get into the RV before I hit the panic button. They took off after that. High-pitched sirens don't seem to be

69

their thing. Victor and Mitch didn't show up until after that. I could describe the three I saw to you. Would that help?"

His mouth twisted into a grim line. "They recorded these attacks?"

She debated telling him the truth but decided to be honest. "Yes."

"Shit."

"Are you going to kill me and my father's team? Last I saw, all three were scared shitless and only wanted to get out of this mess alive. They bit off more than they could chew, pun intended."

"I don't like to kill anyone unless I absolutely have to."

"So what's the verdict on *this* mess?"

"I like you."

"Is that going to save my ass?"

He seemed to relax a little and the harsh expression faded. "That depends on a few things."

"Name them." She didn't want to play games.

"We have laws."

"That's what Club Threads said."

He looked perplexed. "Why do you call him that?"

"Open pirate shirt, slacks and black shoes. He looks like he belongs at a dance club in Miami or something, instead of out in the woods."

He laughed. "His name is actually Kar. Our laws are clear. We can't allow the outside world to know about us. You're smart enough to understand why."

"History," she muttered. "You don't want idiots coming after you, trying to burn you alive. Witch hunts, only the Werewolf updated version."

70

"Exactly. But with modern weapons it would be a lot worse than being tied to a pole and lit on fire. You're taking all of this extremely well."

"You obviously can't read minds or you'd know I'm freaking out on the inside. But it's not a nightmare I can wake up from, and I'd like to survive. That means keeping my shit together."

Lavos stared at her and gripped the bars with both hands. She tensed, expecting him to test their strength. He didn't tug or jerk on the metal though. Instead he loosely held the bars between his fingers.

"We don't kill your kind unless they pose a threat. We protect them from assholes like the one on the floor stirring behind me, or the Vampire masters who made him. Keeping our existence a secret is priority number one. Do you pose a threat to me and mine?"

His words and their meaning sank in. "I see no reason to ever tell anyone what actually happened here tonight. I've heard about Vampires since I was a little girl, and you won't find any news footage of me being interviewed about their existence. I...I'm also pretty sure I've seen a few over the years. I got the hell out of dodge."

"Excuse me?"

"I used to love to go dancing, but not after I thought I'd spotted a couple Vampires. They're hard to distinguish unless you know what you're looking for. I decided club hopping wasn't good for my health, to be on the safe side. I didn't even tell my dad. He and his team would have gone after them—and gotten themselves killed a lot sooner. Live and let live is a good motto. I *still* can't believe they found any out here in the middle of nowhere."

"Your father wanted to prove their existence, right?"

"Yes."

"But you didn't? I find that hard to believe."

"You didn't have my childhood. It was hell. Everyone knew what my dad did for a living. They made fun of me. I was always the freaky kid with the nutjob for a father. I like having a normal life and not being the poster child for weirdness. Is that so tough to understand? The last thing I want is for more people like my father ending up with his fate. I kept telling him it was dangerous." Pain rose and she fought tears. "Look where it got him. That wasn't the man who raised me that you saw. My dad would have done anything to protect me, but that thing wanted to hand me over to the dickhead behind you. He's trying to crawl toward the door, by the way."

Lavos released the bars and strode back down the hallway, grabbing Mitch and hauling him to his feet. He pushed him toward Jadee but stopped at the bathroom. He shoved him inside.

"Stay put and be still or I'll rip your fucking head off." Lavos closed the door, then addressed her. "I'm hoping your father's team aren't immune to my eyes. I can wipe their memories and send them safely home. I'll need to destroy any evidence they have too. Otherwise there's no guarantee how this is going to end. They do this for a living in hopes of proving our existence, but you see the problem with that. I would like your help."

"What do you want me to do?"

"I'd like for you to talk your father's team into calmly meeting me."

She was immediately leery. "You could kill them."

"Your immunity to my eyes is very rare. I'm hoping they're able to be memory wiped." He blew out a breath. "I don't want to kill anyone except bad guys."

72

"I don't trust you," she admitted.

"You don't have a choice. You're intelligent. There's no cell signal in this area so you can't call for help." He touched the bars. "These wouldn't protect you if I really wanted in. That gun would hurt me but I'd survive. You saw how fast those things heal. I'm stronger."

She swallowed hard. "I don't have silver bullets."

He grinned. "That's cute."

"I take it that's a bullshit TV myth too?"

"Bullets hurt no matter what they're made of but I have no allergy to metals." He reached up and gripped a chain around his neck, lifting it from beneath his shirt. A thin silver ring hung from it. "Want to guess what this is made of? It belonged to my grandmother. I wouldn't keep it against my skin if it burned."

She stepped closer but kept out of his reach if he put his arm through the bars. "You actually expect me to open this up so nothing's between us?"

"I'm willing to trust you to keep your silence. You're going to have to trust that I won't hurt you. We need to work together if you want to save your father's friends."

Jadee studied his eyes, trying to judge if she could believe him. It was a tough call. "This is going to suck if you're lying to me."

"I'm not a bloodsucker."

"You know what I mean."

"I promise I won't hurt you."

"What about Club Threads?"

"Kar takes orders from me."

"Can I keep the guns?"

He glanced down at her weapons, then back at her. "Fine, but I'll warn you now that I have no sense of humor when I get shot. Am I clear?"

"Crystal."

"Just the ones in the holsters."

She gave him her back and walked to the other wall. Her heart felt as if it wanted to jump out of her chest. She hesitated over the release button—but then pushed it.

Jadee turned, her entire body tense.

The gate slid open.

Lavos didn't lunge forward, but instead calmly stood there regarding her. "Let me grab this asshole and we'll go outside. We need to find the last soldier. I'd advise you to stick very close to me in case it attacks." He backed up. "And I strongly suggest you start calling Kar by his name. He's been a bit testy tonight. We didn't expect this mess when we were sent out to bring a message to a family that hadn't contacted their mother. We thought a storm must have taken out a few telephone poles."

It was tough to take the first step toward the open doorway. Lavos turned his back on her, opened the bathroom door, and reached inside. He jerked Mitch out and shoved him forward.

"Run and I'll kill you," Lavos threatened.

Jadee wasn't sure if he spoke to her or the dickhead in front of him. She followed anyway.

Chapter Five

Jadee was relieved she didn't spot Victor's body when she climbed down from the RV. Lavos kept a tight hold on Mitch about six feet away. His friend stood alone nearby.

Kar jerked his head in her direction. "What are you going to do with her?"

"Nothing. She's going to help us save more people." Lavos shook his prisoner. "Where's the other one you made?"

"I don't know," Mitch hissed. "Who did you kill?"

"A woman with long dark hair," Lavos stated. "Kar? What did yours look like?"

"Dark hair, a man, shitty breath and bat-shit crazy."

"You're looking for a blond guy," Jadee supplied. "Dark shirt and jeans."

Lavos turned his head, peering at her.

She shrugged. "I said I saw them. One of them was a blond."

"Where's the research team?"

"I'm not sure." She hated to admit that. "I barely found my father's RV from the directions he gave. They always set up in two locations but never too far apart. It will be on or near a road. The trailer they use is towed by a big rig. No way did they take that on uneven or unpacked ground without risking getting it stuck in softer soil or tipping it over. They travel with two other RVs but they're smaller, not like my dad's. Peggy and Mark would have driven those. They used to have a tow car hooked to one, along with this one." She paused, thinking. "Brent would have driven the big rig that pulls the large trailer."

Lavos shook Mitch again. "What direction?"

"I'm not telling you."

"Big mistake," Kar muttered.

"You're not a Vampire." Lavos leaned in, yanking Mitch hard enough to drop the other man to his knees. "You're a soldier. Do you know what that means?"

"I'm a *Vampire*."

"Wrong." Lavos released him with one hand.

Jadee watched as he opened his free hand and his nails grew, shock coursing through her. She managed to smother a gasp and remain still, regardless of the urge to turn tail and rush back inside the RV to lock herself in.

Lavos gripped Mitch's shoulder and dug those claws into his skin.

Mitch screamed. Lavos jerked his hand back, wiping his bloodied claws on the back of the soldier's shirt. He leaned down a little but spoke loud enough for her to hear.

"Every time you're hurt, your body heals too fast. That's the difference between a Vampire and a soldier. Your system is feeding off itself to repair any injures. It makes you go insane faster. Between the bullets she put in you and what I've done to you so far, you'll be lucky to remember who you are by tomorrow night. Am I clear? I could keep going until you totally lose the ability to think anything at all, and then I'll remove your head. You won't come back from *that*."

Mitch looked afraid. "None of that is true."

"Oh, it is." Kar nodded. "Have you noticed those tiny veins across your skin and the blood in your eyes? Vampires don't have those. You're like a hyped-up version of them, but you weren't meant to survive as long."

"Vampires fully heal from injuries but they do it more slowly," Lavos explained. "You recover too fast to mend properly, causing a permanent breakdown of your body in the process. Your mind goes first."

Mitch moaned. "Why would he do this to me?"

"Because Vampires are assholes." Lavos jerked Mitch to his feet. "Take us to where this other group is or I'll have no reason to keep you alive. Don't you want me to go after the bastard who turned you? That means you need to remain sane long enough to tell me everything you know about this asshole, right after you take me to this camp."

"North." Mitch raised a hand, pointing toward a hill. "Right on the other side of that, next to the river. It's probably a mile away."

"Will the blond one you turned be there?"

"Probably. We've taken out everything else in this area. He's got to be hungry."

"Every*one*," Lavos corrected. "They were living beings."

"They were food," Mitch spat.

"What an idiot," Kar muttered. "Shut up and walk, Mitch. You don't want to piss off my friend. He likes humans." He flashed a look at Jadee. "Obviously."

Jadee hoped that was true. Her situation had become dire but it could still get worse. It was possible Lavos had lied to her. She wanted to survive until dawn and make it home at some point. That meant she needed him to keep his word. The guns with ammo still strapped to her didn't make her feel safe.

"Let's go," Lavos said. He pushed Mitch forward.

Jadee wished for a flashlight but her eyes adjusted enough that she felt secure about not walking into a tree. The moon was out enough to show shapes. It also helped that she followed behind Lavos. His friend stayed at her back but she refused to glance over her shoulder. It took a bit for her to relax enough to stop expecting him to do something bad...like stab her in the back with his claws.

They reached the top of the hill and she made out a dark shape that looked like a river flowing into a valley. Kar stepped to her side and pointed. "I see the trailer."

She followed the direction of his finger, squinting a little. It was the black shape of a box a few hundred yards from the water. "I see it too."

"Take hold of this one," Lavos ordered. "I'll help her. The hillside looks steep."

"I can carry her down," Kar offered.

Jadee jerked away from him, not willing to let him touch her. Lavos made an aggravated sound.

"I said take hold of this one, Kar. Now. Keep a firm grip on him. He's stupid and keeps trying to jerk away from me. He obviously hasn't figured out that it would be easy for me to chase him down."

Kar moved away from her, toward the other men. He grabbed Mitch by the back of his neck and the stockier shape of Lavos pulled away, advancing on her. He paused just feet away.

"I don't want you to fall or trip." Lavos spoke softly. "I'm guessing your vision isn't very good right now. Mine is excellent. There's lots of loose rocks and vegetation to trip over going down this hill. Will you allow me to get you down safely?"

"What do you have in mind?" She was still leery but taking a header down the hill didn't sound appealing.

"I'll carry you."

It almost made her laugh but she had a feeling he was serious. "I think I'm a little big for that."

"No you aren't."

"Take my hand and tell me if you see a tripping hazard."

"That's going to be too slow." He stepped closer. "Let me carry you in front. Wrap around me. I can walk easily that way if you just tuck your face against my neck so I can see."

To Jadee, that seemed too intimate.

"Can we get a move on?" Kar sounded irritated. "Decide on something. I'd like to get this over with before someone else dies."

He made a good point. Mark, Peggy, and Brent needed help. There was still one of those things running around. She stepped closer to Lavos. "Are you sure I'm not too heavy?"

Kar snorted. "He's not human, sweetheart. He could toss you about twenty feet without breaking a sweat or pulling a muscle. Carrying you down a hill is nothing."

"Enough," Lavos grumbled. "Don't scare her, Kar." He reached out and touched her arm.

79

She startled and he pulled his hand away.

"I'm not going to hurt you, Jadee. I am a man of honor."

Is he a man? Are Werewolves human? At least the blood on him will be dried by now, I hope. But does it matter?

Nope.

She reached up and carefully placed her hands on his shoulders. They were wide and solidly packed with muscle. He was also like a furnace, putting off a lot of heat. She cleared her throat, nervous. "Okay."

He gripped her hips and lifted. She felt incredibly awkward as she spread her legs and her chest hit his. She did as he'd asked her to do, wrapping her thighs around his waist. He was so warm and firm. Big too. He released her hip to wrap an arm around her middle and adjusted her a little higher. There was no denying his strength.

"Tuck your head," he whispered. "I've got you."

She turned her head and tossed her hair so it wasn't in his face as she pressed closer, until her nose touched his warm throat. She hated that she noticed the soft traces of his cologne. It wasn't one she identified but he smelled good. He shifted his other hand and braced his forearm under her ass. Jadee clenched her teeth, not protesting.

He started to walk and it rubbed their bodies together. She closed her eyes and hoped he could see as well as he'd implied. To fall and have him land on top of her would suck. He was a large man and everything about him seemed hard. She didn't feel any flab on him—and she would know, being this close.

"Can I take a picture of you with her? I doubt anyone will believe me when I tell them about this." Kar laughed.

"Shut up," Lavos ordered. "Keep your phone in your pocket and don't let go of that asshole."

"You're no fun."

"Stop giving her a bad impression of us." Lavos gave her a gentle squeeze around her middle. "We really are law enforcement. It's just that we joke around to handle the stress."

"It's okay." She understood.

"Good."

Rocks slid, the sound of them falling a bit scary. Jadee wrapped her arms tighter around his neck. She didn't want to choke him but the sound of them smashing into other rocks far below frightened her. To die from falling would be a horrible way to go, but better than having her throat torn out by Mitch. She needed a distraction.

"Why does your friend want to take a picture?"

Kar answered first. "Lavos holding a human in his arms is priceless. I'd win so many bets." He laughed. "He was always a little too understanding of his brother and Kira."

"Who's Kira?" she asked, curious.

Lavos sighed. "Enough. Hold on. I need my arms."

He reached up for something and his entire body tensed. He jumped— to Jadee's terror—and she felt as if they were swinging for a second, before they fell. He landed with a jarring impact but his arms wrapped tight around her so she wasn't torn away from him.

"Are you okay?"

"What was that?" She was afraid to look to see for herself.

"A five-foot drop. I had to jump out and grab a branch to avoid landing on a boulder below."

"Never mind." She didn't want to know.

A male shriek started but it cut off abruptly when a heavy weight smashed into something next to them. Jadee gasped, lifting her head and opening her eyes. She couldn't see when she tried to make out what had been the cause.

Lavos sighed again. "You had to throw him? Come on, Kar."

"I'm jumping down." Something else landed next to them and it sounded heavy. "I wasn't going to carry him in my arms." Kar chuckled. "*He's* not cute. Get up, fang boy. Next time, try to land on your feet instead of your head."

"You son of a bitch," Mitch whined. "That hurt."

"Aw," Kar muttered. "What happened to the badass attitude I heard when you were threatening a woman? You're not so tough now when you're dealing with us, are you? Move."

"Don't squeeze so hard. You're going to break my neck," Mitch protested.

"I don't trust you to be smart enough not to run and I'm done chasing shitheads tonight," Kar responded. "We're almost to her people."

Jadee twisted her head and peered toward the water. She saw the dark shape of the trailer. They were farther down the hill than she thought they should be.

She looked up over Lavos's shoulder, seeing the shape of the hill. There was only one tree she could spot above. He lied to her. He had to have jumped more than five feet. It was more like twenty. It gave her chills that anyone could do something like that so easily. It wasn't supposed to be possible but they weren't human.

Lavos walked and she buried her face in his neck, easing her hold around his shoulders. She wanted to freak out but she would do that later. The danger wasn't over and she didn't have the luxury of being able to freak until she was back in her rental and on her way to the airport.

Lavos admitted to being impressed that Jadee was dealing with everything so well. He had expected absolute terror and crying from a human. He kept walking until they reached the back doors of the trailer and he bent a little, relaxing his hold on her.

"We're here," he whispered. "You can get down now."

Jadee released his hips with her thighs and slid down him until she stood. Her arms were slower to let go. She backed away and turned, almost walking right into the back of the trailer. He reacted fast and hooked her around the waist to stop her.

"Easy. It's right in front of you."

"I can't see all that well."

"I can." He felt bad for her. It must be tough to be human.

Jadee cleared her throat. "Mark? Peggy? Brent?" Her chin lifted to stare up at the top of the doors. She lifted one hand, waving it. "Can you see me? Will you please turn on the outside lights if you have them?"

Floodlights lit up from the top of the trailer. Lavos closed his eyes, temporarily blinded. He let go of Jadee's waist and retreated a few steps, blinking to adjust to the brightness. Kar uttered a curse but said nothing more. Lavos glanced at him and saw he gripped Mitch by the back of his neck, keeping him far enough away from Jadee to prevent the soldier from reaching her.

Jadee adjusted her raised arm to shield her eyes from the direct light. "Thank you. I couldn't see anything. I know you're probably worried that I've been made into a Vampire but I'm not." She turned, glancing at him. "They'll be afraid that happened to me."

A soft click sounded and a man's voice with an accent came out of a speaker from somewhere on the underside of the trailer. "Who's with you?"

"The cavalry." She faced the trailer, looking up again. "They saved me and captured the Vampire. Is this tall freaky guy one the Vampires that escaped from you a few days ago?"

"Yes. Where is your father?" It was a woman who spoke.

"Dead." Jadee pointed at Mitch. "That asshole turned him. I let my dad into the trailer but he wasn't the man we knew. I was locked in the cage but then these two showed up. This is Lavos and Kar. They're real Vampire hunters."

That stunned Lavos. He couldn't believe she'd just said that. He schooled his features though. It was obvious there were more cameras. Jadee knew about them, and the location of at least one, since she stared up at something. He couldn't see past the lights to get a clear enough view of the top of the trailer.

"Did you say Vampire hunters?" It was the man with the southern accent.

Jadee nodded. "Yeah. They saved me." She reached up and pulled her hair back, showing off her neck. "See? No bites. I'm still me. It's safe to come out. They won't let the Vampires hurt you. You can open up."

"This is weird," Kar muttered.

"We're not going to do that," the man announced.

"Son of a bitch." Jadee lowered her arms. "Come on, Mark. Stop being such an asshole. What is it going to take to get you to believe me? You're rescued! I'm half tempted to get in my rental and just leave your ass locked inside that container until you starve. Be thankful I like Peggy and Brent. I would never do that to them." Jadee glanced at Lavos over her shoulder. "Can you think of a way we can prove to them we're not Vampires?"

Lavos glanced at Kar. His friend looked as grim as he felt. Lavos bent and yanked up his pant leg, grabbed hold of the dagger strapped to his ankle and straightened. His brother would have a fit if he ever found out what he was about to do in front of cameras, but he needed to get inside that reinforced box to destroy the evidence.

"Yes." He shot another look at Kar. "Hold him tight. He's about to get agitated." He motioned for Jadee to move farther away from Mitch. "You shot him a few times and he hasn't fed." He looked up to the top of the trailer, wondering about the humans inside. "Watch."

He cut his left palm, making sure they could see the exaggerated grimace on his face since a human would probably burst into tears. He wasn't about to go that far but it did hurt to draw a thin, three-inch line across his palm. He opened it, showing everyone the blood.

Mitch sniffed and his eyes widened. He hissed a second later, mouth open and fangs showing. He struggled in Kar's hold, frantic from the smell.

85

The noises he made were animalistic and loud. His hunger had to be causing him agonizing pains.

"Switch your hold on him and give me his arm," Lavos ordered Kar.

His friend jerked Mitch back and got him in a choke hold, making sure his fangs weren't close enough to his skin to bite. Kar twisted his captive and exposed his left side.

Lavos advanced and ripped Mitch's sleeve at his shoulder, shoving it down, then used the dagger to slice open a good six-inch cut above his elbow. The soldier shrieked. It was probably more from hunger and frustration than actual pain. Lavos was glad he'd handcuffed the soldier or he would take any blood source, even cannibalize himself. It sometimes happened with soldiers when they were starved. They'd bite themselves to get blood. He also wanted the humans to have a clear view.

"Watch how fast he heals."

The cut sealed within seconds.

Lavos looked up, trying to gauge where the camera was. "See?"

He backed up, showing his injured palm again. It had stopped bleeding but the cut remained. Nothing could heal as fast as a soldier unless fresh blood and feeding were involved. "I'm not what he is. Kar isn't either. We hunt these things down and stop them. This one is going to lead us to his master so we can take him out." Lavos put away his dagger.

"Happy, Mark? Legend and paranormal hunters, meet actual Vampire hunters." Jadee glared up at the top of the trailer. "Open the damn door. Otherwise I swear I'm going to have them escort me to my rental and I'll just leave you here. There's one more still on the loose. The blond guy

86

hasn't been caught. How long can you stay in there without starving or going crazy?"

Long seconds ticked by, and it irritated Lavos. He didn't have time for bullshit. They did need to find the blond and take him out. They also needed to hunt down the master. He didn't want to babysit the soldier during the day and have to find a safe place to store him so he didn't burn to death. His brother would be worried if they didn't make contact soon. Lorn would send reinforcements. The last thing he wanted at that moment was more of his clan to show up. He liked Jadee but he couldn't guarantee others would be willing to trust her word that she'd never say anything about what she'd seen. And her mind was too strong to wipe...

A bolt slid from inside, then another. Metal scraped as one side of the door opened an inch. He backed up and jerked his head at Kar to do the same with the soldier. Jadee wasn't so cautious. She advanced and curled her fingers around the edge of the door, pulling it back.

Jadee paused. "Are you shitting me?" Then she shoved the door wide open so he could see inside.

Two men and one woman stood inside holding twelve-inch crosses in front of them. Two were made of wood and one looked metal.

Jadee brushed her hands on her pants and gripped her hips. "Wow. I would have packed crossbows and arrows if I'd been you. My eyes aren't burning, guys. I told you, I'm not a Vampire."

Mitch tried to twist out of Kar's hold and avoid looking inside the container. Lavos wanted to roll his eyes. The idiot probably thought crosses would work on him. They wouldn't, nor would they work on pure-blooded Vampires. He kept his mouth shut.

Jadee released her hips and started to climb inside the trailer. He was tempted to stop her but didn't want to frighten the humans. He spotted a few guns on a desk near one of the men. They could shoot Jadee if they panicked.

"I'm going to walk right up to you and touch that thing," Jadee announced. "So you're sure."

"Let me see your teeth," the man with the accent demanded.

Jadee straightened and opened her mouth wide. She stuck out her tongue after she'd given him a few seconds to see that she didn't have fangs. "You're such a dipshit, Mark. No fangs." She approached them, her hands out to her sides. She paused in front of him and slowly lifted her arm. She pushed a fingertip against the wood.

"See? Not a Vampire. I know I don't get a lot of sunbathing in with my night job, but do I look pasty-ass white like the freak outside?"

The woman was the first to lower her cross. She burst into tears and grabbed Jadee, hugging her. "We were so worried. We heard the gunfire and the tablet went dead. We thought they'd killed you."

Jadee hugged her back. "It's okay, Peggy. We're safe now. These guys are going to take us to the truck I rented and I'll drive us out of here." She untangled herself from the woman and backed up, glaring at the man with the accent. "You can lower the cross. You look ridiculous." She glanced at the other man. "It's okay, Brent. These guys killed a few Vampires but are just holding on to that one until they find the master."

"Where's your dad?" the older woman asked.

"He's in a better place now," Jadee answered.

"I need to gather our hard drives and samples." Mark lowered the cross.

"You do that." Jadee glanced at Lavos and winked.

He managed to hide his surprise. She was smart. The man named Mark began to collect things off a desk. That would save Lavos time. The second man, Brent, dropped the cross on the floor. He turned, helping the other one gather their evidence.

"I'm going to take the important data and then lock up the trailer. We'll have to come back in the morning." Mark seemed to be the one in charge. "We'll document everything. We'll bring in Richard Smith and his team. They'll help salvage as much as possible." The guy suddenly turned, staring at Kar. "Could we keep that one? I mean, as evidence? To turn over a live Vampire would prove to everyone they exist."

Kar looked at Lavos. "Um…"

Lavos took control of the situation. He wasn't sure how to respond either. No way would they ever allow that to happen but he needed the humans to relax. "Maybe. We might be able to work out a deal. Vampire hunting can be expensive." Humans liked greed. They understood it.

Mark smiled. "Jadee will pay."

"Excuse me?" Jadee gasped.

Mark glared at her. "Your father is dead and he funded our trips. That means you're in control of the money now. I know he has you on all his accounts and listed as half owner of everything. Pay them whatever they want for that Vampire. Do you know how important this is?"

"Yes." Jadee didn't look happy. "I do." She glanced at Lavos. "But he needs to talk to you first. You know, about the other Vampire on the loose and what happened here."

That was his cue. "I'll talk to them one at a time," he hinted. "So I can get each of their stories. It will help us track the missing one if we get as many details as possible."

"Good plan." Jadee nodded.

Mitch struggled in Kar's hold. "We already broke free from them once. I'll do it again!"

"Shut up," Kar muttered. "You're an idiot."

Lavos hid a smile. He shouldn't be so amused with the situation but he couldn't help it. He watched as the human team collected their belongings. Jadee walked to the back of the trailer and he realized she planned to climb down. He advanced and reached up, holding her gaze.

"Let me."

She only hesitated for a second before she leaned over, placing her hands on his shoulders. He gripped her hips, easily lifting her and placing her on her feet. She didn't seem afraid of him anymore.

"They're all yours," she whispered. "Please don't hurt them. I'm trusting you." She backed away, letting him go.

He waited until the older woman tried to leave the trailer. It stood a good four feet from the ground. He stepped forward, offering to help her out too. She smiled at him and allowed it.

"You're a strong one." She blushed a little when he set her on her feet after lifting her down. "I have a hundred questions to ask you."

"Okay."

"Is it like a family business or did something happen to make you hunt Vampires?"

He hesitated. "Family business."

She looked excited. "How many generations?"

"A few."

"You're like the books!" She grinned. "I want to interview you at length. Can we do that?"

"Sure," he lied. "Do you mind moving so I'm not staring at those bright lights? They're giving me a headache after tracking Vampires in the dark for the past few hours."

"Sure." She stepped around so she faced the trailer instead of him. He turned with her, putting his back to the two humans still moving around inside it. He held her gaze, allowing his power to surge. Her eyes widened in surprise as she watched the blue of his eyes begin to glow.

"Shush," he murmured. "Relax." He was going to have to kill her if he couldn't get inside her mind.

Her features slackened and she didn't make a sound.

"You're safe," he assured her. "Repeat that and speak in a very soft tone."

"I'm safe," she whispered.

Someone stepped closer and he inhaled Jadee's scent. She surprised him when she spoke.

"Is it working on her?"

"Yes."

"Good. I'll watch them and give a warning when they're ready to leave."

She kept close to him, making it appear the three of them were having a discussion. He appreciated it. He needed to focus on Peggy. Kar had his hands full with the soldier.

"You came here to look for Vampires, right?"

"Yes." Peggy suddenly looked frightened. "There were four of them."

He executed a little more force and deepened his voice. "No, there weren't. You arrived here and didn't find anything." He held his breath, waiting to see how she'd respond.

The fear vanished. "We didn't."

"You saw a few bears. A storm came and you parked too close to the river. That's the most frightening thing that happened. The water started to rise and you couldn't get your vehicles out in time." He paused, needing to build a memory for her that would make sense. He'd take care of the trailer and any other evidence in the area.

Jadee put her hand on his arm. "There is a tow car and a rig around here that pulled the trailer, plus the two smaller RVs and the larger one that belonged to my dad. They were all messed with. Maybe you could say she caught a cold and slept a lot. It's best if she thinks she was out of it most of the time from a high fever."

He nodded, letting her know he heard what she'd said.

Not only did Jadee help him do his job but she gave him helpful suggestions about what to put in the human's mind. His admiration for her grew.

92

Chapter Six

It amazed Jadee how easily Lavos manipulated Peggy. His eyes glowed that neon blue and Peggy ate up everything he said as if it were gospel. It left her feeling a little uneasy but it would save the team's lives. She could live with Lavos messing with their memories.

So far he'd kept his word. He said he'd wipe their minds and that's what he was doing. He wouldn't waste his time if he planned to just kill them after all. She gave him more details to help him fill in any gaps she could think of. He was good, coming up with a story to explain how they'd lost their vehicles and the trailer. She cringed a little on the inside. All that money her father had spent would end up at the bottom of the river.

She watched Mark and Brent making extra copies of the videos they must have taken. They put the USB flash drives into their pockets. She'd have to tell Lavos about that. Her father would be disappointed in her for not helping to protect his research, but it had gotten him killed. She didn't want to see that happen to the rest of his team.

"Can you do me a favor?" She leaned closer to Lavos.

He paused in talking to Peggy. "What?"

"Can you tell her this fiasco was an eye opener and she's ready to retire? I don't want them chasing after anything again. She's talked about buying a cabin in Tennessee forever. Brent is her brother. He wouldn't do this without her. There's no changing Mark, since this is who he is, but Peggy loves him. Tell her she's tired of his bullshit. He doesn't deserve her anyway. He hasn't married her in twenty-five years. Can you implant the idea that she's fed up enough to leave him finally?"

"You're sure about that?" He turned his head to peer at her.

His eyes were gorgeous. "Yes. Please. She's like a mother to me. I hate how Mark treats her. She *does* deserve better. She needs to find a man who cares about *her* instead of what he can get her to do for him."

He looked away, staring at Peggy again. She felt relief as he whispered, repeating what she'd said almost word for word. Jadee gave him a little space and approached the trailer to keep the guys distracted. One glance at Kar assured her that he still had a handle on Mitch. She hated that freaky bastard and felt no sympathy for him.

"Make sure you get everything," Jadee called out. "You're representing my dad. This was his big find."

"I know." Mark sounded annoyed. "It's *our* find though. We share the credit."

She rolled her eyes. "Spare me."

"We're going to have to hire tow trucks to locate and pull out our vehicles." Mark didn't even bother to look at her as he checked the sample case he opened. "And we have to buy a new rig to pull this trailer. I want your father's motor home. *You* sure won't use it."

Jadee grit her teeth. "Do you want my bone marrow too, Mark? Maybe a kidney?"

He paused and lifted his head to direct an annoyed look at her. "You know how important this was to your father. Just because he's dead doesn't mean this is over. You also know I can't afford to buy you out. Most of the equipment is owned by your dad."

"Got it. You could at least try to kiss my ass a little when you want something instead of barking out demands."

His anger took over. "I *told* your dad to put me on his accounts and on the titles instead of you so this wouldn't happen."

"Always the asshole, aren't you?"

Brent, the peacemaker, got involved. "He's just upset. It's been a traumatic few days. He doesn't mean to sound so cold, Jadee. You know we loved Vic. We're all grieving."

She believed that. Her father's team was closer to him than she had ever been. It left her feeling a little bitter but she'd swallowed that pill a long time ago, when she'd chosen to live with her grandmother. Her dad could have retired then and stayed with her. He'd kissed her goodbye instead and hit the road. It was little comfort that he'd made sure she was taken care of in case he died by ensuring she had access to his money and putting her name as co-owner on anything he bought.

Lavos approached her side and she looked at him. He gave a slight nod of his head then climbed up inside the trailer. "I need your attention."

Jadee backed up and turned around. Peggy stood motionless a few feet away, her eyes closed.

Kar came closer, keeping Mitch in a chokehold. "She's fine. He put her in a kind of sleep trance while he talks to the other two. He'll bring her out of it when he's done. She'll only respond to his voice until then. She can't hear us."

She hoped Lavos could do his mind magic on the guys and faced the trailer to see how it went. Lavos stood motionless, talking to Brent. "Is it working?"

Kar hesitated. "It seems to be."

"Good."

"Lavos is strong. I'm not good with that shit. I don't have the experience to mess with planting information into minds but he deals with humans more often."

She was interested. "He does?"

"I was never allowed to go on missions far from home, but he has. We test our powers when given the chance. You never know when it's going to come in handy."

A lot of bad scenarios played through her mind. "So you can have sex with women and then make them forget?"

Kar crinkled his nose. "Hell no. Why would we want to do that?"

"Easy sex. You're a man."

"I'm..." He paused, looking uncertain.

"A Werewolf," she supplied.

"We don't have sex with humans. It's frowned upon. We stick to our own kind, and they're immune to mind control."

"Why? Can you accidently transmit what you are to others?"

He shook his head. "No. It's just that..." He hesitated again, glancing down her body.

"What? Will you stop doing that? Spit it out."

"You're too damn fragile." He held her gaze and winked. "I'd break you."

It was her turn to study *him*.

"We're stronger than we look and we'd have to hide what we are. Laws, remember?" He shrugged. "That's the truth. We don't mess with humans or hang around them unless we have to. Our contact is very limited."

"So you just live with other Werewolves in your pack?"

He moved his arm from around Mitch's throat and grabbed the top of his shirt, forcing the jerk to his knees. He gripped the back of his neck. "Try to move and I'll break it. Got it? I'm tired of smelling you." He gave his attention back to Jadee. "Something like that. Are you going to screw us over and tell someone what went down here?"

"No." She meant it. "I'm going back home and forgetting everything. I'll never have my face plastered on the cover of some crazy magazine, right next to the guy who swears he has a three-headed love child with an alien chick."

He chuckled.

"Who's Kira?"

His amusement faded. "Forget that name. You heard Lavos. He didn't want me to say anything else."

"I take it she's human, and you said she was with his brother."

He glanced at Lavos, then her. "Look, I like you, so I'll share this much. Just don't tell him I said anything. Kira's father is one of us, but he mated a human. She was born mostly human without many traits. It made her life a living hell, dwelling with our kind, because weakness is looked down upon in our culture. Is that enough info to curb your curiosity?"

Not by a long shot. She held her questions though. So it was possible for Werewolves and humans to have kids, just not popular or sanctioned by others of their kind. That meant they were sexually compatible.

She stared at Lavos. He was one hot guy.

Dangerous too, and totally not someone to get involved with, she reminded herself.

Jadee shivered. It was growing colder. "How many hours until the sun comes up?"

"Not long enough," Kar muttered. "Summer means the sun isn't down as long as you'd be used to, living in the lower states. We still have to deal with this mess, get you and them on your way, and then track down the blond soldier. We also have to get details from this one about the Vampire who made him. That's one bastard who needs to be stopped."

"Yeah. What went down here? Does this happen often?"

"Never. This is a first. Vampires usually avoid us at all costs. We didn't even know soldiers could make other ones. Apparently, they can. That's disturbing as hell."

She glanced down at Mitch. He seemed paler and a little lethargic. "He's not looking so hot."

"He smells worse. He's been hurt a lot and he's hungry. The longer they go without blood, the crazier they get."

"He seems tame at the moment."

"That's because he knows I'll snap his neck. He'll heal but without a fresh source of blood, it's weakening him every time. I can smell the rot taking hold."

"Rot?"

"His body is feeding off itself and he can't heal fast enough to compensate. His eyes and skin show what he is. His internal organs will look worse. He was made about nine days ago, from what we can figure, by a vampire who'd been part of a nest we took out. And soldiers don't last long without a master Vampire feeding them just enough of their blood to keep them from decaying from the inside out. This one is on his own. He's been feeding off humans but still, it's not enough."

"So he'd die on his own eventually?"

"Worse. They can last months that way but it isn't pretty. The mind is gone but the body isn't. They go after anything living and are totally driven by bloodlust. We call them ghouls at that point. Some human probably saw one once and wrote a zombie story about them. Their skin rots off but they continue to move around. They do get sluggish and slow when they hit that point. It's horrific. Eventually they're so weak and messed up that they usually forget to find shelter before the sun rises. It roasts them. They don't usually turn others though, like in your movies. They take blood, not give it. But this one figured out how to make more of them. That's bad."

She'd never watch another zombie movie again without thinking about Mitch and the others. "Fantastic."

Kar nodded. "Exactly."

"I'm glad I don't have your job if you get to track them down."

Lavos jumped down from the trailer, startling Jadee. She looked at him.

"I put them in a trance until we get them out of here. I'm sorry, but I told them your father tried to save his RV and was washed away down the river. It will explain why they don't have a body."

"I can't bury him, can I?"

He shook his head. "No. Sorry. We'll have to dispose of his body at first light by exposing him to the sun. He was newly made so there are remains until then."

That hurt. "I understand."

Lavos stepped closer, getting in her personal space. His expression softened. "His body will turn to ash in the sun, as if he were cremated. I'm so damn sorry about this, Jadee. You're taking it well."

"It still seems a bit unreal," she confessed. "I'll let it all sink in later and then I probably won't be so okay. I foresee heavy drinking in my near future. Don't worry. I'll do it when I'm alone. I won't tell anyone what happened here."

"You deserve to get drunk. I told them that you came and found them. We'll return you to the truck and get you on your way." He reached out and his hand hovered near her shoulder. He didn't touch her though. He dropped his hand away in the end. "Are you going to keep your word?"

"I will." She held his gaze. "Check their pockets."

He turned away, returning to the trailer.

Jadee blinked back tears. It was almost over, and she just had to hold on a little longer. Then she could fall apart. Her father was dead but she and the others were going to live. That was the important part.

"Jadee?"

She turned her head, staring at Kar. "Yeah?"

"He won't be the one who comes after you if you betray us. Creatures from your worst nightmares will pin a target on your back. You'll have Vamps, Werewolves, and everything else you never want to meet determined to kill you. You'll also get him in deep shit. He's breaking the rules by letting you go with your memory intact. It could mean Lavos being severely punished. He's risking a lot. Do you understand?"

"I do."

Kar studied her.

"I do," she repeated. "I'm never going to tell anyone what happened here. I heard Lavos. My dad called me and I came to visit. I found those three stranded and the river killed my dad. That story won't ever change."

"Good."

Jadee believed Kar and what he said would happen if she ever opened her mouth. She wasn't that stupid. A single night in close contact with Vampires had assured her she never wanted a repeat experience. Once had been more than enough. It would give her plenty of nightmares.

* * * * *

Lavos knew Kar worried about whether they could trust Jadee. He silently admitted his own doubts about depending on a human to keep silent. Kira had been raised with his clan and was trustworthy. Jadee was an unknown, but he thought highly of her spunk. He was almost sorry to say goodbye. He really did like her.

The truck started when he turned the key after reconnecting the battery, and he climbed out of the cab to stand beside Jadee. "It still works."

"At least that went our way. I can't believe those bastards disabled it. Mitch probably did it while my dad was trying to talk his way inside the RV. It will teach me to always lock the doors in the future, even if I'm in the middle of nowhere."

"Drive down this road until you hit the highway. Don't stop for anything. There's a soldier still out there. I doubt he went that way since I found his trail leading toward town. You hit the highway and go right. That will take you in the opposite direction."

"I don't plan to stop until I'm out of Alaska unless I need gas. I was going to fly home but you said you need time to clean up this mess. Driving will waste some days. I can't wait to return to Washington."

"That's where you live?"

"Yeah."

Kar sighed. "I'm getting tired of holding this one. Can we get them on the road? I bet Garson is done with his task and we could use him here. We also have to find the other soldier."

"I know." Lavos didn't look away from Jadee. "Okay. Drive safe and don't stop until you at least hit a larger town. Don't talk to strangers."

She smiled. "Especially pale ones."

He grinned back. "Yes."

She licked her lips and he watched her pink little tongue. The urge to kiss her struck, surprising him. He stiffened, every muscle tensing.

It was probably because he'd carried her and her scent had rubbed off on him. It had been a while since he'd been that close to a woman. The hunt always made him a little horny too. He resisted his instinct to reach out and pull her closer. It was a bad idea.

"Thank you." She glanced at the three still humans. "Too bad I don't have your power. I wish I could keep them like that for the rest of the trip. They're going to argue and bitch. Did you leave them their wallets? We have to cross into Canada and then back into the US. The last thing I want is to be held up at the borders. An unplanned road trip with them is going to be bad enough to deal with."

"Yes."

"You cleaned out their pockets?"

"I asked them to hand over all evidence. They did."

"Okay."

She surprised him when she suddenly leaned forward and wrapped her arms around his waist. The hug was unexpected and fast. She released him and backed up before he could react.

"Good luck and be careful. Did you implant them with the suggestion to wait until we were back in the US before they filed any reports?"

"I did. They're in a sense of shock from your father's death. The authorities should believe that."

"All the bases are covered." She sighed. "Okay. I'm out of here. Thank you." She turned away, climbing into the front of the truck. "Can you ask Peggy to sit with me in the cab and have the guys climb in the back? I don't want to hear them rambling on or bitching about how cramped four of us are on a bench seat. Mark annoys the hell out of me."

He nodded. "Yes."

"Thanks."

She closed the door and he turned away, walking over to the waiting humans. He told the men to climb into the back, that they wanted to sit there. The woman meekly entered the passenger side of the truck.

Lavos backed up and watched Jadee drive away.

Kar shoved the soldier forward and paused at his side. "I hope that wasn't a mistake. You know how risky it was to let Jadee live."

"Where is your compassion?"

103

"Not in my pants."

He growled, narrowing his eyes at Kar. "What the hell does that mean?"

"Give me a break. You wanted to jump on Jadee. You kept sniffing her and staring at her ass. When's the last time you got laid if you were interested in that? I admit she was sexy, but you know better. You were thinking with the head below your belt instead of the one above your shoulders. She couldn't be wiped, Lavos. That makes her dangerous."

"She wasn't a typical human."

"You hope. She was pretty cool and I was impressed by how she handled herself, but she could turn on us."

"She won't."

"I hope not. Our asses would be in deep shit."

"Nobody has to know what happened here."

"I'm sure as hell not going to rat you out. I'd be in trouble too. I let it go down."

"Thanks."

"You should have at least nailed her. I would have."

"Shut up." Lavos turned away, sniffing. "I have a soldier to track. Jadee said he was here. You interrogate that one and get every detail about his maker that you can. I'm tired of dragging him around."

"You're not the one with the cramp in his hand from holding on to him. Next time I'm bringing a leash. What happened to just killing them outright? This one has gone into some kind of catatonic state. It's disturbing."

"Show a little blood and that should snap him out of it to get answers. We need to find the one who did this and make sure it doesn't happen again."

"I know. That's why I haven't killed Mitch here yet. Go track down the blond soldier and I'll get the information we need. I'm hungry. Grab me something if you can."

"Live food?"

"Anything. I missed dinner. I didn't think this was going to be an all-nighter."

"I want my handcuffs back." Lavos handed over the key, then walked the perimeter. "We took out the two that went that way. This one headed back toward town."

"Go."

The faint smell of death helped him track the soldier. He followed it toward the town...but then the scent indicated it had changed direction. A bad feeling sank in.

It headed toward the highway.

"Shit."

Lavos snapped his head up and began to run.

What if the soldier decided to attack any cars on the highway? They seemed stupid, but it was possible one of them wasn't. He and his pals had cleared out the small town of any life. His only blood options had been locked up where he couldn't get at them. That meant Jadee might be headed right into a trap.

He took a shortcut toward the highway.

One soldier could easily attack and kill four humans. They were fast enough to catch a vehicle if it was traveling slower over old roads before it hit the highway. The fact that she was driving a truck made it worse. The soldier could jump into the back and then go through the glass to take out the driver.

It was tempting to shift but he wanted to keep his clothes on. He came across the winding dirt road and entered the woods again to take a direct path to the highway. He didn't see or hear any signs of the soldier or the truck—

He heard a crash. It was a loud, echoing crack, as if something had hit a tree hard enough to split a trunk.

A horn sounded next.

Jadee!

He ran faster, tearing at his shirt to get it out of the way. He didn't care if she saw what he really was, as long as she was alive by the time he reached her. He'd tear the soldier apart if he hurt her.

He opened his mouth, sending out a war cry. It might scare the soldier. Garson and Kar might also hear him and come to his aid, but he doubted it. Garson was too far away and Kar had his hands full with Mitch.

I'm coming, Jadee.

Chapter Seven

Jadee gripped the wheel with both hands. The twisting dirt path someone had dubbed a road needed major repairs. She had to drive slow to prevent jostling the passengers in the back, easing over a big pothole. The highway was just up ahead.

She glanced at Peggy. She worried about her state of mind. She hadn't talked at all since she'd climbed into the cab.

"How are you holding up?"

"I'm hanging in there. I'm so sorry about your dad, honey." Peggy sniffed. "He tried to hook up the rig to the trailer to save it but the water rose too fast."

"It's okay." It was a better story than the truth. She wished she could forget seeing Victor after his attack. Her dad hadn't stepped inside the RV. It had been a stranger with his face and voice.

"It's all gone."

Jadee regretted trying to get Peggy to talk. "It's going to be fine."

"No. Everything is over. We should have stopped investigating this stuff years ago. I'm just so sorry. It shouldn't have ended this way. I'm going to buy that place in Tennessee and try my hand at gardening."

"That's good."

"I don't think Mark is going to give it up. I've been thinking a lot about our relationship lately. I need a change."

Lavos is good. She had to give him credit.

"Do you think it's just the grief talking? I mean, we've been together for so long but I'm just not happy."

"You deserve better." It wasn't the first time she'd said those words to the woman. "Mark is a tool."

"He kind of is, isn't he? I can't believe he still plans to continue without Vic. It just isn't right."

"That's Mark. You should retire and plant a big garden."

"That's what I think too."

"Brent should go with you."

"I'm sure he will. He's as heartbroken as I am over the loss of Vic."

Jadee sped up when the road finally straightened out, spotting a sign warning of upcoming cross traffic. She blew out a relieved breath. They'd hit the highway soon and get the hell out of dodge. *Or Weirdville*. She forgot the small town's name but it might as well have been that. *They have Werewolves.*

"Do you think the guys are too cold back there? You should have rented an extended cab, Jadee. I don't like that the men are in the back. It's kind of dangerous and I'm not even sure if that's legal."

"I didn't exactly foresee all of you needing a ride when I chose this. Dad said I should get something that would be okay off-road. This is what they had. As for having the guys in the back, this is an emergency. I'm sure Mark can rent a car and drive himself home if he doesn't like the truck bed. You and Brent can ride with me all the way back to Washington. We'll get you a nice flight home to California. Then you can go online to hunt for the cabin you always dreamed of."

"I really want to do that. It's important."

"Good."

Something ran into the road ahead of her. The headlights revealed the shape of a man with dark clothes and blond hair. He was directly in her path.

Jadee gasped, and her first instinct was to hit the brakes. She recognized him though as he turned to look at the approaching truck. It was the missing Vampire soldier.

She stomped on the gas instead.

Peggy yelled, "Stop! It's a man!"

Jadee could see him—and planned to run him down. Three thousand pounds of metal slamming into him would at least hurt him enough for them to get away.

Peggy reached across the cab and grabbed the wheel. Jadee hadn't expected that.

It happened fast. She had her foot all the way down on the gas, barreling at the monster trying to stop them. Peggy yanked hard and the wheels hit another pothole. The truck rocketed off the road to the right and the tree seemed to just suddenly appear in the headlights. They hit it hard.

Something smashed into Jadee's face. It threw her back and she slammed against the seat. The horn blared. It cut off fast and Jadee opened her eyes, seeing the air bag deflating that had exploded from the center of the steering column. The headlights were still on, despite the engine being dead. One of the lights pointed up from the hood, crushed at an angle against the tree.

Something was on the hood, and it moved.

Mark groaned, shifting his legs.

Jadee was horrified, realizing in an instant that he'd been thrown forward during the crash, probably hit the tree, and had fallen onto the hood. It was too dark to make out how severe his injuries were but he was alive.

She turned her head, seeing Peggy sagging in her seat. Her belt had kept her in place but the dash over the glove box revealed the other air bag had deployed.

Something moved in the back, bumping against the glass between the cab and the truck bed.

"Peggy?" It was Brent. "Oh shit."

Jadee remembered the blond monster about the time the truck was suddenly jarred. It felt as if something landed on it hard enough to shake the entire thing. Brent made a horrible gasping sound and the truck shifted again.

She turned her head but it was too dark to see. The glass cracked when something hit it. Jadee made out clothing for that flash of an instant.

She was pretty sure Brent's body had just been used to spider-web the glass between the cab and the bed of the truck.

They were under attack.

Jadee frantically reached for her belt to release it, fumbling. It clicked open, releasing the pressure from around her waist. She stared at Peggy's form in the dim interior lights from the dash that were still on. The woman's head remained slumped but her chest moved. She was alive but unconscious.

Someone stomped on the roof of the cab. The metal protested and she looked out the windshield, watching as the blond stepped down onto the hood. He bent, grabbed Mark by his arms, and lifted.

Mark screamed but it was cut off as the thing attacked his neck. Red splattered the windshield. The soldier was killing him right before her eyes, drinking his blood.

Jadee blindly reached over and hit the lock button. It wouldn't keep that thing out for long but it was all she could do. Her wrist brushed across metal and leather, reminding her of the holster strapped there, and the gun.

Peggy moaned, probably coming around. Jadee couldn't look away from the horror taking place on the hood. Mark's legs kicked out, jerking, but the thing had a firm hold on him. The red drops that had stained the windshield were slowly rolling down the glass, reminding Jadee of bloody tears.

Shocked into action, she struggled to get the gun free from the holster. Her left shoulder hurt, probably from the seat belt. She ignored the pain, glad her right hand wasn't injured. She tugged the weapon free, realizing she'd have to shoot through the glass to hit the soldier. She paused.

Mark wasn't moving anymore. The thing just dropped his body and turned.

She couldn't make out the face of the monster at first. The lights were behind him. He shoved Mark right off the hood, crouched down, and peered inside. That close to the glass, his white face was ghastly with dark veins marring the surface. Blood covered his mouth and chin, running down his throat.

She lifted the gun higher, making sure he could see it.

He hissed and was suddenly gone, jumping off the side of the hood.

That made it worse. She frantically glanced around, looking for the blond. It was just too dark to—

Something slammed into the driver's side window. The glass held but it was damaged. The thing punched at it again, making a hole.

Jadee pointed and fired three rapid shots. She yanked on the handle, twisted in her seat and kicked the door as hard as she could. It flew open and hit him, knocking him on his ass. She got out fast, keeping her gun on him. "Fuck you."

He hissed at her, lifting his head. She could make out his face and those fangs. She shot him right in the mouth.

The impact sent him crashing flat to the ground. She swiftly dropped on top of him, straddling his chest, and grabbed his throat with her left hand, digging her nails in.

He choked a little, probably on the blood from the bullet wound through his mouth, rather than from her weak attempt to strangle him. She shoved the gun right below his nose. "Move and I will keep shooting until the top of your head is gone, you murdering bastard."

He jerked once but held still.

Jadee was terrified. He would heal. She'd seen them do it. One of his fangs was gone though. She'd managed to hit it when she'd shot him. Lavos's words came back to her. She'd give anything to trade her gun for a sword to behead the bastard. It wouldn't get up ever again if that were the case.

A loud sound pierced the night, a combo between a howl and some kind of banshee scream. It sent chills down her spine and the thing under her grew totally lax.

"What was that?" She doubted he'd answer her but she still felt the need to ask.

He tried to shake his head, a reminder that she had a firm hold on him. But she was too afraid to let him go. He moved too fast. He could come at her from any angle if he got out from under her. She kept the muzzle of the gun pressed tight to his skin, surprised the primal scream hadn't made her shoot him. No one could blame her for being jumpy.

The thing under her grabbed her leg and she fired instinctively. The bullet tore into his mouth and he bucked under her. It almost unseated her, so Jadee squeezed her legs as tight as possible around his rib cage and dug her heels a little under his hips. She prayed she had more bullets as seconds ticked by while he began to heal.

"I said not to move, dumb-ass."

He made a sickening gurgling noise in his throat. She lowered the gun to right above where her thumb split from her fingers, placing it tight under his jaw.

"You don't have a brain so let's go through your neck to your spine. That put Victor down for a few minutes. Do you know what you *can't* come back from, asshole? Having your head taken off. While you're out, that's what I'll do. There's a shitload of glass around here thanks to you. Don't move again."

She'd have to do something soon. "Peggy?"

The woman groaned from inside the truck.

"Damn it, Peggy!" Her voice rose. "Wake up. I need you."

"Jadee?"

"Yes. Get out of the truck."

"I'm hurt."

The man under her suddenly tensed and grabbed at her again. She fired the gun and he went still, his arms dropping away.

"What was that?" Peggy's voice seemed a little more alert.

Jadee knew the blond would recover fast. They'd both be dead if Peggy didn't do what she asked. "I need you to find something sharp, maybe some metal in the front of the engine area."

Peggy needed to find her something she could use to behead the bastard. It was a disgusting thought but she wanted to survive that bad. She already regretted not carrying a knife or something else sharp enough to cut with.

"Peggy! Damn it, find something sharp and get over here. We're dead if you don't."

"What happened?"

"*Peggy!* Do what I said!"

It was promising when she heard the passenger door open, since she couldn't see inside the cab from the ground just next to the engine area, where she'd jumped on the blond creature.

"Hurry, Peggy."

The thing under her began to recover. She felt his body tense.

"Don't attack me. I'll shoot you again," she warned, just hoping she had another bullet left. She'd lost track of how many she'd fired and she

114

didn't have another spare cartridge. Otherwise she would have already reloaded just to be certain.

"Where's Brent? Mark?"

"Find something sharp, Peggy. Hurry up, damn it!"

"Who was that man in the road? Did we miss him?"

Jadee's frustration swelled. Peggy seemed to be moving around the back of the truck, taking her sweet time.

"Brent! *Oh my God!*" Peggy wailed. "He's here! I found him. He's not moving, Jadee!"

The thing under her picked that moment to buck wildly, and it knocked Jadee off his chest. She slammed into the ground and pulled the trigger just as her other hand tore free from his throat.

The gun clicked but it didn't fire. There were no bullets left.

I'm screwed.

Pain exploded in the side of her face and she realized he'd smacked her. It hurt like a son of a bitch and she struggled to breathe. It felt as if her cheekbone could possibly be broken.

She expected him to rip out her throat next—but it didn't happen. Instead a scream rose from Peggy. Either the soldier was going after her or she was freaking out about Brent.

The gun was still in Jadee's hand and she lifted it, trying to sit up. She couldn't just lay there or she'd die for certain.

Peggy's sobs came from the back of the truck. They were broken, raspy cries. Jadee managed to get to her feet and stumble in that direction. The gun was useless but she could hit the bastard with it. She was willing to club him but didn't think it would do much damage.

She froze when a new sound reached her, and she turned, wondering what other horrible thing was coming. It panted, whatever it was. Loudly. She braced for impact, gripping the gun tighter. It seemed to be coming right for them.

A big, dark shape suddenly came into view, dashing on all fours as it broke from the woods.

It wasn't a Vampire or a soldier. She wasn't sure *what* the hell it was.

It loomed bigger and she threw up her free arm, trying to protect her face and throat. The impact would probably kill her. She even closed her eyes, not wanting to see any more.

The thing passed by so close she felt it brush her leg.

I'm still alive.

She opened her eyes, the image of that beast stuck in her mind. *Werewolf?*

She'd glimpsed something shiny hanging around the thing's throat. The memory of the necklace she'd seen with a silver ring hanging from the chain flashed through her head next...

Lavos!

A shriek hurt her ears, and snarling followed.

Something slammed into the truck hard enough to make metal groan.

Jadee tried to decide what to do. It only took her a second. She jumped inside the cab of the truck and dropped the useless gun. She closed the driver's door then lunged across the seat, having to stretch to close the passenger door. She got it shut and hit the lock button. Sounds of a vicious fight filtered into the truck, reminding her of the hole in the driver's side window, so she scooted over, getting far from the opening. She shoved the broken piece of what used to be the housing for the airbag on the passenger side out of the way.

It took effort to get the jammed glove box open and she gripped the metal flashlight the rental guy had pointed out to her. It was heavy and solid. It would help her see and she could use it as a weapon. She wished she had a shotgun in the truck.

She straightened, bumping her knee on the dash as she curled her legs up. She turned the flashlight on and twisted in the seat, trying to find the source of the fight. It definitely still raged, based on the repeated shrieks and snarls that filled the night.

Jadee found them. The big beasty thing was on top of the blond about twenty feet from the tailgate. It had the soldier pinned to the ground, one of its meaty arms swinging, claws slashing at the thing's throat. Blood sprayed across a nearby tree.

She watched until it was over. The blond's head actually rolled away from the torso.

The beast paused and stared her way. It looked like some kind of messed-up huge demon dog. It wasn't furry like a wolf and it had a more muscular body. She studied his shoulders. They looked more human in shape than canine. Her gaze traveled over the rest of his body. Those thighs were too thick to belong to a dog and he wore black underwear. The small amount of material hid the area between his hips to a few inches down his thighs. She also spotted a tail. The shorts in the back were lower than they should have been, probably to accommodate it.

And she'd seen correctly—a chain with a ring hung around its throat.

She glanced up at the creature's face again. It had the extended jawline and sharp teeth of a wolf but the eyes were wrong. They were more human looking. Their bright blue color and the fact that they glowed caused a sharp pain in her chest. *It is Lavos.*

Beasty version of Lavos stepped off the still body of the soldier and looked away from her, moving toward something out of the line of her flashlight. She moved the beam, following him.

Peggy lay face down and not moving.

Grief struck next. Peggy's normally blonde hair had been turned a bright red and appeared wet. It was blood, so much of it that Jadee knew she was dead without needing to inspect the body.

Lavos sniffed at her then lifted his head again, staring at Jadee. He did a very human thing by shaking his head slightly from side to side to let her know Peggy's fate.

Jadee turned off the flashlight and slumped in the seat. She didn't want to see any more. Tears filled her eyes. Lavos had saved her but no one else had survived. She'd heard Brent being attacked and watched Mark die on the hood of her truck. They were all dead.

Pain lanced through her as she hugged her knees and huddled on the passenger side of the cab. She didn't know what to do...and wasn't sure if she even wanted to do anything at all.

At least the blond monster was dead too. The last soldier had been found. She focused on that bit of good news.

Lavos checked on the three humans, or what was left of them. None of them had survived being attacked. He lifted his head and watched Jadee. She remained inside the truck, unmoving. He put off going to her as long as he could, and then shifted back before slowly approaching the driver's side door. He tried the handle but discovered it locked. He reached inside the broken part and grabbed hold of the inner handle, popping it open.

"Jadee? It's Lavos."

"I know."

He bent down, staring at her. Her eyes were closed, and she held a flashlight as if it were a child's toy, clutched to her chest with both hands. The interior lights of the truck weren't bright but he knew she could see him if she'd just open her eyes. *She might be too afraid.*

"I'm back to normal. It's safe to look at me."

She did. He expected to see horror or revulsion in her eyes, but not the tears. It made him want to climb inside the truck and pull her into his arms. He might have done it except he had blood coating his skin. He glanced down, grimacing at the sight. He probably looked just as bad in skin as he had while shifted.

"I was tracking the soldier into town when I realized he'd turned this way. I came as fast as I could. I had hoped you'd made it to the highway."

"I might have, but the blond jumped in front of the truck. Peggy grabbed the wheel." She released the flashlight with one hand, jerking her thumb toward the front. "I was intent on running that bastard down but instead got a tree."

He tried to make sense of it. He could see damage to her left cheek. She had struck her head at some point. It worried him.

"Running him down?"

"He stood in the middle of the road, probably thinking I'd stop. I stomped on the gas instead. I figured a three-thousand-pound weapon versus one shithead would be a win for the good guys. Why did Peggy have to grab the wheel? We could have made it. I know it. I would have run that bastard over."

Jadee once again proved she was braver than most. "He would have just jumped at the last second and landed on your truck instead."

"Oh."

"There was no real way to avoid this. I'm so sorry. Your friends are gone."

"I know."

"Are you hurt?" He leaned a few inches forward, trying to get a better look at her face. He didn't see any other injuries but she was kind of curled into a ball on the seat.

"He smacked me hard." She tilted her head to show him the red mark. "Better my cheek than my throat, right? I guess he figured I was down for the count so he'd go after Peggy first. Poor Peggy. She didn't deserve to die that way. It's my fault. I shouldn't have asked her to get out of the truck to find me something sharp. I thought I might be able to take off his head."

Her words stunned him, and it must have showed in his expression.

"I know. I was desperate and out of options. The front end was messed up good. I saw that much. I thought it might work to, you know...slash

120

through his throat. I probably would have had an issue when I hit bone, though."

She was in shock. It was obvious. He hesitated, not sure how to deal with that. He needed to get her out of the truck and somewhere safe. The motor home came to mind. It was the closest sound structure. He slowly reached for her jean-clad leg. He'd wiped off as much blood as possible in the grass before he'd shifted back.

"Jadee? None of this is your fault. You didn't kill your friends. That soldier did." She didn't flinch away from him when he curled his fingers around her knee. "We need to get out of here. Can you walk?"

She licked her lips. "I think so."

"Good."

"Are we just going to leave them out there? Will they turn into one of those things? I don't want that. Seeing Victor as a monster was bad enough. I couldn't take that. Maybe Mark. He was always an asshole so I wouldn't feel bad about having to kill him again, but Brent and Peggy would be rough."

"They aren't going to turn."

"You're sure?"

"I only smelled their blood on the bodies. Not his. He didn't try to change them over."

"Being bitten doesn't do it?"

"No. Otherwise the world be overrun with Vampires and soldiers, since they feed off humans. They have to exchange blood."

"Good to know."

She was so pale that he worried. "Did he bite you?" He sniffed but didn't pick up any blood coming off her from an open wound.

"Nope. I was just bitch-slapped by him."

"The motor home is a few miles back. That's where we'll go."

She shook her head, fear showing on her face.

"It's the closest thing to us. Kar is there too."

"So is Mitch."

"He's probably dead by now."

"Kar was going to kill him?"

"He's tired of dragging him around. We just needed every detail we could get about the Vampire who made him. I'm sure Kar was motivated enough to get those answers by now."

"I could walk to the road and hitchhike out of here. I'm sure a car would come by at some point."

"We don't know where the master went. He could be in the next town. That's why I suggested you not make any stops for as long as possible. It's not safe. I want you to survive this, Jadee."

She blinked back tears. "Yeah, I want that too."

"Let's go back to the motor home. I'm sure there's food there, and the soldiers couldn't break into it. It's a safe location. I have things to handle and not a lot of time."

"Clean up."

"Yes. I have to come back here to bury those bodies and dispose of this truck."

"It's a rental. I have to tell them I hit a tree, file an insurance claim and—"

"Stop." He halted her rambling. "We can't leave any sign of what happened. There's blood all over this vehicle. Don't worry about anything, Jadee. We'll handle it all. I'll send Kar to where I left my Jeep and he can drive until he gets a cell signal. More of my people need to come here to wipe away any traces of what really went down. We have some experience at covering all our bases, unfortunately."

"You're going to get help from more Werewolves?" Her heart rate increased and so did her breathing. "They'll come here?"

He wanted to correct her but didn't. It was better if she knew as little as possible. "That's why I want you inside the motor home. You're safest there. I'm going to have you lock in and stay there until they're gone."

"They won't find it?"

"I'll make sure you're safe. Are you sure you can walk?"

"Yes." She squeezed the flashlight she still held with one hand. "Can I bring this? I'm tired of being blind at night."

"Sure."

He didn't mind if that helped her cope with the situation. It would mess with his night vision a little but it would get her moving. Dawn wasn't far off since it was summer, and traffic on the highway would increase during the daylight hours. Someone could make a wrong turn onto the dirt road and come across the truck and the bodies. He couldn't allow that to happen.

"We need to go, Jadee."

"Okay." She straightened in the seat, turning on the flashlight. She opened the passenger door.

He hustled to reach the other side of the truck before she walked to the back section. He used his body to block her view of the carnage as much as possible. *He* didn't even want to see them again, and he'd been raised in an entirely different reality than she had. Violence and death weren't new to him.

She walked slowly but didn't complain as he led her back to the motor home.

Kar pushed away from the front of the RV when they finally approached. The soldier wasn't with him. His friend arched his eyebrows, staring at Lavos's underwear then at Jadee. He uttered a soft curse under his breath.

"Damn. You went after her? I thought I heard gunshots."

"The soldier changed direction and attacked them on the road before they hit the highway."

Kar winced. "Where are the rest of them?"

Lavos shook his head. He didn't need to say they hadn't survived or go into details. Soldiers were killers and they'd already seen what they were capable of.

"Your clothes?"

"I had to shift to run faster to get there in time."

Kar sealed his lips, not looking happy. He glanced at Jadee then Lavos again. There was a questioning look in his eyes.

Lavos nodded. Jadee had seen him when he'd changed forms.

"Shit. This just gets better and better."

"I'm taking her inside. Did you get the information we need?"

"Yes. Full description of the asshole who turned him. It's not a lot to go on though. The suckhead didn't spend much time with him or say much. No name was mentioned either."

"It's done?"

"Yes. His ass is ashed. I guess all those injuries he sustained helped that along, for one so new. No waiting for the sun to rise like the others."

New soldiers left remains behind unless they were rotting faster than normal. Jadee and her bullets had probably helped Mitch get in that shape, since he hadn't been able to feed. Full Vampires turned to ash when they died, but most soldiers needed to be weeks old.

"Give me a few minutes then we'll talk."

"Let's talk now. What's the plan?" Kar directed another glance at Jadee.

"She's going to stay here where she's safe. I'm going to return to where the truck is to take care of that location. I want you to get Garson. It's time to place that call to my brother. We're going to need some help with this mess."

"No shit. We've got bodies and we're going to need a few tow trucks. Do you think we should call Lord Aveoth too?"

Lavos shook his head. No way did he want the GarLycan leader involved. He'd never allow Jadee to return to her world with her memories intact. Since she seemed immune to mind control, the other options weren't good.

"Remember what I said about using the head above your shoulders to think with? I'm saying it again, my man."

"Shut up, Kar. Get Garson and drive until you find a cell signal. Call Lorn. I left the keys to my Jeep in the ignition."

"What do you want me to say to him?"

He paused. "Give him all the facts. Tell him I'm calling in that favor he owes me. He'll understand." He jerked his head. "Go."

Chapter Eight

Jadee felt better after showering. The RV had hot water but she wasn't sure how much longer that would last. She'd have to check the water tanks and batteries. The silence bothered her after Lavos had left her alone. He'd gone to take care of Peggy, Mark, and Brent's bodies.

She felt the worst for Peggy. She'd never have that garden or meet a man who truly loved her. Mark has been a user. Brent had been a devoted brother but he'd been as addicted to the hunt as her father. It had gotten all of them killed. It just proved to her that life was too short and it shouldn't be wasted.

She heated up a can of soup and forced it down. She hadn't eaten since grabbing a microwave burger at some gas station between the airport and her father's camp. She wore one of his button-down shirts. Her backpack was still tucked behind the passenger seat of the rental, all her spare clothes inside.

"Shit. I should have asked Lavos to grab it for me," she muttered aloud. It was too late. She'd have to keep borrowing clothes from her dad's closet or put on her dirty ones. The oversized shirt and the pair of borrowed men's boxer shorts she currently wore wasn't something an airline would appreciate.

Depression set in hard and deep. There would be no funeral for her father or his team. It would be easy enough to trace that she'd gone to Alaska. She'd have to talk to the authorities at some point. It would look suspicious if she never reported them missing, especially since she could spend her dad's money. He had put her on all his accounts. Families and friends of the team would eventually notice they hadn't heard from them either.

She glanced toward the stove. Lavos had been gone for about forty minutes. She wasn't even sure when he would come back. He'd demanded she give him the code to open the RV door. That conversation had been short.

"We have trust, remember?" He'd peered deeply into her eyes. "I'd have killed you already if I wanted to."

He had made a very valid point. He'd saved her ass a few times.

"I don't have time to waste. I need to leave. Give me the code and please don't bar the door from inside."

She rattled off the six digits and nodded, agreeing to his demands. She did have one of her own though. "Just you. I don't want you to tell Kar or anyone else how to get in."

"I wouldn't do that. You're a smart woman, Jadee. Don't open that door to anyone. Do you understand?"

Did that mean she was still in danger? Weren't all those horrific circus acts dead? Was something else lurking out in the woods that would kill her, besides bears? She didn't voice her concerns, already beyond her limit of stuff she never wanted to know.

"Yes. I understand."

He'd left then. She'd picked up some of the mess inside the RV that Mitch had caused with his fit of rage when he couldn't reach her inside the back bedroom. All the broken glass had been disposed of in the trash or vacuumed up. She'd done her best to clean up the bloodstains. The remaining weapons had been returned to their hiding spot in the closet before she took her shower.

Now, every minute seemed to pass at a snail's pace.

The slight beep startled her when it finally sounded, followed by the bolt inside the door sliding. Lavos entered without knocking. He closed the door behind him and she tried not to stare. He dropped something on the floor, distracting her from his body.

She glanced down. "My backpack."

"I found it in the truck."

She studied him again. He still wore just a pair of shorts. They were boxer briefs, made of some satiny material. Dirt coated his hands and almost every other part of his body. It didn't hide the fact he was all muscle and tight skin. She locked her gaze on his face to avoid staring at his abs.

"I'm going to borrow your shower."

Don't look down. "Okay."

He turned away. She watched his beefy ass as he headed toward the bedroom area. He had a firm one, not some flat bottom like most of the men she knew. She resisted the urge to lean over to watch him walk until he entered the bathroom. The door closed and the water came on within seconds.

She figured he wasn't going to like the tiny closet of a shower. He was too tall for the showerhead. He probably wouldn't even be able to bend to scrub his feet in the enclosed space. She'd had a hard time doing that and he was much bigger than her. She got up and passed the bathroom, entering her dad's bedroom.

Victor hadn't been nearly as tall as Lavos but her hero would need clean clothes. She found a pair of cotton gray sweatpants that would stretch to fit. The legs might fall a few inches short of his ankles but she knew he couldn't exactly squeeze into her father's jeans. She placed them on the bed and returned to the living room area.

The bathroom door opened and Jadee called out to him, "I put something on the bed for you to wear."

"Thank you."

She wondered if he walked those few feet naked into the bedroom or had a towel wrapped around his waist. It was tempting to peek but she held still. The bedroom pocket door rolled closed and she waited. It opened seconds later and Lavos came striding down the hall.

The light gray color of the sweatpants flattered his tan skin. He had to spend a lot of time outdoors to get that way. His hair was wet. All the dirt had been scrubbed away. He paused in the kitchen.

"Do you mind if I get a drink?"

"Help yourself."

He yanked open the fridge and took one of her father's bottled waters. He approached her and took a seat across the table. "It's done."

She didn't want to ask about the bodies. "The truck?"

"A casualty of a ravine. I covered it with brush. I doubt anyone will find it for years, if ever. We get a lot of abandoned vehicles up here. People break down on the highway or have accidents. It's too expensive to have them towed to a larger city in some cases. I did grab your purse too. It's outside, since some blood got on it. You can take out the contents but the bag needs to be burned later."

130

"Understood, and thanks. Any suggestions on how I explain a missing truck to the rental place at the airport? They frown on that shit."

He had such striking eyes, and it wasn't fair that a man got such big, stunning blue eyes. "You tell them it was stolen. I'll have one of our people grab a state trooper and a report will be filed. Be vague as hell. You weren't sure where it happened exactly. You had to pee, stopped on the side of the road, and it was gone when you came back."

"That makes me sound kind of stupid. Did I leave the keys in it?"

He chuckled. "Do you care what they think?"

"No. I left the keys in it but took my backpack because I spilled soda on me, wanting to change clothes. I'll say I pulled over on the side of the road to change in the woods. How about that rather than I had to pee? It sounds more believable. Nobody wants to keep driving if they soaked themselves with something sticky."

"Go with that. Say you flagged down a car on the highway and they took you to a state trooper who made the report. I'll have whoever grabs the official contact the rental company."

Jadee gave him the name and location of the one she'd used at the airport. Then they quietly studied each other. There was an elephant in the room and both of them knew it. Jadee wasn't a coward though. She liked to face things head on. The shower and food had helped her recover somewhat.

"So what happens now? How fucked am I when your people come?"

"They don't trust humans."

"I got that."

"You've seen a lot. Too much."

The food in her stomach suddenly made her a bit queasy. "So I'm toast? Is that what you're trying to say?"

"No." He sipped the cold water and set it on the table between them. "Lorn owes me."

"What does that mean?"

"He's my brother, and he now leads our people. I helped him save a woman once. Now it's his turn to help me save you. I'm not going to let you die, Jadee. I believe that you won't repeat anything that happened tonight to anyone."

"I won't. No one would believe me anyway. Hell, I don't even want to believe it. I'd like to just forget." She forced a smile. "Too bad your eyes don't work on me."

He didn't smile back. "That is unfortunate. You're the only human I've ever tried to wipe who ended up being immune."

"My dad always said I was the most stubborn woman he ever met." It made her sad remembering that memory. "I guess he was right."

"It makes you dangerous to my people."

"I'm not going to tell, Lavos. You'll never hear of me ranting about Werewolves."

He broke eye contact. "Good."

The silence stretched until Jadee reached out and brushed her fingers against the back of his hand. He looked up, staring at her.

"I won't, Lavos. You've made it clear and so did Kar. I don't want a target on my back by everything that goes bump in the night or day. My dad had an obsession with proving things like you exist. It got him killed. I'm smart. I also don't have a death wish. I'm going to return to Washington

132

and put all this behind me. I'll just be leery of pale people who come into my bar from now on."

"Bar?"

"I'm a bartender. Mostly we caterer to the blue-collar crowd. It's a small place."

"Blue what?"

She grinned. "People who do physical labor. No business suits. A lot of my customers come from the construction sites some blocks away or are locals. It's a decent area but not touristy. I've never seen anyone I thought might be a Vampire come in there. They'd stick out with all those tanned bodies taking up seats."

"Vamps usually hang out in largely popular spots where they won't be noticed."

"I figured. I told you I thought I'd spotted a few in some dance clubs. Do crosses work?"

"No."

"Holy water?"

He shook his head. "Decapitation is the only way to keep one down, unless you can burn it to ash. That's tough to do, since I doubt you'd be able to get one to walk inside a crematorium and lay down in the nice fire room for you. They'll heal otherwise. I once saw one recover from a house fire. He'd been burned badly but he recovered with some fresh blood and time."

"No wooden stake to the heart, huh?"

"The injury would heal around the wood and the Vamp would get up, completely pissed that you'd hurt it. They don't recover as fast as soldiers do unless they've recently fed. You'd have maybe two minutes to run if you did a lot of damage to it. They have heat-sensory vision and a great sense of smell, especially if you're bleeding. They'd be able to track you."

"Fantastic."

"Ever done any hunting?"

"No. It's not my thing to kill animals. I'd feel guilty. But I do know how to shoot."

"I knew that." He smiled.

She didn't return his smile, not feeling amused by their conversation. "Why did you ask if I hunt?"

"Learn about hiding your scent in case a scenario like that ever happens. Example? If you're ever attacked inside your home, grab a strong-smelling cleaning supply while the bastard is down and splash it around. It will fuck up their sense of smell before you run. It would make it tougher for him to track you and give you more time to escape."

"Thanks for the tip. I do have one more question."

"Ask."

Her gaze lowered to his necklace and the silver ring that hung against his chest. "Aren't you afraid you'll lose that when you turn into someone with four legs and a snout?"

He grinned. "I usually don't wear it if I'm expecting trouble but I can shift without the chain breaking. It took a few times to find one with the right length to accommodate my throat, regardless of my shape."

"Isn't it the same? I just mean I'd be afraid it would break when you're running around on all fours."

"My body thickens a bit more when I'm shifted, including my throat." He reached up and touched the silver ring. "It hangs here when I'm human but rises up a bit when I'm shifted." He shoved it up closer to his throat. "So no, it doesn't bounce around or touch the ground." He released the ring and placed his hand back on the table.

She glanced around, desperate to think of something to say when the silence grew between them. "Maybe I should see if I can fix whatever they did to the RV and drive this home. I might want to start living in it. It's reinforced and I'd feel safer sleeping at night here."

"City Vamps try not to kill when they feed. It draws unwanted attention. They just take blood from their victims and wipe their memories."

"Yeah. Hello. Immune. They'd kill me, wouldn't they?"

His mouth pressed into a tight line and anger narrowed his eyes. "Yes. They would."

"I figured. The whole keep-the-secret thing. So driving this beast home is my best option. It would probably save me more money renting a space for it in an RV park than what I pay for my mobile home. I don't own it. It's a rental."

"Your life is never going to be the same. I'm sorry about that."

"You didn't do this. My dad was the one who had to go chasing after paranormal creatures and spooky legends. I was dumb enough to come here to visit him."

"Why did you?"

She hesitated. "I hadn't seen him in about a year, plus I missed his birthday a few months ago. I felt guilty about that. He just sounded so

135

stressed and he'd already suffered one heart attack. I looked up where he said his camp was. There weren't any hospitals nearby. I was hoping I could talk him into retiring."

"I'm very sorry for your loss."

She appreciated that. "I kind of lost him a long time ago, but I *will* miss hearing from him every so often. I know he probably wouldn't have given this up. He didn't when I was a teenager. He just drove away and left me with my grandma."

"No man should leave his child behind."

"That's kind of what Grandma and I thought too. It is what it is though. Wishing doesn't make it so."

"At least you have her."

"She died a few years ago."

Lavos cocked his head, studying her.

"I'm a realist. I could bitch and whine about how unfair life is but what's a pity party going to do for me? Nada. I'd rather focus on the good stuff. Grandma loved me and she gave me a stable life for the years we had together. I needed that."

"Where is your mother?"

Jadee shrugged. "Honestly? I'm not sure. Dad refused to talk about her. So did Grandma. All I know is she took off when I was a baby after she met a guy. I never looked for her. I figured that was another lost cause. Why chase after someone who didn't give a damn about me? Who could just walk away from their own child? I wouldn't waste my time. As I got older, I kind of understood a little better why she left her husband. *I* couldn't even stick it out with my dad and his lifestyle. She should have taken me with her but didn't. Her new boyfriend probably didn't want to be burdened by me. I stopped being hurt over that a long time ago. It just wasn't worth carrying that pain around inside."

"You're alone now?" Lavos frowned.

"I have friends."

"What about a special man? I noticed you're not wearing a ring."

"Relationships and I don't seem to work out."

"I find that hard to believe. You're beautiful, Jadee."

The compliment was nice, coming from him. "And then I open my mouth." She smiled to soften the harsh words. "I'm too direct. I've been told that often. I make men uncomfortable or piss them off. I was raised too differently to fit in with most people, with the way I traveled around as a kid. Imagine meeting guys' families. I've been there and done that. They ask about my life and I either have to lie so they don't think I'm some weirdo or they instantly dislike me because of the truth. They aren't impressed that I had a mother who abandoned me and a father who spent his life chasing myths and investigating alien sightings. Stress isn't a great relationship-builder when a man's getting pressure from his parents to dump someone he's dating."

"My parents are still alive but I wouldn't give a damn if they didn't approve of a woman in my life. We don't have a close relationship to begin with."

"What's wrong with your parents?" She was curious.

"My mother is old school. My father would say jump and she asked how high. She always sided with him until recently, regardless of whether she knew he was right or wrong. The jury is still out on how this new twist

137

in their relationship will play out, but Mom finally stood up to him. They are together but I'm sure it's tense. He's an asshole, always has been and always will be." He paused. "He was never the most supportive or loving of fathers. He used his sons to get whatever he wanted, regardless of what it cost us. Lorn and I had to stand against him, so we're not even on speaking terms."

"I'm sorry. That must be rough."

"It's kind of a relief. I don't have to pretend to give a damn about what he wants anymore. As I said, he's an asshole. He and my mother just moved to a new location. That's the only down side. I love and miss her. She's stuck with him."

"I'm not really sure what that means."

"They are linked on a very intimate level for life. She can see good in him where others can't. She would have a near impossible time cutting those bonds, even though he's massively flawed."

"Is he good to her?"

"He usually is. I give him credit for that but he's lacking a lot when it comes to being a father or a decent person as a whole."

"Are you close to your brother? I always wanted a sibling. I imagined it would be terrific."

"Lorn is my best friend. We never fought like most brothers do. I guess you could say we bonded so close since we had to support each other against our father. Dad was tough on us growing up. He's got this strong belief that weakness of any kind is a flaw."

"He *does* sound like an asshole." She bit her lip. "Was he abusive?"

"He was harsher than most parents."

138

She'd take that for a yes. It horrified her. "I'm so sorry."

"We're very loving as a people but my father lacked that trait when it came to his sons. It wasn't as bad as you might imagine, but he treated us as if we were adults instead of children. His expectations were too high for our ages. Most of our men start their training at around ten years old. He had us sparring by the time we could walk."

"Sparring?"

"Fighting."

That stunned her.

"I'm not like you, Jadee. You've seen me shifted. We need to learn discipline and how to protect ourselves at a younger age than your children do. We don't play in a safe environment as youths. Our backyard comes with predators."

"Discipline?"

"Can you remember when you were about ten years old?"

She nodded. "Sure."

"Ever fight with another child over something trivial?"

"Of course."

"Now imagine if you'd had the ability to claw or bite into another child, and the kind of damage you could do, not really meaning to, in a fit of anger. Our children can't fully shift until they hit puberty but we get some of our abilities earlier than that. Like extending our claws and fangs. We need to learn young to control our tempers and think before we act."

She looked down at his hand. "Can you show me?"

He twisted his wrist until his palm was face up but didn't do anything else.

She peered into his eyes. "The cut is gone. That was the hand you sliced open last night, wasn't it?"

"I heal fast. Jadee...I don't want to frighten you."

"You won't. I asked. Can I see your claws? I mean, can you do that?"

"Watch."

She focused on his hand again. He moved it a few inches from hers and curled his fingers upward. His fingernails began to grow. They got longer, until they were about an inch in length. It amazed her. They had sharp-looking tips and were thick.

"You can touch them if you want but don't cut yourself."

She hesitantly used her fingertip to feel the side of one nail. It was smooth, almost like bone. She smiled and looked up at him. "Very cool."

He smiled and retracted them. "Thank you."

"What else can you do besides grow claws, fangs, and get your neon eyes on?"

He had a great laugh. She liked hearing it when he chuckled. "I shift. You saw that already."

"Does it hurt when you do?"

"It's painful at first but over time, it's just what it is. It happens faster and you become accustomed to the shape of your body changing without discomfort."

"Do you ever accidently shift? Like if you're having a bad dream and then boom, you wake up with a tail?"

He laughed again. "I did that a few times when I first started shifting but then you learn to control it better. There are no accidental transformations now."

She grew serious. "Thank you for saving me."

He reached over and gently took her hand in his. "You're welcome." He let her go. "You should try to get some sleep. You probably aren't used to staying up all night. I need to go out there and help with cleanup. Promise me that you won't go outside. Stay inside where you're safe. I'll come back later and we'll figure out what's wrong with the vehicle to get you on your way home."

"My father's team said they thought the Vampires had torn out the oil pan."

"That won't be too difficult to fix."

"Is your pack going to want to hurt me?"

"I won't allow it to happen, Jadee. Lorn does owe me a debt. He won't let me down. We are very close and he'll know how important this is to me."

"Thank you. I realize it would be so much easier to kill me, rather than risk your ass."

"I think the world would be a much less interesting place without you in it."

The way he looked at her in that moment left her reeling a little. She worked in bars. It was obvious when a man was interested in her—and that intense stare of his indicated he saw her as a woman he wanted.

He suddenly slid out of his seat. "I have to get to work. Sleep. I'll be back later."

"Thanks again. There's plenty of food if you get hungry so help yourself."

"I appreciate that." He left fast, closing the door firmly behind him.

Jadee sighed. It figured that she'd finally found a guy she was interested in and he wasn't a type she could get involved with. He sometimes had a tail, claws, and he turned into some scary beast-looking thing when he shifted. His pack was also anti-human. Life just wasn't fair.

* * * * *

Lavos located two of the cars in a ravine and managed to push them into the river before assistance arrived. Lorn found him first. His brother strode toward him quickly with a grim expression.

"Kar filled me in. Where is the human?"

"Sleeping inside the motor home. It's about a mile to the south."

"She's a risk. Kar said she's immune to you. Let me try to wipe her mind."

Lorn was stronger than him. He debated it. His brother wouldn't hurt Jadee...but did he want her to forget all about him?

The answer came fast. "No. Leave her be."

"It's too dangerous. She knows too much. Kar told me *everything*, Lavos—including the fact that you seem to be attracted to her. He thinks your reasoning is compromised."

He felt a little betrayed that Kar had shared that with his brother, but Lorn was their clan leader. Part of Kar's job was being honest. He couldn't fault him for that. "She knows enough to keep herself safe when she returns to her normal life."

142

"Damn it, Lavos. What are you thinking?"

"She's different, Lorn. Special. I trust her."

"I don't."

"You owe me." His temper flared. "I helped you protect Kira."

"She was raised with us and I love her. This human is irrelevant when it comes to safeguarding our people."

Lavos stepped closer. "Don't do this. Don't be like *him*. You're channeling our father. You don't know Jadee. She's brave and smart." He reached up and almost ran his fingers through his hair in frustration, then saw how dirty they'd become. He brushed his palm over the sweatpants he'd borrowed instead. "I like her, Lorn. Yes, I *am* attracted to her, but I'm not planning on trying to take her to bed. It can't work out. I just want to see her go free. She's got spirit and spunk. You'd like her too if you got to know her. She reminds me of Kira."

"Damn." Lorn's expression softened. "That's low, comparing this human to my mate."

"But effective." Lavos relaxed.

Worry creased Lorn's features. "Is she...you know?"

He masked his features to hide his emotions. "My mate? I'm not testing her blood to see. I won't even kiss her."

"It's just that—"

Lavos cut him off. "I already know. Let me save you the trouble. I'm not Veso. He'd already made enemies as soon as they realized he wasn't loyal to Decker, so him taking a human mate wasn't much worse in the clan's eyes. He's also antisocial. I'm your lead enforcer. Having a human mate would stir the shit with the clan in a massive way because they'd have

143

to deal with her all the time. I doubt Veso will even allow Glen out of his cabin unless he's ordered by you to bring her in."

"Our people need more time. I'm balancing a fine line of trying to ease them into a new way of living but I don't want to break their minds in the process."

"You're a good leader, Lorn. You're thinking about your clan. Don't look so torn up. I just like her. I do have to tell you that she thinks we're *Werewolves*. I didn't correct her."

"Do you honestly believe she won't reveal anything?"

"She's not going to tell anyone what happened. She's seen too much. That's why I'm so certain I can trust her. She never wants to cross paths with anything nonhuman again. It will help keep her safe if anything ever goes after her. I want her to live, damn it."

"Fine. I'm surprised you didn't hustle her out of here before we arrived."

"I tried. She came to visit her father in a rental but it was in a wreck when that last soldier attacked. Can you have Digger come out here to get the motor home up and running? There's oil all over the ground under it. It looks as if the soldiers tore open the oil pan and probably fucked up some wiring. She can drive that home."

"Sure."

"Thank you."

Lorn glanced around. "What a mess. Kar said the master wasn't found."

"He already fled. We have a description of him though."

"I'm going to have to assign some enforcers to track him down. He's long gone from this area if he's intelligent and not totally insane."

"I agree. You could send me."

Lorn scowled. "No."

"You don't think I can handle one moron? I've been out in the human world before."

"I think it would give you an excuse to spend more time with this human you've grown an attachment to. I'll call a council meeting between the clans to give them an amended version of what happened and they can decide who to send after this son of a bitch, to make certain it never happens again. It affects us all."

"Don't tell them the truth about Jadee."

"Like I'm a moron." Lorn snorted. "That's why I said amended. They might assign someone to go silence her for good if I told them everything."

"I knew I could count on you."

"You knew comparing her to Kira would work."

"Guilty."

"Are you *sure* you can trust her?"

Lavos didn't have to think about it. "Stop worrying so much. Yes."

"Fine. I'm going to want to meet her though, and I'll tell everyone that I was able to wipe her mind. Kar might slip up at some point. He's got a mouth on him when he wants to impress women. This way our bases are covered. She'll be safe from reprisals."

"Thank you—but don't mess with her head."

"I give you my word."

"I appreciate it."

Lorn glanced around again. "What a damn headache. We have the death toll at almost three dozen in all. I brought ten of our clan with me and we located a few cars that they probably lured into pulling off the highway to attack the drivers."

"Son of a bitch."

"I know. We're still looking." Lorn withdrew his satellite phone when it rang, answering it. "Yes?" He paused, listening. "Great. Clean it up." He ended the call. "They just found another car with a body. It happened about two days ago. At least they didn't leave the vehicles within sight of the road."

"Damn."

"I think this master is trying to start a war by leaving this mess on our doorstep. It's as if he's trying to push the blame on us for these murders. The idiot. If the humans discover what *we* are, they'll be hunting Vampires next."

"Jadee is the least of our worries."

"I hope so." Lorn glanced down at his phone. "I'll call Digger. He can fix anything on four wheels. Take me to your human and we'll keep her out of sight when Digger arrives, or tell her to pretend to be under my control. He tends to gossip. The last thing I need is anyone doubting my leadership. She'd better be worth this, bro."

"She is."

Lorn didn't look convinced but Lavos had no doubts. Jadee was innocent and needed to be protected. He couldn't stand the thought of any harm coming to her. He wanted her to live. Even if that meant never seeing her again.

Chapter Nine

Thirteen days later

Jadee hated Friday evenings. The bar was packed with drunken idiots and their favorite sports team had lost. It meant a bunch of unhappy customers with little to no common sense. She swept the last of the broken glass into a dustpan. One guy had decided to smash his drink in frustration. It probably wouldn't be the only time she had to clean up a mess before her shift ended.

She straightened and caught Bob's eye. He was her backup behind the bar. "I'm taking out the trash."

"I can do it."

"I want to get a little fresh air," she admitted. "I'm getting a headache."

"Go ahead. Take five. I'll handle this."

"Thanks."

She removed the plastic bag and replaced it with a new one, then lifted the trash. The back door beckoned. She picked up the pace and exited, happier the second the door closed. The noise from inside could no longer be heard. She had to cross the alley to reach the Dumpster, and the narrow lane was blocked off at both ends every evening so she didn't bother to pause to check for cars. There wouldn't be any. Deliveries were only made in the mornings. The two big gates also kept the homeless from ransacking their Dumpsters and sleeping behind the bar and the stores attached to each side of it. It meant she was safe from anyone bothering her.

Jadee threw the bag inside and dropped the lid. She looked up. It was a full moon. "All the crazies are out. No wonder," she muttered, thinking about her customers. They were an unusually rowdy bunch.

She strolled slowly toward the back door, in no hurry to enter. Her threshold of dealing with bullshit had to be at an all-time low. One customer had already tried to lean across the bar in a sad attempt to kiss her. He'd ended up with a stern warning that he'd be cut off if he tried it again. She hadn't been talking about beers. His nuts had come to mind. She leaned against the building and closed her eyes.

Lavos's image popped up. It happened often since she'd left Alaska. She thought about him more than she wanted to. He was very memorable. She hugged her waist and crossed one ankle over the other. He'd been a hell of a man, unlike the ones she dealt with at work.

He probably had forgotten her as soon as she'd driven away, but he'd starred in many of her dreams when she slept. Some of them had caused her to wake up with a sense of loss, while others had been of the highly sexual nature. Either way, they'd left her frustrated and missing him.

It could never happen between them, though. Kar had admitted it was a big no-no for Werewolves to hook up with humans. Lavos's pack would likely have a bone to pick with them having any kind of relationship— probably one from her dead carcass.

Her pocket buzzed and she reached down, sliding her cell phone out. She opened her eyes but didn't take the time to look at who called. "Hello?"

"Can you talk or are you swamped?"

She smiled, identifying her friend's voice. "I'm taking a break. What's up, Maria?"

"I wanted to invite you to a barbeque on Sunday."

"No way. This is another setup, isn't it?"

"He's nice. His name is Mitch and he's hot. He also has a good job, no mommy issues, and his family lives in New York so you won't face a firing squad anytime soon."

Jadee winced. "No." The last Mitch she'd met had been a killer. It was the night she'd lost her father and met up with a stranger walking around inside his body.

"I want you to be happy." Concern laced Maria's voice. "I worry about you."

"I'm okay."

"Have they found the bodies?"

She tilted her head up, staring at the moon. "No. They probably never will. The entire camp washed into the river when that storm hit. It's remote up there and they may never surface, or if they do, they won't be easy to find. It's miles of endless woods. I'm just glad my dad had parked his RV away from the rest of their camp."

"What were they looking for?"

"Some kind of tree beast," she lied. "Think of a devil in the body of a tree. Someone said they saw a moving tree walking around. I'm sure they were just drunk and it was windy." She wasn't sure if that was a legend but it didn't matter. Her friend wouldn't waste the time to look it up.

"Why are you working? I know you already talked to your father's lawyer and the police. Megan told me she'd gone with you to do all that. She also told me the lawyer called yesterday, saying your father had left you everything, but the call was just a formality since he'd already put you

150

on all his bank accounts. You have access to his money. He left you set for life."

"Bartending keeps me busy."

"You should take some time off to grieve."

"I need to stay occupied."

"I can't believe they let you return to work."

"I didn't tell them about my dad." Jadee sighed. "For that reason."

"I understand. You want to try to keep things as normal as possible but you've got to be hurting. Mitch is a nice guy. My husband works with him. I just can't stand you being alone. Everyone is worried about you, Jadee. I'm surprised you even answered your phone. I usually get your voicemail; you're bad about returning calls ever since you got back from Alaska. It's like you're avoiding us."

"I've had a lot on my plate. I don't want to be a downer. You just got married four months ago and Tina is expecting her first baby."

"We love you. Come to the barbeque. Hang out with the people who care about you. We'll worry less."

She'd have to smile and act as if her life hadn't been altered in ways that could never be changed. Some guy named Mitch would be there, and Maria was about as subtle as a tank when it came to trying to play matchmaker. "I have to work," she lied. "Sorry. Maybe another time."

"It wouldn't kill you to call in sick."

"I'm just not ready to deal with everyone yet. I hate pity."

"I know but we should talk about holding a memorial or something for your dad."

"I don't want to do that."

"You plan to wait until they find his body to do it?"

Jadee was fed up and decided to be blunt. "This is why I've been avoiding calls. It's too raw right now, okay?" She didn't want to admit that she'd decided not to hold any kind of funeral. "I don't want to discuss any of this."

"I'm sorry. I'm being thoughtless. Will you at least have lunch with me next week? I promise I won't bring up your dad or men in general. I just want to see your mug."

Jadee grinned. "Only if something deep fried and greasy is involved."

"Fried mushrooms, fries and bacon cheeseburgers?"

"Deal. I'll call you Monday to set up a time. I'd better get back inside before Bob sends out a search party. It's a zoo tonight."

"Don't go home with any drunks."

She laughed. "Not a problem. Love you." She ended the call and shoved her phone back inside her pocket. She pushed off the wall and almost tripped on a wooden pallet on the ground next to her. She shot it a glare and then reached for the handle of the door.

"Hello."

The man's voice startled her and she spun around. No one should be in the alley at that time of the night. The other shops on the strip closed at eight but it was well past ten.

The sight of the man's pale, semi good-looking face had mental alarm bells screaming the second she looked at him. He wore a black dress shirt and slacks. They only accented his white skin.

"You're not allowed back here."

He tilted his head slightly. His eyes were a light color, probably a shade of blue or perhaps green. They started to glow and her heart pounded. That wasn't natural—and she knew what he was. *A fucking Vampire. Shit!*

"I was out for a walk along the rooftops and spotted you." He gave a smile. "It's your lucky night, my dear. Tell me you're grateful."

He was probably trying to control her mind. She *was* grateful—grateful she'd seen Lavos in action and knew how to respond appropriately.

"I'm grateful," she managed to get out. He'd kill her if he realized she was immune. It seemed safer to play along. It also meant he probably planned to bite her. Lavos said city Vamps weren't killers, they just stole some blood from their victims and left them alive afterward. Dread pitted her stomach. She'd have to let the son of a bitch bite her without putting up a fight to fool him into believing he could make her forget what he'd done.

It was a horrible choice to make but she'd seen what Vampires could do. There were no bars separating her from the monster now. She didn't have an assault rifle either. All she had was an ice pick tucked into the back pocket of her jeans. It was handy since their ice machine tended to let the ice melt a little bit when the door was left open for a minute or two, then freeze it solid fast, lumping it together. She also never worked in the bar without something to defend herself.

The Vampire reached down and unfastened his slacks, shoving them over his thighs until they pooled at his ankles. He wasn't wearing underwear and he had a hard-on.

Jadee's fear intensified. So did her anger.

153

"Drop to your knees," he demanded.

He wasn't after just her neck. It pissed her off. *Does he do this to other women? Order them to blow him? What a sick pervert. Like stealing blood isn't enough.*

She lowered to her knees while slowly reaching behind her, lifting up the edge of her sweater to grip the wooden handle of the ice pick.

"Tell me my dick is big."

She studied his dick, since it was right in front of her face. He *wasn't* big, or even on the average side. It explained why he felt the need to force poor women into sexual submission. "Huge," she murmured, glancing to both sides of her without moving her head.

"Open your mouth," he hissed.

It wasn't going to happen. She'd rather die than follow through with his instructions. She slid the ice pick out and fisted it tight in her hand. She had something hard for him too…and it had a sharp tip. She lifted her chin and glared at him, adjusting her hand to her hip, hiding the weapon.

"Fuck off, perv."

She rammed the ice pick into his nuts.

He shrieked, throwing himself back. His pants around his ankles tripped him and he went down hard, frantically reaching for his injured crotch.

Jadee shot to her feet and grabbed the door, yanking it open. She saw him sit up just as she threw her body inside. The door closed and she slid the dead bolt across.

She backed up, realizing he might be able to break through it. It was reinforced to protect the bar against break-ins from humans, not super-strong Vampire freaks. He could also avoid the back and enter through the front, coming after her from that direction.

She reached for her phone, her first instinct to dial 9-1-1.

She froze. It wouldn't work. He could just wipe the cops' minds or freeze them in place while he killed her in front of everyone. "Fuck!"

Something hit the door and she gasped as a crack split the painted white wood near the doorjamb. A frantic search around her revealed nothing she could use to attack him with—but then the glass fire case caught her attention. An axe and a fire extinguisher were inside.

She moved quickly as the door suffered another blow from the Vampire. She hoped no one inside the bar could hear it over the loud music coming from the main room.

She threw up her arm and twisted her head in the opposite direction, slamming her elbow into the glass. It triggered the fire alarm the second she breached the glass. She'd forgotten it was wired to go off in case of that happening. Bob would start to clear the bar and the fire department would be notified. Cops and firemen would arrive but she'd probably be dead by then. It was possible that the Vampire might take off.

He hit the door again and more cracks appeared in the wood. Worse, the section of frame with the dead bolt splintered. He was about to bust the thing in.

She grabbed the fire extinguisher and was grateful the owner was almost anal about safety. He always kept the extinguishers filled. Some drunks smoked in the bathrooms and had caused a few small trash fires by not completely putting out the butts before they tossed them away. She removed the pin and pointed the hose toward the door. She stepped to the

155

side and glanced at the axe, then prepared to squeeze the lever to spray the fire retardant.

Two more hits and the door was torn open. The pale freak entered. His eyes still glowed but he'd taken the time to pull up his pants. They looked wet near his crotch, a dark stain proof of the blood she'd spilled. She hoped it hurt like hell.

She let loose with the spray, hitting him in the face. She aimed for his eyes.

He threw up his hand, roaring out in surprise, hopefully blinded. She pitched the entire container at him. It hit him in the chest, knocking him over since he was already off balance and scrambling backward, and he landed back in the alley.

She lunged, grabbing for the axe.

He was still on the ground, wiping at his eyes when she ran out the door after him. Vampires recovered fast. It was something she'd never forget. She didn't want to die but she still paused when she raised the weapon, gripping the handle with both hands. It was gruesome to consider chopping off someone's head, regardless of the dire circumstances.

"You bitch!" he yelled. "I'm going to take you to my nest and we're going to tear you apart limb by limb. You'll die screaming! I'll—"

She swung for all she was worth the second he lowered his arm and opened his eyes.

He must have seen the blade coming, because he jerked before she struck his neck. The sharp metal sliced through and she saw his head come off his body in that split second. Blood gushed—but then his entire body seemed to explode.

Ash flew into the air, almost like a big balloon popping, filled with the stuff. It surprised her, and she almost tripped over her own feet to jump back. The axe clattered to the ground and she felt tears burn behind her eyelids from something irritating them. She rapidly blinked and was able to see again.

Ash covered the ground where his body should have been. The wind blew, stirring some of it enough to see a dark stain where he'd bleed. The ash stuck to it, looking like a gross gray-and-red mixture of mud.

Jadee was in a state of shock as she looked down. Ash had landed on her sweater too.

"Oh fuck!" She frantically slapped at her clothes, the urge to puke strong.

Loud sirens penetrated her awareness and she realized the fire truck and police were close. *How in the hell am I going to explain this?* They would think she was insane if she told them a Vampire had attacked her. They'd lock her up in a mental ward. Other Vampires would come after her, and God only knew what else.

She had to act fast. She forced her body to move as she bent, picking up the axe, the ice pick and grabbing the fire extinguisher. She entered the bar, closing the busted door as much as she could. She set everything down and tore off her sweater, grateful she'd worn a tank top underneath. She turned it inside out and used the sleeves to frantically wipe off anywhere her fingerprints might be on the extinguisher, replacing it in the casing. The axe and ice pick had blood and ash stuck to them. She gripped both and ran into the hallway off the back area.

The music still played in the front of the bar but the tables she could see were clear of customers. She shoved at the door to the large closet where they kept cleaning supplies and scanned the top shelf. She grabbed the bleach and tossed the weapons into the small sink that sat in the corner. She doused them and then turned on the water to rinse the bleach away when the strong chemical began to sting her eyes.

The sirens stopped, telling her the police had reached the front of the bar. The inside fire alarm still droned on. She replaced the near-empty bottle of bleach and used her sweater to grab hold of the axe, trying to dry it and wipe off her prints if any remained after the bleaching it had taken. The blood was gone from the blade. She shoved the ice pick back into her pocket after wiping it down too. She yanked open a storage cabinet, shoving her sweater under a stack of bar towels, then rushed out of the closet and replaced the axe.

Jadee hesitated, glancing around, trying to think of what to do next. Her mind blanked until she stared at the damaged door. The Vampire remains were still out there. They might test them or something.

She exited through the back door. There was a water hose a few feet away attached to the building, to wash chairs and tables down in case someone puked. She turned it on and directed it at the ash. It turned into a gray mess but she hit the blood area the most, then turned the hose elsewhere, spraying it in every direction it could reach. She also bent, took out the ice pick, and shoved it behind the wooden pallet, out of sight.

The back door was shoved open and a cop with his gun drawn stepped out. He pointed it at her and she froze, only easing her thumb off the sprayer so the water stopped.

"I work in the bar," she told him.

He didn't lower the gun. "What are you doing?"

"I went to take out the trash and got a phone call from a friend. I was talking to her when I heard someone kicking at the back door and stepped out from over there." She jerked her head toward the Dumpster. "It was some guy wearing a baseball cap. He went inside and then the fire alarm went off. I was afraid but I snuck over here and grabbed the hose. He ran outside and I nailed him with water. He ran that way." She jerked her head toward the main street. "He's wet."

A fireman and Bob stepped outside. Bob looked relieved. "Thank God you're okay, Jadee. I got everyone out front but then realized you weren't there. I remembered you'd taken out the trash."

Bless you for having good timing, Bob.

The cop holstered his weapon. He grabbed his radio as he peered at the busted back door. "I'll call it in and we'll look for the perp. Did you see his face?"

"No. He had his hat tugged low and it happened so fast. I was terrified." She purposely tried to look confused and a little scared. "It's a blur. I was just so freaked out."

The fireman bent a little, frowning at the ground. "What is this?"

It was the gray, watery mess that had once been a Vampire. "Oh that. I saw it when I came out. I think someone must have burned some boxes or something. We get a lot of homeless who try to come back here to sleep. Sometimes they'll burn stuff to keep warm or cook food. They climb the gates."

The cop walked down the alley and the fireman returned inside. The fire alarm shut off. Bob approached her. "Are you okay?"

"Yeah. I can't believe some thug tried to break into the bar."

"I can. People are nuts." Bob pulled her into a hug. "Where's your sweater? You always say you're cold with the air conditioning on inside."

"I was hot outside so I took it off." She wasn't about to admit it was covered in Vampire dust and damp from her using it to wipe down items she'd used as weapons. "What a night. It's a full moon."

He kissed the top of her head. "Never confront a robber. Damn, you could have been hurt. A hose? You think water is a weapon?"

"It was all I could think of."

The fireman returned. "It looks like the burglar broke the glass, trying to get the extinguisher or maybe the axe to use as a weapon in a robbery. The alarm going off probably scared the hell out of him. He didn't steal anything."

Bob loosened his hold but kept his arm around her. "I'll call the boss and we'll fix this door. The bar is closed for the night." He gave her a squeeze. "Go home after we wrap this up."

The cop returned. "I'm going to need a statement from you."

She nodded. "Of course."

Jadee glanced up, feeling a chill along her spine. Two men stood on a roof down the alleyway. They wore black clothing and were pale skinned. She dropped her gaze before they realized she'd seen them, terror hitting hard.

They had to be Vampires. Normal people didn't hang out on rooftops, and her attacker had said he'd spotted her from one. Had they seen what she'd done?

Oh shit. She needed to get out of there before they came after her. The pervert with fangs had said he belonged to a nest. That had to mean there were more of them.

* * * * *

Jadee had a headache by the time the cops left and the owner had sent out a few guys to repair the back door and frame. She'd left the pick in the alley, not willing to go out there to retrieve it with Vampires hanging around on rooftops. She could say she must have dropped it in all the confusion, if they were able to figure out it was hers. She was also grateful no one had asked why the door had been locked when she'd supposedly taken out the trash, since the guy had supposedly bust in the door. They might think of it later but she had time to think up a lie.

Bob led everyone outside when they finished and locked the front door. The repair guys walked toward their truck at the curb, talking to each other. The fire truck had gone and so had the two cop cars.

"What a night."

She looked up at Bob next to her. "You're telling me."

"At least it wasn't a real fire. That's an upside. I about shit when that alarm went off. I rushed into the bathrooms but nothing was smoking. Then I cleared the bar. One guy was so drunk I had to damn near carry him out. I'll walk you to your car."

"You did good." She moved, Bob staying next to her.

161

He stopped at her car. "Are you okay to drive? I could drop you off at home. We're working the same schedule tomorrow so we could ride to work together." He looked hopeful. "You shouldn't be alone."

Jadee knew he was interested in her; he had asked her out a few times. "I'm fine but thanks."

"Oh. Okay."

She withdrew her keys and forced a smile. "I appreciate it though."

"Anytime. I mean that. I'd do anything for you, Jadee."

She felt bad. He was a nice guy but she wasn't attracted to him. *He's no Lavos.* She inwardly flinched at making the comparison. "Good night."

She unlocked her car and climbed inside, starting the engine. Bob backed up and waved. She lifted her hand and waved back. She clipped her belt with her right hand and pressed down on the brake before shifting the gear into drive. One glance in the side mirror to check for traffic and then she pulled away from the curb.

The streetlight half a block down was red so she came to a stop. It was just after midnight and traffic was still heavy since it was a weekend. Another car pulled up next to her and she glanced over. It was a couple and they seemed deep in conversation. She smiled. It looked as if they were arguing. She faced forward, staring at the light and tapping the wheel as cars passed in front of her. She glanced toward the sidewalk...

And almost forgot how to breathe when she met the gaze of a man standing at the crosswalk. He was staring right at her.

It wasn't the fact that she'd caught the attention of a stranger that had that effect on her. It was the fact he was pale and wore all black clothes.

He stepped off the curb, coming toward her car.

Jadee's heart pounded and she darted a look at the light. It was still red. She glanced back at the man. He was definitely coming her way. He stepped out of the painted pedestrian lines to reach her passenger door. He leaned down and his eyes began to glow. He gripped the door handle and gave it a yank.

She'd never been so grateful for a feature on her car. The locks had auto-engaged when she'd put it in drive, so he wasn't able to get inside. But she couldn't look away from his eyes. They were getting brighter.

"Open the door," he demanded.

He was attempting to control her mind. She glanced at the light, finally breaking eye contact with him. It turned green.

She stomped on the gas, taking off. Her tires protested but the car shot forward. Jadee trembled as she kept her foot pressed hard on the accelerator.

Those Vampires had to know what she'd done. She wasn't sure if he'd been one of the two she'd seen on the roof. It was possible. One thing was certain though—they'd come after her.

She glanced in the rearview mirror as she made it through the intersection.

The guy in the dark clothes ran after her.

He was fast—too fast—but she was able to put distance between them. She gripped the wheel tighter and ignored the speed limit until she didn't see him anymore. She took a few turns, eventually feeling safe that she'd lost him.

The RV she'd gotten back from the repair shop days before came into view and she sagged with relief. She'd quit her job in the morning. They knew where she worked. Would they learn her name? It was a grim concept. The Vampire she'd killed couldn't tell anyone she was immune to mind control but the one at the red light could. She'd refused his order to let him inside her car.

I'm in deep shit. She parked her car next to her father's RV and ran inside. She locked the door and rushed to the panel in the front. She twisted the key to bring the shutters down. The loud motor came on and they lowered, sealing the windows. It was the first time she'd used them since she'd returned home with her father's tank on wheels and had one of the damaged windows replaced. It had seemed like paranoia to think Vampires were ever going to come after her once she'd left Alaska.

"I'll be paranoid now, happily," she muttered.

She dropped her purse on the table and took a seat. It reminded her that she needed to wash her sweater. It was balled up inside her purse, where she'd snuck it earlier when she'd gotten a chance.

The memory of that Vampire exploding into dust made her grimace. She stood and started to strip. A shower was in order, and then washing her clothes.

A slight noise startled her and she stopped unzipping her jeans. The handle on the side door turned but the locks held. She released the metal tab on her pants and backed up, trying to remain quiet. She reached the front and flipped on the monitors. She'd gotten familiar with the new camera setup, which she'd had replaced along with the damaged window.

The man from the intersection stood outside the side door.

Jadee's knees almost buckled. She had no idea how he'd managed to follow her home but there was no denying the truth.

164

He turned his head and nodded to someone off camera.

"Shit," she mouthed. She lifted the remote and changed the camera feed to show the front of the RV. Two more Vampires stood there. They stared at the windshield. One of them approached the driver's side door and tried it. She turned her head, looking at it, already knowing it wouldn't open for them, locked. Her gaze returned to the screen. Another Vampire arrived and he tested the passenger door.

A creak overhead had her jerking her chin up. It had almost sounded like a footstep. She changed the feed again until she found the camera that showed the roof. A woman had somehow gotten up there. She wore tight black clothing. That made a total of five Vampires outside. The woman moved slowly to the side and jumped off.

Jadee strained to hear anything but it was too quiet. She stared at the screen, flipping the channels to watch them from different views. A sixth one arrived. It was another woman. All of them wore black and they gathered near the side door. She wished she'd had sound wired with the cameras to hear what they said. They spoke too softly for her to hear them from where she stood. They split up again, surrounding the RV on all sides.

One of the women knocked on the side door. "Hello?"

Jadee sealed her lips and set the remote down. She lifted a leg and tore off one shoe, then the other. She was careful to stay very quiet as she tiptoed down the aisle to the door. She reached out and eased the bars down over the door as carefully as she could, timing her movements with the woman's knocks, hoping they wouldn't hear. The extra bolts were slid into place next. One of them made a slight scratching sound, and Jadee winced.

165

The Vampire knocked harder. "Hello inside. Can you help me? My boyfriend beat me up. I just need to use your phone."

Jadee backed up and took a few slow, steady breathes. They couldn't break in. The shutters were down.

The woman Vampire pounded on the door. "Hello? I need help!"

They clearly thought she'd fall for it. The strong desire to grab weapons surfaced but she hadn't bought more ammo. The guns were useless, hidden inside the hallway closet. She could call the cops but it might get them hurt. It would be like ordering delivery food for her unwanted visitors.

She turned her head and stared at the television mounted by the front. The Vampire woman wasn't alone for long. A guy with blond hair joined her. He was new—and that meant there were now seven Vampires.

"Her name is Jadee Trollis."

She could hear him speaking softly outside. She crouched down when her legs threatened to turn to jelly. They knew where she worked, where she lived, and now they had her name.

"I grabbed one of her neighbors and ripped into his mind. He was very helpful." He paused. "She moved here a few days ago and keeps to herself so far. No husband or kids that he knows of. The engine of her car is still warm so she must be inside. He didn't see her come home but he was watching television."

"Lower your voice," the woman whispered.

"Maybe she's deaf," the guy stated.

"I said lower your voice!" the woman repeated.

Jadee closed her eyes and leaned forward until her head nearly touched the door. She was tempted to press her ear against it but what if they heard her breathing? She wasn't willing to risk it.

They tried the door again, the handle wiggling. She opened her eyes and turned her head, watching the monitor. The woman lifted one foot and planted it on the side of the RV. She pulled, gripping the handle. It might have normally worked to rip the door open if it weren't reinforced. The metal creaked a little but it didn't budge otherwise.

Huff and puff, Jadee silently taunted. *But you can't get in.*

Jadee realized in that instant that she had to leave town. They knew her name though. Did one nest of Vampires talk to others? Would they be searching for her no matter where she went? They might put word out to others to hunt her down.

Lavos came to mind. He could help her. *Maybe.* He had before.

She chewed on her lip, watching the two Vamps on the screen softly talking just feet from her side door. They were probably plotting how to kill her.

How could she find Lavos?

That Digger guy had fixed the RV. She'd seen the name of his business printed on his T-shirt. He'd had to come inside to start the engine and check a few things on the dash. He knew Lavos. If she could find the mechanic, he could send a message. She just had to wait for the sun to rise and then hit the road.

Chapter Ten

Lavos didn't feel like being sociable. His brother depended upon him though to stay at his side and help host the festivities. It was the first time they were officially welcoming visitors for a social event since his brother had taken leadership. It would help strengthen the bonds between the four clans, something that had been lacking when Decker ruled.

They were using the lodge for a meet and greet. He forced a smile as he entered the foyer, seeing some familiar faces but a lot of new ones. His brother stood near the bar and motioned him over the second he spotted him.

"This is my brother, Lavos." Lorn looked relaxed, a group of people surrounding him.

"Hello." Lavos twisted his lips upward in a forced smile.

A woman caught his attention when she reached out and ran a hand over his arm. "You're single."

He couldn't deny it. He'd seen her nostrils flare so she'd taken in his scent. "I am."

She possessed big dark brown eyes and long matching hair. "Lorn was just telling us that you're his lead enforcer." She batted her eyelashes. "That's impressive."

He kept his muscles relaxed. She was obviously hunting for a mate with status. "Well, it's a perk of being the brother to the new clan leader."

"You're being modest." Lorn shot him a look. "Lavos is an excellent fighter."

The woman ran her hand up Lavos's biceps, squeezing them. "He's a strong one." She stepped closer and pushed out her breasts when she shoved her shoulders back. "I am looking for a mate. We should go somewhere more private and get to know each other."

She was a beautiful woman but he felt no desire to have sex. His brother would encourage a mating between the clans but Lavos had no interest in her.

He'd had that problem ever since he'd met Jadee.

He couldn't forget her. She'd haunted his dreams for the past two weeks since they'd parted ways. He'd wake with painful hard-ons, wishing she were naked in his bed.

"My brother has a beautiful house not too far from here. You should ask him for a tour."

Lavos wanted to kick Lorn. It was his turn to shoot him a look.

His brother smiled, not upset or taking the hint when he continued to speak. "I'm mated, so now it's his turn."

The woman rubbed up against Lavos's side and leaned closer. "I would love to see your home."

"I have duties to perform first. I'm going to be free later." He didn't want to offend her by flat-out refusing to take her to bed, but he silently plotted to avoid her for the rest of the day and evening.

Lorn let it go and helped get him off the hook. "Speaking of, could you please find Brista and make certain she's prepared to watch all the children for the feast tonight?" Lorn addressed the others. "She's the clan caretaker for our young. We were told some guests might bring their children and we thought it would be nice for her to entertain them."

169

"Of course." Lavos bowed and untangled his arm from the woman. "I'll see you later."

"I'm Mya."

"Until later, Mya."

He fled and yanked out his phone the moment he walked outside, calling Brista to relay the message. He knew Lorn wasn't a fan of the woman but she was well liked by some of the clan, enough that it had assured she held her position when Lorn had taken over, at least for the time being. But he doubted Lorn would ever entrust his own future children to Brista's care, not after the way she'd mistreated Kira for being so human when they were kids.

He closed his phone when the call ended and marched toward the gas station. He entered and sighed when he saw Volti behind the counter.

"Kill me," Lavos demanded.

His friend grinned. "I take it you met the delegates from the other clans and it's a bore?"

"One of them wanted to tour my house. She's looking for a mate."

"My heart is bleeding for you." His friend rolled his eyes. "I'd trade jobs with you in a heartbeat. I'll go fuck her to test our compatibility and you can clean the bathroom, after you restock the shelves."

Lavos assessed the small store. "Deal."

Volti shook his head. "I wish."

"I mean it. You make her happy and I'll take over here."

"Don't mess with me. It's cruel."

"I'm not." Lavos rounded the counter. "Show me the basics of a cash register since I've never done this before."

Volti shoved him back. "No way. Lorn would kick both of our asses. It's too important that we make a good impression on our visitors. They don't trust us because of Decker. Not that we can blame them. Our previous leader was a total dickhead. Your job is to kiss ass and mine is to make sure any humans dropping in to fill up their tanks don't decide to stroll around town." His eyes brightened, glowing. "You're in a hurry to get where you're going so gas up, take a piss, and hit the road. You saw nothing of interest here and it was just a small town. It wasn't even memorable. Leave."

"How many vehicles have stopped so far today?"

Volti's eyes dulled in brilliance. "Three. One family is sightseeing as they travel to visit an uncle. They wanted to check out Janella's store but I told them it's closed. They'd bought some jewelry from her online. One guy was heading to a new job. He wanted in and out of here as fast as possible, so I didn't have to mess with his mind. Then there was a trucker. He's a regular so no problem there. We're along his route and he stops in a few times a week."

"That's good."

"Janella was a little upset at losing prospective tourist business but today's too important to risk someone seeing something they shouldn't. Lorn purposely planned this for midweek since the weekends bring in more traffic. The delegates will be gone quick enough and life can resume as normal once the other clans feel comfortable with Lorn in charge."

Lavos knew he needed to get back to the lodge to help Lorn give a good impression but he lingered. "Where's Kar?"

171

"On patrol up the hill. He wrestled with Garson for the assignment and won."

"Why?"

"There are new women in town to flirt with." Volti grinned. "Why else? He didn't want to be stuck doing perimeter duty. Garson was dumb enough to take that bet."

"Horny bastard."

"It's totally natural. Our heat cycle is coming on soon. It's better to find someone to spend it with now than have to travel around, hoping to catch the eye of some babe who isn't hooked up with someone already. Spending it alone is hellish. This is the first year that other clans might welcome us with open arms instead of suspicion that we've come to spy on them, or worse."

Anger stirred. "I'd almost forgotten that Decker sent one of our women to kill Velder's son."

"It wasn't as if we knew about it until after the fact. Can you imagine? What a messed-up way to get an enforcer's guard down. She got him into bed and then tried to cut out his heart. I'm glad she failed."

"Decker had no honor."

"Is Lorn going to get rid of that law that prevents us from sexual contact with humans? There are a lot of hot babes a few towns over that I'd like to get to know better."

"It's never safe when we interact with them."

"I'm not looking to mate with one. I'd just like to be able to say yes when a cute human wants to jump my bones. It happens sometimes when it's my turn to go pick up store supplies. It just feels so damn wrong to say no. I want to make them happy and I'm perfectly willing to use condoms."

Lavos laughed. "Only doing your civic duty to be polite to humans, right?"

"Hell yes! They think we're gay."

"That impression keeps them from coming into our town to seek out our males."

"Hey, I won't tell them where I live and I'll make it clear it's a one-time deal."

"I'll bring it up to Lorn next time we're discussing laws."

"Thanks."

Lavos turned away. "I better get back to the lodge."

"See you later. I'll be at the feast."

Lavos avoided the main entrance of the lodge and went in through the kitchen. It had become a hive of activity. He talked to everyone working to make sure there were no problems. Davis, Kira's father, had everything running smoothly. He had to finally return to Lorn's side.

Mya ended her conversation with a tall male and came straight to him, gripping his arm. "You're back."

"I made my rounds. Everything is going well."

"Can you leave? I want to see your house." She licked her lips. "Everyone I've spoken to has said nice things about you. My father would approve. He wants me to find a strong mate."

He had to give her points for persistence. "I'm on duty until this evening."

She pouted. "Your brother is the clan leader here. I'm sure he'll be more than happy to get someone to cover for you."

"He's depending on me for his support. I wouldn't ask him to do that." He hoped she'd take the hint.

"I want to test a mating. I'm attracted to you, and you're strong enough to be worthy of me."

He'd have to be blunter. He didn't want to offend her but he wasn't going to fuck her either. He felt no attraction. "I'm flattered but right now isn't a good time."

Anger glinted in her eyes. "I see." She released his arm.

Shit. Lorn would kick his ass if the woman called her father to complain that someone had been rude to her. "Later tonight I'll be free." He winked, hoping he gave the impression he wasn't flat-out refusing her offer.

She rewarded him with a smile. "Business first. I respect that. I'll see you later." She blew him a kiss and returned to the tall man she'd been speaking to before.

He withdrew his phone, calling Volti.

His friend answered right away. "What's up, Lavos? Didn't I just see you?"

"Dress to impress for that feast."

"Are you seeing a lot of hot babes?"

"One. Her name is Mya. Remember it. She's beautiful and really wants to test a mating with an enforcer."

"Was she running a fever? There's nothing better than sex with a woman in heat."

"She's hot all right."

"Thanks."

He hung up and sighed. Lorn caught his attention and he had a feeling it was going to be a long afternoon. One of the men standing next to his brother was Velder, another clan leader. Velder knew they owed him. He'd supported Lorn taking over the clan from Decker.

It was time to kiss some ass. He could do it.

* * * * *

Jadee's shoulders hurt and her eyes burned. It was from exhaustion. She'd spent almost four entire days driving with only a few hours of sleep for breaks. She reached over to take a sip of coffee. It wasn't hot anymore but it helped her stay awake. She glanced at the top monitor on the dash. The GPS said she had nearly reached the town.

"I want to be there already!"

I thought leaving Alaska and driving home had been rough. She'd at least stopped for entire nights to sleep six to eight hours that first time. She'd also pulled over to stretch her legs at rest stops. But the return trip had just been brutal.

It hadn't helped that she'd started her journey already tired. It wasn't as if she'd gotten much sleep while she'd waited for dawn to come the night the Vamps had followed her home. She'd dozed off for a few minutes, only to be woken by noises. They had tried to get inside the RV all night but had given up right before the sun rose. She'd showered to wake up some, then hooked up the trailer to haul her car.

Jadee glanced at the dash to the second monitor, the one under the GPS. The sight of her little red car being pulled behind the RV was reassuring. She also checked out traffic. She'd been paranoid that someone would follow her but she felt secure it hadn't happened. They would have tried to attack her at night already.

She tapped the volume control embedded in the steering wheel for the CD player, heavy metal music blaring from the speakers. It helped her stay awake too. Bone tiredness had hit about the time she'd left Canada and driven into Alaska. She was used to spending eight hours a day on her feet tending bar, not sixteen hours a day with her butt planted on a seat as she drove. Her entire body felt stiff.

Digger's Auto Repair and Garage had been easy to locate. It was located in some tiny town she'd never heard of. She only hoped he knew how to get ahold of Lavos. She'd been certain Digger was a Werewolf too.

She flashed back to meeting the big mechanic. He'd been a bit cold and distant to her but seemed at ease with Lavos. She'd stayed inside the RV once he'd arrived but his nostrils had flared, as if he were sniffing around, when he'd come to start the engine. She'd noticed.

For at least the hundredth time, she reconsidered her actions. Would Lavos be annoyed that she'd sought him out for help? She just wasn't sure what else to do. He might have answers, knowing a lot more about Vampires than she did. All the movie and book facts she'd learned seemed like bullshit. He could probably tell her if every nest of Vampires was looking for her or if she just had to avoid Washington. It was information she needed. Otherwise she'd never know if she was safe or not.

He could also clue her into whether Vampires would tell Werewolves about her. The latter could come at her during the daytime. That would shoot her plan to hell to just lock herself inside the RV when the sun went down. She'd be at risk during the day too, and she had no idea how to spot Werewolves.

She tapped the wheel to the beat of the music and glanced at the GPS again. She'd find out soon enough if Digger could relay a message and if Lavos would speak to her. He might be pissed.

Would he kill her? She softly cursed.

No. He won't do that. He kept me alive before.

She also had to admit that seeing him again was something she longed to do. He wasn't forgettable in any way. She'd had a hard time saying goodbye to him. He hadn't seemed eager to let her drive off either. They'd stared at each other until his brother had ordered her to go. Lorn hadn't been rude but he hadn't been overly friendly either. The guy frowned a lot.

A sign caught her attention on the right side of the road. It stated gas was just ahead. Her heart sped up a little and it helped her get a second wind. Some of the tiredness faded. It was possible Lavos lived in that town too, along with Digger. She might see him faster than she'd anticipated.

She straightened in the seat until she got a look at her face in the rearview mirror. Her hair was a mess from opening up the windows a few times to allow air to blow inside and her eyes were bloodshot.

"Great," she muttered. "I look like hell. What's new?" It wasn't as if Lavos had met her at her best.

Jadee slowed when she saw the town. It was as small as the map implied, with several buildings on one side of the road. There was a gas station with a mini market and a few tiny tourist shops. A large barn, with Digger's name painted in red on the wooden side, sat at the end of the strip, beyond the gas station's pumps and parking lot.

She spotted another structure off the road, lurking behind the buildings and up a high hill. It had to be the biggest log cabin she'd ever seen, but it seemed to be a private home, since there were no signs near or on it. The road leading to it wasn't even in view.

Jadee parked at Digger's Auto Repair and Garage, maneuvering into the wide space beside the building. She noted the main doors were shut as she peered out her passenger-side window. A closed sign was displayed. "Shit." It was just her luck that he wasn't there when she arrived.

She turned off the engine and glanced at the sky. It would get dark soon but she had a bit of time. She removed the keys and unlocked the door, climbing out. Her legs protested when she put weight on them but she ignored the achy muscles, stretching. She leaned in and grabbed her purse off the floor under the seat where she'd stored it.

The gas station/mini-mart was open. She slammed the door and hit the remote lock on the RV door, heading that way. No other customers were in the small parking lot and she didn't see anyone inside except the clerk. He was a handsome guy in his twenties. The music inside was a little loud.

He stopped sweeping the floor and grinned at her. "Hello." He had a nice voice.

"Hi."

He turned his head, staring out the windows. "You need gas? I don't see your vehicle."

"I parked next door. Do you know when Digger's auto shop is going to be open?"

"Are you having car trouble? I can call him. He doesn't live far."

She hadn't expected that. "Thank you. That would be great."

"No problem." He set down the broom and walked over to the counter. He leaned across and lifted up the receiver of the phone. He flashed her another grin. "We'll get you up and running fast enough. Digger is magic with anything on four wheels."

He turned away and dialed. Jadee noticed a small display of hot dogs and walked over. The breakfast bars she'd eaten as road snacks had been tasteless after the first few. She started making two dogs.

"We have a code red," the clerk said. "A woman has car problems. Get here." He paused. "Thanks."

Jadee was surprised at his words. *Code red?* She met his gaze when he hung up.

He grinned again. "He's on his way."

"What's a code red?"

"That little engine light going off, of course. It's an inside joke. You know. He's a mechanic."

"Got it." She wasn't about to correct him on the car trouble. She faced the food stand and put ketchup on her dogs, then put them in their little pouches. She grabbed a bag of chips, a soda, and a candy bar. She went to the counter and set everything down.

"This is a small town."

179

"Yes." He stepped behind the cash register. "We don't get that many visitors. It's boring as hell around here." He started to ring up her purchases.

It was tempting to ask him about Lavos but she didn't dare. Instead, she studied the man. He was a very muscular guy for a store clerk. Was he a Werewolf who belonged to the pack? Did Werewolves work in gas station convenient stores? Did they even hold real jobs or just run around the vast woods all day, hunting for food? She slid her hand inside her purse and pulled out cash.

"Where are you heading?"

"I'm not sure yet."

One of his eyebrows lifted. "That's an odd answer."

"It was an unplanned trip." She struggled to come up with something to say that wouldn't give away too much information. "Ever just want to hit the road and drive? That's what I did."

"I wish." His features relaxed. "That sounds like fun." His nostrils flared. "You traveling alone?"

She'd seen that move. He was sniffing her. "Yes."

"That's brave. I mean, most women don't do that. It's a dangerous world. You're safe here but you know what I mean."

"I do." She was afraid to bring up Lavos but all those dire warnings he'd given her resurfaced. She wasn't sure if she could trust the clerk or if he'd lunge across the counter to try to kill her if he thought she knew he was a Werewolf. She glanced at his name tag. "Volti. That's a cool name. I've never met someone with that one before."

"It's Russian," he mumbled. "You'll find a lot of us in this area."

"Ah." *Russian Werewolves, or is that just an excuse for the odd name?* "Very cool."

"Thanks." His gaze darted down her body and then back up. "What's your name?"

"Jadee."

"What do the initials stand for?"

"It's just Jadee." She spelled it. "My parents weren't exactly the types to do the norm, including give me a name like Mary or Tammy."

"Hippies? We get some of them in the summer. They come out here saying they're trying to communicate with nature or find their karma or some such shit. No offense."

She laughed. "None taken. I bet you do get some odd visitors. This is far off the main highways."

"Yes, it is. You should have stuck to them though. The next motel is about thirty miles down the road and it's kind of a dive."

"I have an RV. I can sleep in it."

"I like those." He stepped out from behind the counter and walked to the door, peering toward Digger's. "Nice. It's a big sucker." He came back to her. "I don't see too many women driving them."

"It belonged to my father. I inherited it."

"I'm sorry." His features softened. "I'd be bummed if I lost my dad. We're close."

The front door of the store swung open and Digger came inside. He recognized her right away—his mouth fell open and his eyes widened. "Shit."

"What's wrong?" Volti's voice took on a deeper tone.

"Um…" Digger gave her a once over. "Nothing. This is the lady with the engine troubles?"

"Yes."

Digger took a few hesitant steps, giving her a suspicious look. "You ever been in this area before?"

He'd definitely recognized her. She was certain of that. He knew she had, so why did he ask? It might be because it wasn't safe to talk in front of the clerk. She'd play along. "Not this town but some of the ones nearby."

Digger's dark eyes started to lighten and he advanced fast, gripping her by her arms. She dropped her purse, stunned. He was trying to control her mind. His eyes didn't exactly glow. They were a dark, deep brown but they looked eerie as hell with some yellow lighting them up.

"Goddamn," Digger hissed. "She wasn't supposed to come back."

"Who is she?"

"She's the only survivor from when those bloodsuckers took out that small human town. Lorn said he wiped her mind and sent her back to the lower forty-eight. I was sure he'd told her to never return to Alaska, so what the hell is she doing here?" He kept his gaze locked on her. "You'd better call Lorn, Volti."

"Are you sure she's the right one?"

They were talking as if Jadee wasn't there. Did that mean that Digger thought he had her under his control? Was she supposed to be like some breathing, brainless doll? He looked furious and scary. She masked her features and held very still, prepared to pretend. She didn't know what he'd do if he realized she was more than aware of what was going on, in control of her body and thoughts.

"I thought that damn RV looked familiar but I didn't walk up and inspect it. It'll have California plates but the tow car had Washington ones. That's why I didn't put it together." Digger leaned in a little. "Hold real still, sweetheart. No need to be afraid. We're going to send you home so we don't have to kill you. Her heart is racing."

She tried to slow that down. He either had super-good hearing or he could feel her pulse.

"Lorn is busy. The delegates from the clans are here. They arrived this morning. They're all up the hill at the lodge. I'm supposed to send any humans on their way so they don't stick around."

"Call Lavos then."

"He's up there too. He dropped in about half an hour ago and said he had to go kiss some ass. I think we should handle this. Put her to sleep and I'll carry her to the back storeroom while you go find out what's wrong with her engine. We'll wake her up and send her on her way as soon as you get it running right. I'll even fill her tank. She'll just remember it was something trivial you fixed fast, she pumped her own gas, and took off."

"She got food."

"Not a problem. I saw how she likes her hot dogs. I'll just get her fresh ones. She won't even notice a time gap if we implant that she arrived here whenever you get her engine going."

"Sleep," Digger ordered.

Jadee closed her eyes and let her body slump. It was going to hurt if she hit the floor but the idea of letting the two Werewolves know she was immune might be more painful, since Digger mentioned killing her.

The mechanic didn't allow her fall. He held her up until Volti walked up behind her and grabbed her under her arms. He lifted her off her feet, against his solid body.

"Her keys are on the counter." Volti turned with her. She let her head fall forward, playing dead to the world. He adjusted his hold on her to free a hand when they must have reached a door. He bent back to keep her body against his front. Then he eased her down on something soft. She waited until she heard a door close before she peeked.

It was a small storage room and there was a sleeping bag on the floor, where she'd been gently dumped. She listened, hearing Volti and Digger softly speaking from the other room. She just couldn't make out what they said. She sat up when she realized she was alone.

She saw the back door and rose up, walking toward it. There was a glass window and she peeked out. The big log cabin up the hill was within sight. That had to be the lodge they'd talked about. Lavos would be there.

She glanced at the other door that led into the store. She could lie back down and play along until they sent her on her way. It would mean she couldn't return. Digger and Volti would know she'd fooled them then for sure.

She looked out the window again, watching the line of trees. No one else was around. She glanced at the log structure. It wasn't too far away and thick trees covered most of the hill. She debated her options.

It would be stupid to make a dash for that lodge to find Lavos on her own. They'd mentioned delegates from other clans. She could guess what that meant. Werewolves from other packs had come to visit. The woods could literally be crawling with them. The memory of what Lavos looked like while shifted sent a chill down her spine.

Her other alternative would be to forget about trying to gain his help by meekly leaving town. But she'd come a long way. It was a hell of a choice.

The memory of those Vampires flashed in her mind. What if they *did* send out messages to other Vampire nests? Lavos said they loved to live in cities. She'd be safe if she avoided any large ones, probably.

"Damn," she muttered.

What if Vampires and Werewolf packs talked to share information? They knew she was immune to mind control. Was there already some alert going out for her? Would everything that went bump in the night and day be after her ass? Paranoia could only go so far to keep her safe. She needed to know what she was up against if she wanted a chance at surviving. That meant she'd have to get answers.

She could kidnap a Werewolf and make him talk. She ditched that idea as soon as it formed. She wasn't about to kill someone like Lavos, regardless of what they wanted to do to her. They were just trying to protect their secrets, unlike Vampires, who were bloodthirsty perverts who attacked women for no good reason. The two men in the store had just wanted to wipe her memory and send her on her way. Neither one had demanded she perform sexual acts on them.

Her last option would be to change her looks, ditch the RV and her car. That RV was her only protection though. Her dad had left her a lot of money. She could order another RV that wasn't traceable, but it would take months to have all the special features added to it. Months she'd be sleeping in motels with cheap doors and easy access to her if something wanted in.

Fuck. She stared up at that lodge. She needed to talk to Lavos. She didn't want to die. Digger was going to go play with her engine and he'd figure out fast that there wasn't anything wrong with it. He'd come back and she'd have to leave town. Her only chance at finding Lavos would be gone.

She gripped the handle of the door but examined the frame first. There was no alarm hooked to it. It wasn't even a sturdy security door. The town must not have much crime. She twisted the knob and it turned. She opened the door an inch.

"Damn," she hissed. "This is stupid—but what choice do I have?"

She eased the door open and stepped outside. She froze momentarily, looking at the woods once more, not seeing any other people or hairy beasts. She pushed off the wall and ran for all she was worth to the line of trees.

Chapter Eleven

Jadee peeked out from behind a big tree trunk, staring at the building. No one lounged outside but she couldn't exactly just stroll inside the double doors. Her heart pounded and she turned her head, looking down the hill she'd just climbed. The small town sat below. Her RV remained parked at the garage. Digger had lifted the hood up and stood on something to reach the engine. Volti hadn't charged out of the store to search for her so far. At least she hadn't seen him.

How easy would it be for them to track her?

They're like dogs. Probably as simple as pie. She clenched her teeth.

A noise behind her made her startle and turn her head. The double doors opened and a few men stepped outside of the lodge. They weren't Lavos but they looked badass. Were all the men in town muscular and large? It seemed that way, since all of Lavos's pack she'd seen so far fit that exact description.

One of them jogged down the steps and headed into the woods behind the lodge. The other one withdrew his phone, dialed, and then held it up to his ear. His voice didn't carry to her but he seemed to be amused by whoever he spoke to.

The guy strolled toward the side of the building, still talking on his phone. He disappeared around the corner.

Jadee looked down the hill. Digger had closed the hood on her RV and carried his toolbox inside his garage.

"Shit." Time wasn't on her side.

The doors opened behind her again. She knew the sound now. She peered around the tree trunk...

And relief flooded her as Lavos stepped out.

He talked to someone inside, his body turned sideways. She drank in his profile. He wore a nice T-shirt and faded jeans. He looked really good. He even wore the biker boots still.

Close the door so I can step out and you can see me, she thought his way. *Come on. Stop talking so I can let you know I'm here.*

He closed the door and took a few steps down the stairs. Jadee sucked in a deep breath and almost moved when the door opened again. A tall, beautiful dark-haired woman wearing a green formal dress exited.

"Wait!"

Lavos spun, giving Jadee his back. The woman stopped at the top of the stairs. Her mouth moved but Jadee had no idea what she said. She wished she could hear them. Lavos stayed at the bottom of the steps.

Jadee glanced down the hill. Digger had left his garage and walked toward the gas station. He would go in there and they'd know she had escaped.

Panic hit. They'd hunt for her.

She twisted her head, irritated that the woman and Lavos still yakked away as if they didn't have a care in the world.

The woman gripped the railing of the stairs and gracefully made her way down each step. Jadee didn't miss the way she seemed to be looking at Lavos as if he were a meat stick she wanted to eat. She proved Jadee's theory by stopping one step up so her and Lavos were the same height. The bitch put her hands on the tops of his shoulders and leaned in. Her dress was so low cut her boobs almost spilled out.

Jealousy struck but Jadee pushed it back. She had bigger worries—like the fact that Digger was now inside the store and they'd probably noticed she wasn't still inside that storage room.

She looked down in time to see the back door being thrown open and Volti rushing outside.

The jig is up. Damn. She watched Digger join Volti behind the store. The clerk crouched, bracing his hand on the ground. He was either sniffing it or looking for footprints. His head snapped up and he seemed to be staring right in her direction.

Jadee ducked fast, hoping he hadn't spotted her. There was a lot of vegetation between him and her. She turned her head, looking at the lodge.

Lavos had backed away from the woman. He turned in Jadee's direction and advanced with long-legged strides. The woman called out loud enough for her words to carry.

"When *is* a good time, Lavos?"

He paused and glanced back. "Later. I have to make rounds."

He faced Jadee's way and started walking again. The woman grabbed her skirt and hiked it up a few inches, rushing after him. She got in front of Lavos, released her skirt and put both of her hands on his chest to prevent him from getting around her.

"You don't need to play hard to get to hold my interest. I think we're a perfect match." The woman sounded angry. "I don't enjoy games."

Jadee leaned up a little, hoping to catch a glimpse of where Digger and Volti were. She spotted them coming up the hill. They'd reach her within minutes. She didn't have any time left.

She just straightened and stepped out.

The woman's back was to her and Lavos's focus was on the woman, so he didn't spot Jadee. She waved her arms, and he must have seen the motion because his gaze lifted. His surprise was evident when they made eye contact. His mouth fell open.

The woman started to turn but Lavos suddenly gripped her arms.

"Later. We got an alert and I'm on duty. You need to go inside. You don't want the enemy to see you." He spoke loudly.

Jadee got the message. She ducked behind the tree and stared down the hill. She caught a glimpse of Digger and took a seat on the ground. They were coming right at her, moving way faster than she had. And it was a steep hill.

Lavos's boots crunched on the ground as he drew closer. She held still but lifted her chin when he entered the woods and stepped right in front of her.

"What in the hell?"

He looked good. Angry but as handsome as ever. "Hi." She lifted her hand to give him a tiny wave.

He crouched, spreading his thighs on both sides of her and bracing his hands on the tree above her head. "Are you insane? How did you get here? How were you able to get past the enforcers?"

"I think two of them are coming after me right now. I mean that literally. Digger and Volti are almost here."

190

A deep snarl tore from him and he twisted his head. He sniffed the air. "I smell them." He focused on her. "Don't say a word. Not one. I'll handle this. Don't move either."

"Okay."

He rose to his full height and turned, planting his booted feet right in front of her bent knees. She leaned a little to the right to see around him.

Volti arrived first, with Digger right on his heels.

"We have a problem," Volti growled.

"I'm aware." Lavos's tone sounded calmer.

"It's that human from the campsite." Digger sounded a little out of breath. "You found her."

"Yes. I did. Return to your posts. I'll handle this."

"I put her to sleep but she woke and took off. Something is wrong with her."

"Digger." Lavos paused. "Listen to me. I want you to drive her motor home out to my place. I see it from here. Then I want both of you to keep damn quiet about her being here."

"Did you hear me? She woke and took off!" Digger seemed worked up.

"I implanted orders in her. She was to find me if she had any information about the Vampires who want to start a war."

"You didn't tell me that." Volti stepped to the side, frowning at Jadee. "She's human."

"A smart one who is very receptive to taking orders." Lavos inched back, putting his body closer to hers. "She's our spy. We have other clans here, though, and I don't want them to know about her."

191

"Does Lorn know about this?" Volti scowled at Lavos.

"Of course. It was his idea. I need to get the information from her but I don't want anyone alarmed that there's a human in town. And I don't have time to argue with the two of you. I'm issuing you orders. Hide any trace that she was here and keep your mouths shut. Drive her motor home to my house and hide it around back. Lorn is busy right now so I'm handling this on my own. Go!"

Both men took off fast. Jadee relaxed. Lavos held still, seeming to watch them until they were far down the hill. He turned, then glared down at her. "Do you have any idea what kind of shit storm this could start? What are you doing here? What possessed you to find me? *How* did you find me? Do you have a death wish?"

"That's a lot of questions."

He crouched and leaned forward, bracing his hands on the tree again. It put their faces about a foot apart. "I told you how dangerous it would be if anyone figured out you were immune to our eyes."

Speaking of, she stared into his. They were still as beautiful as she remembered. "Is that woman your girlfriend or something?"

She couldn't believe that popped out of her mouth. She sealed her lips.

He blinked a few times. "No. Do you know what? Be quiet." He glanced around the area. "The meet and greet is officially about to begin soon. That means everyone will be heading this way. I need to get you out of here. Roll in the dirt."

"What?"

He stood, backing away. "To cover your scent. You reek of human. Roll in the dirt. Just do it. We don't have much time. You can clean up once I have you inside my house. *Roll*, Jadee—do you want to survive or not?"

"Great." She was close to the ground already, at least. She leaned forward and flattened onto her belly. She rolled, squeezing her eyes closed. The earth was loose and dry. The strong smell of it filled her nose.

"A few more times," he ordered. "You need to be coated to hide your scent."

She rolled again and wiggled against the ground, then stopped and sat up. "I feel like that old cartoon character who throws off grime when he walks."

Lavos grinned and offered her a hand. "You can have a hot shower soon."

She gripped it and he pulled her to her feet. He was strong, and that smile of his made her belly quiver. He was just too good-looking. "That's not how I imagined it would be if you ever asked me to get down and dirty."

His eyes lit up, glowing. "Don't flirt with a predator, Jadee. I bite." He released her hand and suddenly bent, snagging her around her knees with one arm.

She gasped when he lifted her right off her feet and her world turned upside down. He wrapped his other arm around the back of her thighs.

"Be quiet and still. I'm going to move fast to avoid everyone."

He lunged into the woods. She made no protests but she did wonder about that bite reference he'd mentioned. Would he actually bite her? It didn't sound as scary as it might have once. Lavos was extremely hot. It wasn't as if she hadn't fantasized about him nibbling on her a few times since they'd met.

Lavos paused and sniffed the air. He scented some of his clan nearby. He turned left, skirting one of the trails that would lead to the lodge. He could still faintly smell Jadee but he had her slung over his shoulder. The dirt smell was stronger, tickling his nose almost into a sneeze.

What in the hell is she doing here? He had a hundred questions but couldn't ask them until he got her safely inside his house. Lorn would shit a brick when he found out Jadee had entered their territory. The timing couldn't have been worse. They were supposed to be showing the other clans that they were strong and able to hold their own clan together. It would be bad if anyone found out not only had they allowed Jadee to keep her memories, but she'd hunted down where they lived.

Jadee kept silent. He was grateful for that. Humans weren't known for following orders well unless they were being made to. He reached his land and relaxed a little. He'd taken the long way to get there and come around the back. Her motor home and trailered car had already been parked behind his house. He marched to the back door of his home and entered, slamming and locking it behind him. He kept her over his shoulder. He took the stairs two at a time and didn't stop until he entered the master bathroom. He supported her back and bent, depositing her gently on his counter.

She took in his bathroom and smiled. "Nice."

He had no idea what to say to her first. Dirt covered her but she was still as appealing as hell. "Why did you come here, Jadee?"

"I'm in trouble. I didn't know where else to go."

That suddenly made him feel more concern than irritation over her bad timing. "What kind of trouble?"

"Can I shower first? It's kind of a long story." She touched her jeans and grimaced. "I stink."

"Yes. I have to make a call." He'd have to tell Lorn he wasn't returning to the lodge, and why. He backed up. "Do it fast. I'll be waiting in the bedroom." He entered his room and closed the door between them. He used his cell phone to contact his brother.

"Where are you?" Lorn didn't sound happy.

"Can you be heard?"

"Yes."

"Walk away and find some privacy."

"Of course." His voice grew a little distant, as if he'd lowered the phone away from his mouth. "Excuse me. I have to take this call." Long seconds ticked by and Lorn sighed into the phone. "Okay. I'm in the bathroom and no one else is in here. Is there a problem?"

Lavos closed his eyes, dreading his next words. "I'll handle it. It's just that I won't be at the feast later."

"You have to be here," Lorn growled. "I need you."

"Don't blow your top—but Jadee is in my bathroom."

Lorn said nothing.

Lavos winced. "I'll figure out how she found us and why she's here. She just said she's in trouble. That's why I need to stay here. No one can see her."

195

"I knew it was a mistake to let her go," Lorn said.

"Saving her wasn't a mistake. I know you don't mean that. You're just under a lot of stress right now. I'll handle this. Make my excuses to your guests."

"And tell them what? My lead enforcer has better things to do than spend time with them?" Lorn growled. "Do you know how the rest of our clan is going to react when they find out you're harboring a human inside your home? There'll be more challenges for leadership. Decker made them hate humans too much. They'll believe I'm weak."

"I supported you being with Kira."

"I love Kira, and she's not exactly weak now, is she? She was also raised in this clan. You barely know Jadee."

"They haven't bitched too much about Veso and Glen."

"He's not my lead enforcer and brother."

Lavos reached up and fisted his hair. He knew Lorn made valid points. "Look, she's in trouble. I like her. She found us and she's here. I'm not going to send her on her way until I find out what the hell is going on. I can come for the feast but that means I leave her here alone. Is that okay with you?" He released his hair and let his hand drop to his side.

"No! What if she goes outside? What if someone sees her? What if she strolls right in here and introduces herself to everyone? She obviously doesn't have much common sense if she came back after she was given her freedom."

"I'll explain things to her."

"You did that once, yet she's here." Lorn calmed. "Okay. I'll tell them there was a Vampire sighting near one of our borders last night and we just heard about it. That will excuse you from the feast since I'd send you to check that out. Just deal with her and get her on her way by morning. Am I clear?"

"Very."

"And Lavos?"

"What?"

"Fuck her and get it over with. Your fascination with her isn't healthy for either of us." Lorn ended the call.

Chapter Twelve

Lavos paced the bedroom until the water shut off in the other room. He waited for her to come out. Jadee didn't belong in their territory. He and Lorn were cool with humans but the rest of the clan wouldn't be okay with their leader's brother taking a human mate. They would see it as a weakness and a reason to challenge. Old-school thinking wasn't going to easily change.

The door opened and Jadee stepped out wearing just a towel around her middle. He swallowed hard, trying but failing not to stare at the tops of her breasts or those shapely legs of hers. For a short woman, she had a great body.

"I didn't want to put my dirty clothes back on."

"I should have remembered to give you something." He knew he should offer her clothes to wear but his boots seemed glued to the floor. He'd wanted Jadee naked in his bed, and it was just across the room. It would be easy to snatch that towel away and carry her there.

She kept hold of the towel with one hand and leaned against the doorjamb. "How mad at me are you?"

"Not very. I'm more surprised than anything."

"I bet. Should I start at the beginning or just get to the point?"

"You said you were in trouble." He locked gazes with her to avoid getting turned-on more by ogling her body. "Why?"

"A Vampire attacked me."

His gaze lowered to her neck. He didn't see any wounds there. He took a step closer, alarmed.

"I killed him. I mean, I would have just let him bite me so he thought his eyes were working, but...my blood wasn't the only thing he wanted."

He glanced down her body. "He wanted sex?" He couldn't blame the Vampire. She was very attractive. But it also pissed him off. She was too good for one of those damn bloodbags. Then her other statement registered. "You killed him?"

"Yes."

"How did you do that?" He drew even closer, wanting to pull her into his arms. The thought of her fighting off a Vampire chilled his blood. She could have been killed. She was too small to be a fighter. Humans rarely survived facing off against a Vamp.

"I think the ice pick I shoved into his nuts gave me the advantage."

His leg automatically twitched, wanting to protect his own. *Ouch.*

"He ordered me to get down on my knees and blow him. He let them hang out in the breeze. I just aimed for the closest body part. They were a bigger target than his dick. It was sad. I could almost understand why he felt the need to mind warp women so they wouldn't laugh when he unzipped. I've seen bigger ones when I changed diapers."

Lavos would have laughed but he saw the haunted look in her eyes. He also noticed how tired she looked for the first time. She'd been traumatized by the ordeal she spoke of, probably tormented by nightmares when she slept.

"Come here." He opened his arms.

She did, to his surprise. He pulled her into a hug. She was damp and smelled like him, since she'd used his shampoo and conditioner. He lowered his chin until it rested on top of her head, not minding the wet strands. She could have been killed.

"He exploded on me, just not the way he meant to. How can one body make so much ash?"

He closed his eyes and held her tighter when she shivered. He doubted she was cold; it was more from the trauma she must have suffered. "How did you kill him?"

"Fire axe to the throat. I thought I'd have to chop at him a bit but one swing did it." She shuddered in his arms. "His head came off and boom — ash explosion."

He rubbed her back. "My brave Jadee. It sounds as if you got lucky and hit his neck just right. They have stronger bones than humans but they weaken if he hasn't fed for a while."

"Then his nest came after me. They must have seen what happened and somehow followed me home. A bunch of them surrounded my place. They couldn't get in since I had started living in the RV, but at dawn I got the hell out of there. I didn't know if more of them would come after me. They knew my name. I'm fucked, aren't I?"

He picked her up. She tensed in his arms but didn't struggle. He carried her to the bed and eased her back onto her feet. "Sit." He let her go. It was difficult. He liked holding her.

She sat on the edge of his bed and he crouched in front of her, bracing her knees between his spread ones. It put them at face level. "It depends. Were they rogues?"

"How can you tell?"

"Did the one you kill smell bad, as if he hadn't bathed in a while?"

She shook her head. "He was a well-dressed perv."

"Rogues tend to be a little nuts and they don't live the way humans do. The organized Vamps pretend they're human. They keep homes and take care of their appearances to avoid drawing attention."

"These Vampires seemed organized. The two women and five guys were dressed almost in uniform, in all-black clothes."

He sighed. "It means they're members of a nest, and probably associated with the Vampire Council if they weren't rogues."

"They have a council?"

"Yes."

"That means they can tell other nests about me, right? What about your Werewolf packs? Will they be sending out alerts about me to them too? Can you check to see if you've gotten one yet?"

He hated to see the fear in her eyes. The Vampire Council *would* spread the word to other nests if one of them reported Jadee. "Do they know you're immune to their eyes?"

"Yes." She swallowed hard. "I didn't blow the perv, and another one demanded I unlock my car door to let him in at a red light after I left work. I took off like a bat out of hell and left rubber on the streets in my wake. Then those other ones showed up at my place. Did I mention they know my name?"

He let that sink in. It was bad. Vampire nests would be looking for her. She'd killed one of them. That was enough to stir their wrath. A human killing a Vampire tended to be a crime they wanted punished. The fact that

201

she was immune to them controlling her mind and erasing her memories would make them fear her.

"You probably think I should have just given the pervert a blow job, right?"

"No." The desire to rip apart the Vamp who had come after Jadee surged but he was already dead. "You had every right to defend yourself. I'm just glad you were able to. You're lucky to be alive."

"I won't be for long if more Vampires find me. Is anywhere safe for me to go? I was thinking about avoiding big cities but then I realized they could send your kind after me too. Is that how it works? I needed to know so I came to you for answers. Will I be safe if I just lock down at night and only go out during the day?"

"I need to tell you something, Jadee."

"It's bad, isn't it? I'm toast, aren't I? Spit it out. Can you put in a good word for me with these packs so they don't come after me? Tell them I'm dog friendly or something?"

"I'm not a Werewolf."

Her eyebrows shot up. "You're not a Vamp. We were just outside. The sun burns them."

"I'm something else."

"But I saw you. You were a big...dog."

"I'm both."

She frowned.

"I'm a VampLycan. Long story short, Vampires and Lycans once held alliances but it turned out bad. The male Vampires figured out they could

202

get the female Lycans pregnant. They attacked the women, willing or not. I'm a result of both races."

She chewed on her bottom lip.

"I can't tell packs to leave you alone. We're not in control of them, and we don't have sway with the Vampire Council. They hate and fear us. We avoid them too so they don't think we're trying to start another war. Vampires can be paranoid about that shit."

Jadee leaned back a few inches, staring at his mouth with a little trepidation. "You drink blood? I hope you're not hungry."

She wasn't screaming or trying to get away. Her mild reaction amused him. "Your neck is safe." He glanced down at the towel. Her body was another matter. He swallowed, attempting to ignore how easy it would be to strip her. "We get the ability to control minds from Vampires. We shift forms thanks to our Lycan blood. It pretty much means we got the better qualities of the two, and far fewer weaknesses."

"Do you have a council?"

"No. We have four clans, with a leader for each one."

"Will they get notified about me and start trying to take me out?"

"Not if I can help it."

"I'm starting to feel like a unicorn."

He laughed, her response totally unanticipated. "Why is that?"

"It seems it's pretty rare to be immune to your eyes. I must be unique if this many people want to kill me."

"The Vampires will fear that you'll start hunting and taking out their nests. There are other humans like you who are immune, and in the past they became Vampire hunters. The council used to actively track and take them out in the old days. It's probably why there aren't as many of your kind as there used to be. They'd slaughter entire families so their children couldn't continue the tradition of becoming hunters. They believed it could be a hereditary trait."

"I just want to live and let live. I have no intention of becoming a Vampire slayer. I wouldn't have used an axe on that jerk except he came after me. I was just taking out the trash at work, not asking for him to flash me his goods and order me to blow him."

"I understand, but you have to remember that a lot of these masters are hundreds of years old, if not thousands. They run the council, and therefore, they rarely change the way they think."

"Thousands?"

He nodded. "Some are. My Vampire ancestor was over two thousand years old. I never met him but I heard the stories. He was one of the few ancients who came to America once it was discovered. Most stayed in Europe, since travel was highly dangerous for day sleepers. They'd starve or be discovered by humans during the long journeys by ship if they fed from passengers."

"They didn't have redeye flights."

He chuckled. "No, they didn't."

"Where is this antique Vampire ancestor of yours?"

"It's uncertain. He may have been killed during the war."

"The civil war?"

"The war between Vampires and Lycans."

"I missed reading about that one in my history books."

Jadee amused him; he enjoyed her sense of humor. "Humans who did know wished they hadn't. Most didn't survive. They were food for Vampires."

"Who won?"

"We did, obviously, considering we're not under the control of Vampires. They wanted to use Lycan women as breeders to create an army of children like what I am. They believed they could control them the way they do their nests."

"How is that?"

"A master rules everyone in his nest to an almost slave-like degree. They planned to use the children to protect them during the day, and Vampires can also survive off Lycan blood."

"Dual purpose. It sounds great for the Vampires but not so much for the kids. Slave labor and blood donors."

"Exactly. The Lycan women weren't too thrilled either. Vampires didn't care if they were willing to become breeders or even if they were already mated. They just attacked them once they realized they could get them pregnant under certain conditions. The Lycan men defended their women. That started the war. The Lycans fought while the women of breeding age ran away. Then the children were born...and the Vampires had something to fear as we matured."

"You *are* a badass."

He grinned. "We have their strengths but not their weaknesses. Let's just say the war was over once we grew up. It's against the law for a Vampire to force a Lycan to breed anymore. If they tried, we can hunt them down during their day sleep and take them out. We have claws to rip their heads off. They just have fangs and sharp fingernails, *if* they let them grow out. They tend to avoid us to stay alive. The Lycans avoid us because we upset their pack structures."

"English?"

"Almost every VampLycan is considered an alpha because of our strengths and abilities. A Lycan pack exists because a single alpha holds them together. They survive by living in small groups to help keep them stronger as a unit. We show up and it makes them nervous."

"They're afraid you'll take over their packs?"

"Yes."

"How do your clans work?"

He sighed. "It's complicated. It not only takes strength to lead a clan but respect." He paused, instantly thinking of Decker. "Or fear."

"It *sounds* complicated." She broke eye contact with him and glanced at his arms. "So who was that woman?"

"The one at the lodge? No one."

She locked gazes with him. "She looked like someone."

Lavos knew she wasn't the type to just drop something. It was one of the things he liked about Jadee. "She's visiting from another clan."

"Have you ever slept with her?"

"No."

"Ever wanted to?"

She was bold. He liked it. "No."

"Ah. Okay. Does she want to sleep with you?"

"Yes."

Her mouth compressed into a tight line. "I knew it. She seems really interested."

"It isn't going to happen. I'm not interested in *her*."

"Do you already have a girlfriend?" She glanced around. "I haven't seen anything to indicate you're dating someone. There's no women's stuff in your bathroom."

She'd looked. He was flattered. "I met someone recently that I'm attracted to. I can't get her out of my thoughts. I don't want to settle for someone else when I only seem to want one woman."

She stared into his eyes. "Does she have a name?"

He almost laughed. "Yes. Everyone does."

"Want to tell me what it is?"

"Do you want to keep playing this game?" He leaned in closer, inhaling through his nose. He wanted her badly.

"I'm not playing. I'm just curious."

A soft growl rumbled from him. "Are you going to deny the attraction between us?"

"No. I just wasn't sure if it was mutual."

"Do you think I would have brought you into my home and protected you from my clan when you trespassed if I didn't want you right where you are?"

She glanced down at his bed, then looked at him. "Nice."

"I'm not sure how to take that response." He wanted to kiss her. "You don't look afraid."

"Should I be?"

"Possibly. You know what I am and that I want you."

"I'm not feeling any fear."

He inched closer, until their breaths mingled. "Are you on anything?"

"I don't do drugs."

He tilted his head, wondering if she was joking or being serious. "Birth control."

"No. Is that an issue?"

"It might be if I take that towel off you and do what I've wanted to since we met."

Her tongue darted out and she licked her lips. "I thought your kind couldn't get my kind pregnant unless we were the same species."

"Wrong." He glanced down. "You'd have to be ovulating though."

"I can't tell."

"I can. Get rid of the towel."

"How would you know?"

"I'd taste it."

Her eyes widened just slightly, then heat crept up into her cheeks. He thought the fact that she blushed was telling. His Jadee was less sophisticated than she pretended to be if oral sex caused that reaction from her.

"Toss the towel and lie back, Jadee."

He held his breath, waiting to see how she'd respond. He was keeping his lust in check to prevent his eyes from glowing and proving how much he wanted her. He thought about warning her but then figured it was best not to remind her of how different they truly were.

She reached up and tugged the towel free where she'd tucked it over her breasts to keep the seams together. He tried not to stare as she parted it, revealing her creamy skin and lush breasts. Their size wasn't too large, nor too small. They were perfect. She tugged the towel open more to show off her belly, then finally her lap and the top of her thighs. It took restraint for him to hold still while she lifted up and leaned back, tugging the damp material out from under her. She just blindly threw it in the direction of the bathroom.

She shaved almost all of her hair off her mound, just a small, closely cut strip to accent her pussy. Jadee lay flat on his bed, and then surprised him when she spread her thighs, bracing one of her feet against his chest near his shoulder, while placing her other heel firmly on the edge of the bed.

Lavos looked at the foot she'd rested on him, amused with the red toenail polish he hadn't noticed before. His attention traveled over her calf, to her bent knee, down her thigh, right back to her pussy.

"I have one rule."

He lifted his head, staring at her. She intrigued him and he became very interested in learning what it would be. He could guess her greatest worry. "I'll be gentle."

"That's not it. You already warned me that you bite. Could you avoid fang damage down there? I'm not a fan of clit piercings or pain."

He admired her courage for taking him on. "That's not where I'd bite you if I sink my teeth in."

He tried to lean forward but she pushed against his chest with her foot, so he held her gaze. She opened her mouth but he spoke first. "What?"

209

"Where would you bite?"

"I'd roll you over, fuck you from behind until you screamed my name, and then go for your shoulder."

"No neck? You said you were part Vampire."

"I don't crave blood and I'd never bite into a main artery. The fleshy part of your shoulder wouldn't bleed much, and it's a convenient place to go for in that position."

"Why bite at all if you don't crave blood?"

"That's a discussion for another time. I won't bite you, Jadee."

She eased her foot off him and lowered it, her heel resting on the bed. She spread her legs more, an invitation he wasn't about to resist. He did surprise her when he slid his arms under her thighs and cupped her ass with both hands, lifting her lower half a few inches off the bed. She gasped but he wanted to taste her too much to waste another second.

The scent of her was making his dick hurt. He stopped holding back the lust, letting it flow. He opened his mouth and ran his tongue along her clit in one slow, long lick. She wasn't prepared for him to fuck her yet but she would be. Her moan was music to his ears.

He growled deeply, hoping it wouldn't scare her. She didn't seem the type to easily frighten. She'd proven that to him a few times already.

She tensed...but then she understood why he did it. She moaned.

"You vibrate when you do that! Do it again."

He almost laughed. His Jadee was brave and adventurous. He growled louder, sliding his tongue against the bundle of nerves. She tried to wiggle in his hold, spreading her thighs more. Her breathing increased, and so did

210

the sounds of her pleasure. The scent of her desire rose as she started to get wet. All amusement died inside him.

He snarled, wanting to fuck her so bad it caused him real pain. He became merciless with his mouth, intent on making her come hard and fast. She arched and cried out his name. Her hips bucked in his hold and he tore his mouth away, staring down at her sex.

Her pussy appeared small and fragile, but so wet. He lowered her ass to the bed and didn't bother with his shirt. He tore at the front of his pants instead, freeing his straining cock. He looked at the size of it, and then again at the small slit of her pussy. Frustration rose with a fury.

Who the hell has she been fucking?

He leaned forward, rubbing the head of his dick against her slit until he was right where he wanted to be. He gently pushed. Her slick flesh parted for him but it was a tight fit. Her pussy squeezed the head of his dick. He let go of his shaft and gripped her calf, lifting her leg to spread her open more. One glance at her face told him she was still recovering from her climax. Her eyes were closed and her mouth parted as she tried to catch her breath.

He leaned over her, letting gravity help him enter her body. He clenched his teeth, caught between heaven and hell. She felt amazing but he didn't want to risk hurting either of them by making her take his wide girth too fast. She moaned and he looked at her face. Her eyes opened, gaze locking with his.

"Relax."

She nodded and reached out to him. Her fingers curled around his arm, braced on the bed next to her waist. He pushed in more when her muscles

211

relaxed just a tiny bit, the firm grip her pussy had on him easing. She was hot, wet, and tight. *Perfect.*

He withdrew a little, then pushed in again. She took more of him. He worked back and forth in a torturously slow rhythm that seemed to affect them both as she dug her nails into his skin and moaned his name.

He was going to come before he ever got fully seated inside her. He'd wanted her too much and for too long. His balls drew up tight and he felt the muscles in his lower stomach tensing. Jadee arched her hips when he moved forward and he was all inside her on that last thrust. He had to close his eyes to break their connection. His fangs shot out and he opened his mouth to prevent them from piercing his lower lip. He held still, fighting for control.

Jadee bucked her hips, moving him. That slight friction was too much and he snarled, knowing he was lost.

He came down over her, pinning her to the bed. He wanted to bite her shoulder but twisted his head, keeping his fangs away. He couldn't hold back, fucking her without restraint as ecstasy ripped through him. He came deep inside her, not caring if she was ovulating or not, though he hadn't tasted it on her.

Lavos rolled so he didn't crush her, keeping her locked to him so his dick remained buried inside her pussy. She clawed at his shoulder, her nails scratching against skin through his shirt. Her ragged cry hopefully wasn't one from pain. He felt her muscles squeezing around his dick and it set him off more, another jet of his sperm shooting inside her.

He groaned, turning his head and burying his nose against her throat. His fangs touched her skin but he didn't bite.

Chapter Thirteen

Jadee knew she'd have bruises but she didn't care. She was on her side pressed tight against Lavos. One of her legs was hooked over his hip, the other one tangled under one of his against the bed and off the side of it. The sexy guy had a good firm hold on her ass cheek. He had big hands, big feet, and the saying was true in his case. Lavos was hung.

Who's the big dog? Lavos.

She almost laughed at that thought. It was one she wouldn't share in case it insulted him. She caught her breath and tried to make her mind work. It was tough to do after he'd just made her come twice in a row.

She became aware of more things. He had fangs and they were touching her throat. She didn't feel any pain but it was impossible to miss the feel of them with his open mouth on the area just under her ear. He could bite her. She didn't jerk away, not willing to move yet. His heavy breathing tickled a little.

She eased her death grip on his shoulder. She must have done that in the heat of the moment. She let her hand trail down his biceps, liking the feeling of them. It was a pity he wore a shirt. She wanted to touch him all over.

The man had a wicked mouth and no one had ever blown her mind better than he had. He'd growled and vibrated as he'd gone down on her. That was an amazing sensation while being licked. It also made her feel a tiny bit embarrassed. She hadn't lasted more than a minute. He'd be disappointed if he wanted to play with her for a while.

Lavos made a low rumbling sound and his chest vibrated against hers. She liked that. He licked her throat. It was a little odd but nice. His fangs scraped against her and then he closed his mouth, pressing a tiny kiss on that same spot.

"Next time we'll do this a bit slower." He lifted his head and she opened her eyes, loving the sight of his. They were that beautiful, vividly bright blue she found fascinating. They glowed a little but not too much. He studied her, his expression serious. "Did I hurt you at all?"

"Nope." She wasn't going to complain about a few bruises from his hands digging into her various body parts or the tenderness she felt because he was a bit of a stallion.

"I wasn't too rough?"

She knew what it meant to be fucked like an animal in those last few minutes. He'd gone at her with wild abandon. "I liked that part."

His smile erased the tension from his features. "Was there anything you didn't like?"

She glanced at his shirt. "You're overdressed."

"I can fix that."

"I want to touch you." She hoped he wouldn't back off, hearing those words. Some men liked to detach themselves from a woman after sex.

"I'm all yours." He pulled away a little. "Hold that thought and don't go anywhere."

Jadee hated the feeling of him pulling his cock out of her. He still felt hard though, a surprise since she knew he'd come. He was vocal about his pleasure and she liked that. It was sexy hearing him groan her name, and all that snarling. Most women probably would have been unnerved by those almost vicious sounds, but not her.

He rolled onto his back and sat up. Jadee scooted on her side to the center of his bed. It was kind of awkward as he stood, undressing.

This is why I don't do one-night stands, she reminded herself. They were highly attracted to each other but they weren't yet at a stage where she felt totally comfortable with him. But as Lavos stripped off his clothes, she still admired his beefy ass. He had no tan lines.

He turned, presenting her with his front.

She could stare at him all day. He had broad shoulders, muscular arms, and his stomach was lined with killer abs. Her attention lowered, taking in what she'd felt firsthand. His cock was big and thick. She was grateful they'd already had sex or she might have been intimidated enough to feel a little leery of that bad boy. He kept the hair around his groin neatly trimmed.

She noticed something when she admired his chest again. "You're not wearing your grandma's ring."

"I took it off because I was expecting some trouble today."

"At the lodge? I know I was a surprise."

"The lodge meeting. I hoped no fights would break out but I wanted to be prepared just in case." Lavos got on the bed. He caught her gaze with his. "Any regrets for what we just did?"

"No."

"You look a little stunned."

"You're big *all* over."

He laughed, lying down on his side, facing her. Only inches separated their bodies from touching. "I have good genes."

Yes, you do. Animal magnetism too. She smiled, keeping that to herself.

He smiled in return and used his arm to prop his head up. He reached out, playing with her hair. He wrapped a damp lock of it around his finger. "We need to talk."

Her good mood died. "Already?"

He unwound her hair from his finger. "You know what I'm going to say?"

"Yes. This was a one-day-stand kind of deal. Don't get attached. You want me to understand that this isn't going to lead anywhere. I'm human. You're not. Yada, yada, yada."

His eyebrows shot up. "Is that how you feel?"

"No. But you're still a man. I almost forgot that, despite what we just did." She felt disappointed, and worse, disgusted with them both. Him for hurting her feelings by seeming to think what they'd done was just sex, and her for not expecting it.

She rolled, preparing to get out of bed. She'd borrow something to wear from him that wasn't covered in dirt and then leave. Maybe she could move to Siberia or Antarctica. She doubted Werewolves or Vampires would hang out in either place. She'd freeze her ass off but she'd live longer.

She'd almost reached the edge of the bed when Lavos lunged, wrapping an arm around her waist and dragging her back to the center. She twisted her head, gaping at him. He looked pissed.

"Where are you going?"

"I'm leaving."

"You're not going anywhere."

His gall pissed her off. "I had questions and you answered them. I can kiss my ass goodbye if that nest contacts their council and has other nests hunting for me, thinking I'm some Vampire slayer. I got it. Avoid all Vampires. You have no pull with Werewolves, so avoid the woods and big parks, in case they hang out there. Maybe I can drive my RV into the middle of the desert. Do wolves like blasting heat and miles of cactus?"

"Why are you so angry with me?"

"It's mostly at myself, Lavos. I don't know what I was thinking. You get close to me and I turn stupid. That's the problem. Couldn't you have at least waited until tomorrow to pull that 'we need to talk' crap?"

"I wasn't going to say what you think I was."

She took a deep breath. "Okay. Spill it. I'm waiting with bated breath."

His eyes narrowed and he still looked pissed. "I was going to say that what happened between us changes everything."

That stumped her. She didn't know what to think. The silence stretched between them until she got irritated. "Do you want to expand on that?"

He sat up and let go of her waist. "How about I show you?"

He opened his mouth and his fangs grew as she watched. They were menacing, even scary, considering the thunderous look on his face.

He moved fast, startling her. She found herself flat on her back, Lavos coming down on top of her. He grabbed her wrists before she could react, jerking them up to the sides of her head, and he held on to them as he settled his body over hers.

"I want to bite you."

This is what happens when you get into bed with a predator. He'd warned her about flirting with him, and that he would bite. Her heart rate increased, and Jadee knew she was about to die. How could she be so wrong about Lavos? It leveled her, and left her feeling more bewildered than terrified.

His tone softened, and so did his harsh features. "The urge to bite strikes a VampLycan when he thinks a woman could possibly be his mate."

Never saw that one coming.

"And I want to bite *you*, Jadee." He inhaled. "You smell right to me. I've been attracted to you since we met, and it only grows stronger every moment we spend together. I missed you. Now that I have you in my bed, I can't imagine you not being here." He growled and his eyes began to glow neon blue. "I can't get enough of you." He shifted his legs, pressing his stiff cock against her thigh. "*That's* what I wanted to talk about."

He felt hard and big. "Oh."

"I'm trying to be reasonable, telling myself all the reasons why I shouldn't do it." He paused. "This clan hates humans. Our old leader was a real asshole who would have killed you before he allowed one of us to mate with one of your kind. He shared that belief long enough that a lot of members bought into his bullshit. He preached that humans would be the downfall of us all. I never believed it, nor did my brother. Lorn leads the clan now but he just took the job. If I test your blood, and you taste perfect to me, it's going to force him to have to fight to remain in control of the clan. But I will claim you regardless of the consequences, if you're my mate. I'll never let you go."

Jadee managed to open her mouth but no words came out. She was too stunned. How had they gone from her thinking he was going to say they meant nothing to each other, to him saying he might want a future with her? Mates sounded serious. Movies were bullshit on getting facts straight, they'd established that, but him saying he'd never let her go sounded really permanent.

"You were raised in a human world, so adjusting to life with VampLycans is going to be tough on you. I'm considering that but I have to admit, it's not really bothering me too much, since I'd kick anyone's ass who looked at you wrong. And I'd keep you very busy." His gaze lowered, his look heated as he admired her breasts. "Maybe even keep you tied to my bed and just fuck you every day until you couldn't move, so you never wanted to leave me."

She swallowed, then cleared her throat. She still wasn't sure what to say but her body was responding to the image of him doing just that. It was a shitty threat, if that was what he'd intended it to be, especially right after he'd just shown her how incredibly talented he was with his mouth and what it felt like to have him inside her. She'd let him tie her to his bed and do his worst. It sounded hot, and the idea turned her on.

He eased his hold on her wrists but didn't let them go. He gazed into her eyes. "Worst case, my brother will ask me to live with another clan. I'd hate to leave him but he's smart, and has discovered he has more support than we believed possible. He knows I'd have his back if he needed me, regardless of where I go."

She finally had something to say. "That would suck to lose your home."

"It would but he might need me to leave for the good of the clan." He ran his tongue over the tips of his fangs. "Then I think about the up sides of tasting your blood to see if you're my mate. Want to hear them?"

"Yes."

"I'd get to keep you if you're my mate. You'd be mine, and that wouldn't suck. Well, there would be some sucking involved, but only the kind that would have us both panting and pleasured." He leaned closer, inhaling. "I could become addicted to you. Not a bad thing. You're alone in the world, so you could live with me without having to leave anyone behind. There would be no guilt on your part to start a new life."

"That's true."

"No Vampires or Lycans would dare come hunting for you here. I'd hang their heads and bags of their ashes on the walls of our den."

"That's kind of disturbing."

He laughed. "You wouldn't feel that way if they came to kill you."

"I agree."

"I'd know you were always safe because I'd make damn certain of it."

"You're such a badass."

"I can be, and you motivate me." He sobered. "So, are you willing to take the risk? I *will* mate you if your blood reveals that you're my mate— and I'm certain you are, Jadee. Hit me with your questions. I know you that well. You've probably got dozens of them."

She might get to stay with Lavos. He'd be hers. But they barely knew each other. It had to be a sign of insanity to say yes. It would almost be like marrying a stranger, if her thoughts on what a mate was were correct.

220

"Jadee? I'm not a patient man. Right now, I'm not even all man. My Lycan side is raising hell because it senses you're mine."

"How many mates do you get?"

That seemed to surprise him. "One."

"You wouldn't cheat on a mate? And to be clear, that's the actual definition, not the politician one of 'it's not sex unless my dick is inside a vagina' bullshit."

"You'd be it for me, and if you even look at another man, I'll kill him."

"Would you be looking at other women?"

"No."

She chewed on her bottom lip, trying to think.

"Faster, Jadee."

"Don't rush me."

He closed his mouth and growled.

"You're impatient. I got it. It's hard to think when you're naked and on top of me."

"Are you attracted to me?"

"You know I am or I wouldn't be in your bed."

"Do I frighten you?"

"Would you ever hurt me?"

"Never."

He said it with such vehemence that she believed him. He looked offended that she'd even ask. She took a deep breath. It caused her breasts to brush against his chest. He glanced down, and she did too. The view of them so intimately pressed together made her want to touch him again, but he kept hold of her wrists. She could probably jerk free but didn't try. He wanted to bite her and was waiting for her to decide if he could. He got points for at least asking. He seemed the type to just take what he wanted but he was leaving it up to her.

"Can we get to know each other a little better?"

"Lorn wants you gone tomorrow morning. And he does lead this clan. Time isn't something we have a lot of. We need to figure this out before then."

"It's like marriage, right?"

"Without divorce."

"That's a big decision to make on short notice."

"I missed you the second you were gone. Did you miss me?"

She wasn't going to lie. "I thought about you all the time."

Lavos licked his lips and glanced at her shoulder, then held her gaze again. "You're the bravest human I've ever met, Jadee. You've got such courage." He grinned. "You killed a Vampire with an ice pick and an axe. What's so bad about a little bite compared to that? Say yes and let's find out if we're mates. You have nothing to lose and everything to gain if I'm right. We'll have each other." He grew serious. "Aren't you ever lonely? I am. We know we're good in bed together and I'm so drawn to you. I think we could make it work, and we'd be happy."

She had a feeling he'd be winning most of their arguments if they did end up being mates. The whole pinning her down while naked and talking in that sexy, raspy voice worked. She wanted to take the leap by letting him bite her.

She took another deep breath. *I'm not a coward.* "Do it." She tilted her head to give him more room. "Now I'm almost afraid I *won't* be your mate. You'd make a hell of a salesman, sweetheart. You have me sold on this insane concept."

He didn't laugh at her attempted humor. He released her wrists and suddenly lifted off her. "Get on your hands and knees in front of me."

She was starting to suspect he was always going to be surprising her. She'd expected him to just bite, not get off her and demand she change positions. "Okay. Can I ask why?"

"I don't want it to hurt when I bite you. Trust me. This is going to be pleasurable."

She sat up and eyed his fangs. They looked painful. Just like everything else on the man, they were big. "Yeah. Good luck with that." She rolled, going onto her hands and knees on the bed. "Don't expect me to always be this compliant. I'm kind of in shock so I'll do it your way."

Lavos chuckled and adjusted his legs on the outside of hers. She tossed her hair over one shoulder and looked back at him as he stood on his knees right behind her ass. He reached between them and gripped the shaft of his cock. He adjusted and she moaned at the feel of him entering her. She was still wet and ready to take him. He released himself and came down over her, falling forward. His arms braced his upper weight so his chest didn't slam against her back.

He slid into her deeper and she almost closed her eyes, but she liked to stare into his. They were glowing neon still. She'd never get tired of how striking and gorgeous they were. It was a reminder that he wasn't anything like other men.

"Ready?"

"You could have asked that before you entered me. Not that I'm bitching about it."

He growled low and lifted one arm, hooking it around her waist. He didn't just hold her in place but instead slid his hand down her belly to her clit. He rubbed against the sensitive nub with two fingers. Jadee moaned and turned her head, lowering it a little because it was hard to focus on anything but how big he felt inside her and the way he intimately massaged her with those fingers of his.

"You know how I said next time we'd take it slower?"

She gave a slight nod. "Yes."

"*Next* next time."

Chapter Fourteen

Jadee couldn't think when Lavos started to move inside her in deep, fast thrusts. He pressed his fingers against her clit, rubbing furiously. She cried out, reeling from the overload on her senses. She clawed the bed and braced her arms because otherwise her upper body would have collapsed. His arm around her helped keep her in place as he hammered her from behind.

The world fell away and there was only Lavos. He started to kiss her shoulder with his hot, wet mouth. He bit down but it didn't hurt. It was just a nip. It sent a jolt through her already overstimulated body.

He was all around her, with his body curled over hers, his cock pounding in and out of her pussy at a rapid pace, and his fingers playing hell with her clit. It was too much but she wouldn't do anything to slow it down. She moaned louder, feeling the climax building.

"Oh God!" she yelled, right before her entire body seized and she started coming so hard she worried she might die from the sheer magnitude of it. A white haze of heat and ecstasy slammed through her. She did manage to frantically make a grab for his wrist with one of her hands, latching on to him.

Lavos snarled and bit her. It wasn't exactly painful at that moment, but noticeable. She did feel his fangs sink into her skin, and the strong clamp of his jaws as he locked on to her shoulder. He released her clit and jerked his arm upward to flatten his palm right above her breasts. He cradled her that way so she didn't fall forward onto her face.

He took her with him when he sat back on his legs. His cock was buried even deeper inside her in that position, Jadee almost sitting on his lap, her legs trapped between his. He violently jerked, shaking both of them with the force of it. Lavos whimpered, almost crushing her when his arm around her tightened and his other one wrapped fully around her waist. He held her in a near bear hug from behind. He shook again, making another pained sound.

It alarmed her. She released his wrist and grabbed hold of his arms, worried about him. She tried to turn her head but she couldn't with his face buried against her shoulder, his fangs still locked in her flesh. It was starting to hurt, and he eased his hold with his mouth—but then locked it down again. She gasped.

The other sensation she became aware of was Lavos's cock felt bigger inside her, and rock hard. He whimpered louder but eased his hold on her just slightly.

"Lavos?" Her voice was a little raspy. "Are you okay?"

He suddenly stopped biting her. The feeling of his fangs pulling out of her skin wasn't the most pleasant sensation. He licked her, keeping his head tucked. He ran his tongue over her skin a few times, and then lifted his head.

His eyes startled her when she got a look at them. They weren't bright blue anymore. They had turned pitch black. There was no variation between his pupils and irises. He had more facial hair too. Dark hairs had grown along his jawline and up his checks.

Shock held her still, or she might have fought to get away from him, despite the fact that she was on his lap and he had her trapped in his arms. The urge was there but she just couldn't move.

He released her around her chest and yanked his arm up, opening his mouth. He savagely bit into his forearm. The sight of that, then the blood when he stopped, had her mouth falling open. A scream wanted to rise but she couldn't get it out.

Lavos shoved his bleeding arm over her lips. The taste of blood was instant, flowing into her mouth.

"Drink!" he snarled. "Swallow. You're mine!"

Oh shit! She tried to turn her head, panicked. He hadn't told her to expect his eyes to go all evil looking or that he'd make her drink his blood. She'd agreed to let him taste hers, not the other way around.

He used his head and shoulder to prevent her from moving away from his arm. His blood totally filled her mouth, and she had to swallow or choke on it when it started to go down her throat anyway. Some of it seeped out the sides of her mouth, dripping down her chin and landing on her breasts.

His hand around her waist adjusted and he caressed her. Some of the neon blue bled back into his eyes. "Drink, baby," he urged, his speech a bit more understandable and less ferocious. "It will bond us. You're my mate. I'm yours."

She wanted a time out but he wasn't having any of it. His arm was bleeding into her mouth and she couldn't move her head with the way he held her. His arm was wedged between her lips so her jaw was forced open. She breathed through her nose and swallowed again. The coppery taste barely registered over the adrenaline and fear she experienced. The whole situation was surreal.

He rubbed her stomach. "That's it, Jadee. Bond to me. Relax. We're sharing blood." He used his face to nuzzle against her cheek, his breath warm. "I've got you. It's okay. Take a few more swallows. I want our bond to be strong."

She desperately tried to relax. It was tough to do. She swallowed, almost choking since it sank in again that it was blood. *I'm drinking blood. Oh fuck, what did I get myself into?*

"It's okay." Lavos's eyes became neon, the black now contained to his pupils. "I'm sorry. I see your fear. Never be afraid of me. I just lost my mind when I tasted you. You have no idea how it feels. I'm so sorry…"

The regret was clear in his tormented tone. She would have told him she was calming down a bit and that she'd be okay, but that would have meant he needed to move his arm away for her mouth.

Tears filled his eyes. It stunned her since she couldn't imagine someone as strong and tough as him crying. He didn't even try to hide it from her or blink them away. "I'm so sorry, Jadee. Forgive me." He lowered his arm from her mouth, dropping his gaze to her chin and then her breasts. "Oh fuck."

She glanced down. Blood had spilled onto her chest. It wasn't a lot but enough that it ran over his hand on her stomach and even to her thighs. The bright red was a drastic contrast against her pale skin.

She looked back at him and licked her lips. They were coated with blood. "I'm okay."

One tear fell, sliding down his cheek. "I planned how to bond to a mate most of my life. I worked it out in my head so it would be sexy and not traumatic. Then I just totally lost control and my Lycan side took over. It was this overpowering desire I couldn't suppress to make you accept my blood. I fucked this up so bad! Please don't hate me."

"It's okay, Lavos." She was more worried about him than about what had just happened. She reached up, cupping the side of his face she could reach. "I'm fine."

He closed his eyes.

"Hey, look at me."

He opened them back up. The neon had faded but the tears remained.

"It's just a little blood. It washes off." She forced a smile, trying to use her sense of humor. It always came in handy in tough situations. "I could never hate you. I knew what you were before we did this, and while a heads-up about the sharing blood would have been nice beforehand, nobody died." She actually laughed. "That's a bonus, right?"

"You're amazing." He rested his forehead against hers. "You forgive me?"

"We're good." Then it hit her. "We're mated, aren't we?"

All the tension eased from his face and he smiled. "Yes. You're my mate, Jadee. No doubt about it."

"Okay." She glanced down her front. She was mated to a guy who was part Vampire and Werewolf. Some blood being spilled should have been expected. "We should probably take a shower, and then you can tell me all about mates."

He leaned in and brushed his mouth over hers. It was probably the weirdest kiss she'd ever received, since his lips were bloody too. "I'm going to make you happy. This will be great."

"I hope so. You said we can't get divorced."

He suddenly tensed and anger narrowed his eyes. "We won't."

"I was teasing."

"It's not that. It just hit me that a nest of Vampires wants you dead. They're after my mate." He growled. "I'll kill them all."

Her eyebrows shot up. "Feeling a little overprotective?"

"You have no idea. Nobody is ever going to hurt you."

"Okay. Take a deep breath. We're in Alaska. I think I'm safe."

"I have to tell my brother we're mated." His voice deepened into a snarl. "This clan will accept you or we'll leave tonight. I won't permit you to be in danger. I'll kill anyone who even *thinks* about doing you harm."

She wiggled in his arms and he released her. She sat up, carefully unlinking their bodies where they were still intimately joined. She turned, facing him on her knees. "This is new to us both. Come on." She extended her hand. "We need a shower. Maybe some food too. Lots of deep breaths for us both."

He took her hand but he tugged her back when she tried to climb off the bed, drawing her full attention. His expression appeared grave.

"I'm going to be the best mate to you, Jadee. You're everything to me. I want you to know that. No one is more important to me than you are. Nothing is."

She stared into his eyes and realized he meant every word. Her life had changed forever. She tried to judge how she felt about that. Staring at Lavos helped. She was with him and they were going to face whatever their future held together. She decided to be brutally honest.

"I think I'm falling in love with you."

He grinned. "I've already fallen for *you*. I'll help you catch up."

Her gaze traveled down his body, ignoring the blood. He still looked super-hot. "I don't think you'll have to try too hard. You're irresistible."

"So are you."

"Let's shower. You're hot. Blood is not."

"We're going to share blood often."

"That's not a selling point."

He grinned. "I won't mess it up next time. You'll enjoy it."

"I think you could make me like anything if you set your mind to it."

"I'm motivated."

Lavos led Jadee into his bathroom and turned on the water. Regret over losing his mind surfaced again but the gorgeous woman who stepped under the hot water in front of him had accepted his apology.

He'd been warned how his instincts would burst to life when he found his mate. He'd thought he'd be prepared for it but when he'd gotten a taste of Jadee's blood, he hadn't been able to think. The Lycan side of him had taken over completely. *Mine! Bond us now!* Then he'd realized what he'd done when he calmed enough after she'd drank some of his blood.

After he'd forced her to.

231

He would make it up to his mate. He grabbed body wash and squeezed some into his hands, gently washing the blood off her chest and throat as she ducked her face under the spray to rinse off her chin and lips. He just wanted to touch her all over and his dick hardened. He could fuck her for days, weeks, and want nothing but her. Forget food and everything else. It was part of finding his mate. She was human though. He needed to remember that.

She needed food and rest between bouts of sex. He ran his hands over her breasts again, loving how her nipples hardened. He lowered his fingers to her stomach, imagining when she would be ovulating. He'd fuck her until his seed took. He wanted to see her pregnant with his child. He hadn't ever had a desire to become a father but that changed the moment he knew Jadee was his. He closed his eyes and just held her, trying to get a handle on his raging emotions.

"Are you okay?"

He nodded. "Yes."

"You look ready to kill something. Still upset about the Vampires?"

He opened his eyes. "I'm having Lycan issues right now."

She turned in his arms, her hands bracing his shoulders. She glanced down at his stiff cock pressed against her belly, then lifted her chin. She smiled. "A constant hard-on doesn't seem like an issue."

"All these instincts are hitting me. I'm trying to be rational."

"What kind of instincts?"

There was so much she didn't understand about him. He spotted no fear though as he studied her face. His Jadee wasn't like any human he'd

232

ever met. "You know, making our bond stronger by getting you pregnant. Wanting to make you mine in every way possible."

Her eyebrows lifted.

"The urge will pass soon. I hope it's normal. I don't think you're ovulating yet. I can't smell or taste it on you. I'm going a little crazy inside but I know it's hormones. I'm amped up on them right now."

She massaged him. "Okay. So you're saying it's like a really bad case of PMS, only the Werewolf version that involves knocking me up instead of being bitchy and bloated?"

He chuckled. "That's a unique way to put it but yes."

"What can I do to help?"

Vivid, erotic images of all the things he'd like to do with her streamed through his mind. "Let me take you back to bed for a good week."

She pressed tighter against his body. "Sold."

He understood now they had started to bond together the night they'd met. He'd liked her already, and had wished he could keep her in his life. He'd suffered regret after she had driven away. She'd remained in his thoughts, even haunting his dreams. He'd been too damn happy to see her again, despite his shock at the time, and now he realized why. Some bonds snapped into place quickly for his kind. He already loved Jadee.

He just hoped she could love him as deeply as he did her. Her human side might resist the fast, intense bond. They didn't listen to their instincts, instead tending to ignore them in favor of rationalization. He backed away from her.

"Let me wash off the blood."

Her smile faded. "You're not regretting what we did, are you?"

233

"No." He cupped her face and leaned down to put them closer together. "I won't let you, either. Lycan PMS, remember?" He used her own words to make her understand he was on an emotional roller coaster. "Never regret. Don't question my commitment to you and making our mating work, Jadee. I'm going to be sane within a few hours." He hoped.

"You just look angry."

"Vampires want you dead. I don't know how this clan is going to react to you being human. I've got to keep you safe, yet all I can think about is fucking you for days. That's the anger you're seeing. It's not directed at you. I'm pissed that I can't just lock us inside our home and spend every second showing you how much you mean to me."

"Okay."

"Nobody is going to hurt you, and I'm so glad you're my mate."

Her smile returned. "I'm glad too. Wash up. You mentioned food. I'm actually a good cook. Do you mind if I find your kitchen?"

"What's mine is yours. This is our home." *At least for the time being.* He didn't mention that again. They might be moving soon. He let her go. "That's a good idea. Otherwise I'll fuck you where you stand."

"You're horrible at threatening me, if that's what you were aiming for."

He laughed. "I want to take you on the bed, slower this time. After we eat." She was human, not used to spending hours having sex. Her body would ache and she'd pay for it if he didn't take it easy on her. Of course, he could have her drink more of his blood. It would heal her. "Go. I'll be out in a few minutes."

She rinsed off once more and then stepped around him, leaving the shower. She dried off fast. He couldn't take his eyes off her until she left the bathroom, going out of his sight. He grabbed the body wash again and quickly showered.

Jadee wasn't in his bedroom when he stepped out there. He located his phone and dialed. Lorn wasn't going to be happy but it didn't matter. He had a mate.

"What now?" His brother sounded frustrated.

"Can you speak freely?"

"Not yet. You did see signs of a Vampire?" His brother cleared his throat. "Let me go take a look at that map." Seconds ticked by. Lorn closed a door. "So what kind of trouble is she in? Is it heading our way?"

"A nest of Vampires attacked her. She killed one of them. They followed her home and she came to me to find out where it would be safe for her to go."

"Damn. She isn't our problem, Lavos."

He took a deep breath. "Remember when you told me to fuck her?"

"Yes."

"I did."

"Good. Now she'll be out of your system."

"Never. She's my mate. We shared blood."

Lorn didn't say a word but Lavos could hear him breathing.

"Did you hear me? Jadee is my mate, Lorn. I got the overwhelming urge to bite and she agreed to let me test her blood. One taste and it was a done deal. We've already exchanged blood."

235

Lorn remained silent.

"Do you want me out of your territory?" Lavos braced for the answer. "I'll understand. I know how much trouble this will cause you. I can have us out of here by sunrise. Tell everyone at the lodge that I'm tracking Vampires, and I'll even wait a few days before approaching another clan to ask them to take us in. I'll make it seem as though I ran into her outside of our territory. That way, no one from another clan will know she was ever here. I thought Velder might be receptive since both his sons mated mostly human women."

"Don't you dare go anywhere," Lorn barked. "We'll work this out. You're my brother and my lead enforcer. This is your clan too."

"There will be challenges if I stay. They'll question your leadership."

"Then you'd better be prepared to fight at my side. You aren't leaving. You swore to help me keep the clan together and I'm holding you to it. That's an order from your clan leader and your brother...but I'm also your best friend, Lavos. Congratulations on finding your mate."

Lavos relaxed. "Thank you."

"We wanted changes and to bring our clan into more modern times. This just means getting them onboard faster. How is she accepting it?"

"She's amazing. Jadee just takes things in stride and rolls with it. It probably helps that she was raised by a human who believed in the existence of Vampires and Lycans. Less shocking to her."

"Good. Keep her at your house until the delegates are out of town. Shit, speaking of, that Mya is becoming a pain. She asked me where you'd gone to."

"You encouraged that shit, not me. I wasn't interested. Could I have been any clearer?"

"I just wanted you as happy as I am. A mate is everything."

"All I could think about was Jadee. I told you that."

"I didn't understand you were *that* drawn to her."

"Now we know why."

"This Mya is damn persistent. The news might upset her, since she made it clear she was interested and believed you were single."

"Too bad for her. Volti's an enforcer, and he'd love to test out a mating. Kar wasn't looking for a mate but he's definitely horny. Both of them are good options. Gar wanted a mate but he's doing territory patrol."

"I'll shove them at her."

"Thanks."

"I need you here when the main meal is served. Can you drop your mate off with mine? They'll be safe together and Kira would appreciate the company. We discussed it and I don't want her there. I trust the other clans not to attack my mate but it would be a perfect time while we're distracted for any Decker sympathizers to go after her. The other clan leaders agreed with me."

"Kira was okay with that?"

"Yes. She understands."

"Can do, but you know everyone is going to smell Jadee on me."

"I realize, but it's important my lead enforcer be at my side, Lavos. Human mate or not. We'll say you mated Jadee and brought her home when you checked out that report of a Vampire sighting. Maybe she could be the one who saw the Vamp, and you interviewed her. There is such a thing as instant bonding. Be vague with the details. You're good at that."

"Understood. An hour?"

"Make it an hour and a half so it's believable. Appetizers are just being served. Davis figured passing around trays of them would help relax everyone and ease us into conversations before we're seated. He called it 'mingling.' You supposedly left our territory, so you'd need time to return. I'll try to pull our enforcers aside so they don't seem shocked when you arrive, scenting like you've just mated a human."

"Can you send Davis to your home? I know Kira can defend herself but Jadee can't."

"You're a pain the ass, but yeah, I'll see what I can do."

"Thanks, Lorn. You took it better than I thought you would. You're a good brother."

"You're an idiot if you thought I'd accept your offer to leave. I'd rather not have a clan than lose my brother. We've always stood together. See you soon." Lorn disconnected the call.

Lavos grinned.

Chapter Fifteen

Jadee felt nervous. "So this Kira was a human, then a Vampire, but now she's a VampLycan?"

"Her father is a VampLycan but her mother was human. Kira was born mostly human like her mother."

"Then she was attacked, turned into a Vampire, but drinking blood from your brother helped her become more Lycan than Vampire?"

"She's almost equally both now. She can withstand the sun and eat food."

"This is so complicated."

"You're doing great." Lavos smiled.

"I feel like I'm cramming for a test no one told me about and I have an hour to learn it all or I fail."

"There's no failing. I'm just getting you acquainted with facts about your new family. I'm sorry I have to go to the lodge but you can't come with me. And I don't want to leave you alone. You'll be safe with Kira."

"She won't want to bite my neck, right?"

"She only feeds off my brother, Lorn. Mates share blood."

"Am I going to turn into something from drinking your blood? Will you turn partly human?"

He chuckled. "I have the dominant traits in our relationship. I won't turn human, but some things about you will become different over time."

She felt the blood drain from her face. "Am I going to turn into a Vampire?"

"No." He shook his head, looking far too amused. "My Lycan blood will protect you from my Vampire genes. You'll get a better immune system to fight off colds and other things humans suffer from. It will also greatly slow your aging. You'll heal faster from drinking my blood, too."

"That doesn't sound so bad. It probably accounts for how awake I feel. I was exhausted when I arrived but now I'm almost hyper."

His gaze lowered to her belly. "Every child you carry will help. Some humans who mate with Lycans tend to become Lycan over time." His voice deepened. "We could have lots of children."

"Eyes up here, sexy."

He held her gaze.

"Still fixated on the babies, huh?"

"Sorry."

"It's okay." She took his hand. "Is the PMS a little better?"

"Not by much. I resent having to be dressed right now when all I want to do is keep you naked in my bed."

"I wouldn't complain. I love sex with you."

He growled, the blue of his eyes brightening.

"Horny, huh?"

"You have no damn idea. I'm rock hard."

She glanced at his groin, the bulge detectable. "How long do you have to spend with your brother?"

"A few hours at most. I'll return and pick you up as soon as possible."

She focused on his face. "You said Lorn just took control of the clan and the other ones are worried about that. Why?"

"We were led by Decker. He had no honor and tried to cause friction with the other clans." He licked his lips, his gaze wandering over her body. "Everyone hated him, including most of his own clan."

"He was like a corrupt politician?"

"Worse." The blue faded from his eyes and darkened to near black. The evil look returned. "He murdered innocents and wanted to start a war."

"What's going on with your eye color?"

He blinked a few times. "Sorry. It's a VampLycan thing. They lighten when I'm using Vampire traits or thinking about sex. They darken when I feel rage and my Lycan side is bleeding through."

"Okay." It would take time to adjust to those abilities. "Thanks for clearing that up."

"The other clans need assurances that Lorn is nothing similar to Decker."

"Is he?"

"Hell no!" he snarled.

Jadee startled at his sudden outburst.

"Sorry." Lavos lowered his tone, softened it. "I hated Decker."

"You said he was a murderer?"

"Any children in our clan who presented too many Vampire traits were killed, along with their parents if they tried to protect them from Decker and his enforcers. He didn't like humans either, and kept my brother from claiming Kira because he saw her as too weak to matter. The bastard would have killed her if he could have. It just pisses me off to think anyone could compare my brother to that bastard."

241

"I'm glad Lorn isn't upset that you mated me."

"He understands." He reached out, stroking her. "He had to resist the urge to claim his mate for a long time. They both suffered for it."

"It worked out okay though, right? They're mated now."

"Yes, but we expect problems. That's why Kira usually has a guard when Lorn isn't with her. Davis is her father, and he'll fight to the death to keep her safe too."

"What does she need to be protected from?"

"Some of our clan are paranoid and racist against anyone not clan."

"But she's not human anymore, right?"

"Yes, but she was turned into a Vampire. Some won't trust her because of it."

"But…VampLycans are half Vampire!"

"That's true. Though Decker taught them to hate anyone with too much Vampire blood."

"He sounds like a dick."

"He was much worse."

"Was? So he's dead?"

"We wish, but no. He's gone though, and he can't ever come back. The other clans would kill him on sight."

"That's good."

"We need to show the other clans that Lorn wants peace with them and alleviate their concerns."

"That should be easy enough. He mated Kira and you said Decker kept them apart. That sounds like proof to me that they aren't the same types of men."

He grinned. "True." He let her go. "I wish logic played a part in this but we're talking about almost two centuries of Decker fucking with the other clans. It's going to take time to build and strengthen our bonds with them again."

That stunned her. "Two centuries?"

"Vampires don't age, and Lycans age much slower than humans. Decker had ruled this clan since he became strong enough to shift and fight. He chased off the full-blooded Lycans and bullied the other VampLycans into following him."

She let that sink in. "How old are you?"

"I'm second generation...and it took a long time for my father to find his mate, and then decide to have children."

"He didn't want to knock up your mother right off the bat?"

"No. We've never been anything alike."

"You didn't answer my question."

"How old do you believe I am?"

"Mid-twenties?"

He leaned in and stared into her eyes. "Add a few years."

"You look good."

"I'm considered young. That's another strike against Lorn. He's only three years my senior. He's second generation too, and just a baby compared to the other leaders. The other three clans are still being run by first-generation VampLycans who took control from the beginning."

"But he's not Decker, so that has to make him a huge improvement."

He brushed his mouth over hers, kissing her. "Yes."

"Point that out to everyone."

He grinned. "I will. I wish I could take you with me."

"I'm kind of curious now to meet this Kira. I'll be fine."

"You will be. Her father swore he'd protect you with his life. Davis has honor and he's human friendly. I trust him. He just left the lodge so he'll be the one guarding you."

"Let's go. Avoid that woman, please. She looked determined earlier to get you into bed."

He nodded. "I'm not interested in anyone but you. Remember, I'm a VampLycan."

"I'm still trying to figure out what exactly that is."

"Would you settle for eating dirt-covered live snails if you were craving chocolate?"

Jadee grimaced. "Ewww."

"That's how I feel about other women. You're mine, Jadee. No one else will do."

She relaxed, willing to trust him. "Okay."

"Time to go. Lorn will be eager for me to join him at the lodge."

Jadee gripped his hand tight. "You're sure Kira won't want to bite me?"

"Positive."

"Let's go."

* * * * *

Lavos pretended to ignore the shocked gasps and the few openly hostile stares as he stood next to his brother. He'd purposely hugged Jadee and rubbed against her when he'd dropped her off at Lorn's home. It made her scent cling to him strongly. No one would doubt he'd taken a human mate.

Lorn glanced at him, giving him a knowing look. "Blatant," he said drily.

"So what? We want to make a stand and change things."

"True." Lorn smiled, glancing around. "I noticed you turned on the overhead fans."

"It helps scents mingle and spread."

"As I said, blatant. You've got balls, bro."

"My situation is different from yours. You had to hide it when you first mated Kira. I want everyone to know Jadee is mine."

"They will. I'm certain the gossips will spread it to our members who aren't present as soon as the meal ends. I didn't have a chance to warn anyone. Sorry. The clan leaders have been talking to me."

"That's why I asked for Davis to protect her. Sorry to take him from the lodge."

"Perri said she could handle the kitchen, and I feel better with Davis watching over my mate too."

The bell rang, announcing dinner. Lorn sighed. "Try not to start any fights with the other enforcers."

"Good luck eating with the other leaders. No fighting for you, either."

"We're here to keep the peace."

Lavos didn't need the reminder. He turned, making his way to the table he'd been assigned. Kar and Garson were already seated, along with nine enforcers from the other three VampLycan clans. Every man there watched him as he took his assigned place.

"I'm Lavos, Lorn's brother," he announced. He glanced at Garson. "I take it Lorn invited you?"

"Yes. I got a text from him."

Kar sniffed, then smirked. "I know that scent."

"Shut up," Lavos ordered his friend.

"I don't." Garson inhaled, his eyes widening. "You're mated? When the hell did that happen? I just saw you this morning."

"Long story. Drop it," Lavos ordered.

"She's human." The deep voice came from a dark-headed hulk of a man. "Maku," he introduced himself. "From Velder's clan."

"Do you have a problem with that?" Lavos tensed, trying to stifle his instant anger.

"No. Two of Velder's sons mated mostly human-blooded women. They are good women with big hearts."

Lavos breathed easier. "I heard about that. Decker's granddaughters, right?"

Maku nodded. "They take after their grandmother. She was from our clan."

It was meant to be an insult to the previous clan leader. "My father swore loyalty to Decker long before we were born. Lorn and I hated him." Lavos decided it was best to be clear and break the tension. "My brother

246

and I weren't his enforcers, nor were *any* of Lorn's current enforcers. We all refused to do his bidding and would only take patrols to keep the rest of our clan safe." Lavos addressed the rest of the table. "I refuse to apologize that my mate is human. We can take it outside if anyone has a problem with it."

"My clan won't," another dark-haired enforcer announced. "The name's Frack, and I'm the lead enforcer for Crocker. We don't allow our members to casually fuck humans just for the sex, but if someone finds their mate by feeling a strong urge to bite one, bloodlines don't matter."

The man seated next to him nodded. "I'm Brody. Crocker will have no problem with it."

An unusually tall enforcer leaned forward, openly studying him. "I'm Wen, from Trayis's clan. Don't be so defensive, Lavos. Only Decker fiercely opposed other races being mates. We've had a few of our men mate humans. In my clan, only first sons are expected to keep the bloodlines pure VampLycan—and only if their parents demand it. Trayis is open to accepting human and Lycan purebloods as mates if they are willing to swear allegiance."

The man to Wen's left nodded. "I'm mated to a Lycan. The name's Denno; I'm one of Trayis's enforcers."

Wen spoke again. "We kept close ties with the pack that protected the first generations, before it left here and settled somewhere else. Family is important to us."

"That's how I met my mate." Denno grinned. "I helped our Lycan family deal with a group of renegade Lycans who'd made a habit out of raiding packs to steal breeders. One of those bastards had forced her to be

247

his mate. I took his ass out and expected her to try to kill me in revenge. Imagine my surprise when she thanked me instead. She asked for my protection, since the renegades had murdered her entire pack when she'd been taken. I brought her home. We fell in love and now she's mine."

Wen lifted his drink and took a sip. "We're not the ones who have a problem with you taking a human mate." He stared pointedly across the room. "It's your own clan you should be worried about."

Lavos followed his gaze and caught a few of his clan members glaring in his direction. "Those three are first-generation elders who were loyal to Decker."

"I could stick around for a few days," Wen offered. "I'm not mated, and Trayis wants to see your brother succeed. We sure as hell don't want one of *them* to take over your clan."

"We can handle our own people," Garson protested.

Lavos waved him silent. "That's a nice offer."

"Nice, hell." Wen snorted. "Nobody wants another Decker in charge over here. I'd be willing to fight to keep that from happening."

"That's appreciated." Lavos inclined his head.

"We're doing fine," Garson muttered.

Lavos kicked him under the table and shot him a warning look. "Enough." He turned his attention back to Wen. "I need to take a perimeter walk. Would you like to join me?"

"Sure."

"I'll go too," Kar offered.

"Sit," Lavos ordered.

His friend sat hard, not looking happy. Lavos led the way, giving his brother a nod that stated everything was fine. The taller enforcer followed him outside and they both studied the area.

"What did you want to talk about in private?" Wen got right to the point.

Lavos faced him. "You said some of your men mated humans. I have some questions, if you don't mind me asking them. Decker didn't allow it and other clans barely spoke to us. Not that we blamed them. You should never have trusted anyone he sent to visit your people. He mostly ordered his loyal enforcers to go spy for him. I'd like to know what to expect between a VampLycan and a human."

"Gotcha." Wen shifted his stance and leaned against one of the porch posts. "I'll tell you what I know. Hit me with your questions."

"Just between us?"

"Sure. I don't see any reason to share what we discuss of a personal nature. Trayis wouldn't ask me to either."

"I want to get her pregnant," Lavos confessed. "It's an almost overriding desire. My brother and other mated couples I've known didn't seem to experience this."

"I've seen it before. Blame the Lycan side. First off, she's the weakest species. Humans are fragile. It's going to cause you to fear losing her, which riles up the beast. Second, it's harder to form a mating bond. It's always a coin toss on the links we can establish with them."

"What does that mean?"

Wen crossed his arms over his chest and sighed. "Damn. Decker *did* keep you in the dark. Okay, it's just a maybe on being able to link thoughts

249

and feelings when you mate a pure human. It certainly doesn't happen right away. It can take years of blood exchanges."

That news wasn't welcome, but it didn't matter. Jadee belonged to him.

"Your Lycan side can suffer insecurities. Humans often divorce. As a man, you can reason that you'll keep her happy enough to never want another, but the beast isn't always logical. That might be a big part of why you're craving seeing her pregnant quickly. Not to mention, humans have no natural birth control. You'll probably get her pregnant regardless of trying or not if she's fertile."

"What about human birth control options?"

"It's iffy on birth control pills. No glove, no love is the best way to avoid a pregnancy if she's ovulating."

Lavos flinched. "Condoms?"

"Never used one before?" Wen grinned. "They aren't so bad. I've had human lovers. You adjust. They sound far worse than they are." His humor faded. "It's better than ending up having to mate a woman you accidentally got pregnant. I've had nightmares about that."

"You wouldn't consider having a human mate?" It disappointed Lavos. He'd started to like Wen.

"I would have been very open to it…but it's not an option anymore." His features turned harsh. "My older brother died. I'm first son now, and my parents demand I mate a VampLycan to ensure pure bloodlines."

That forced Lavos to think about his father. "I don't give a shit what my father thinks. Jadee is mine, and anyone who doesn't like it can fuck off."

"I've hinted to my parents that they should have more children because I wish to shun the first-son responsibilities." Wen straightened, pushing away from the post. "We'll see if they listen. I've always been their problem child."

"Are you close to them?"

Wen nodded. "Sometimes that's a curse. Guilt is a shitty thing to feel when they depend on you to keep them happy. They even drag the memory of my brother into it occasionally, telling me what *he'd* do if he were still alive. I just wish for the freedom I once had as second son."

"I totally understand that. I never envied Lorn his position in the family. Our father has always been an asshole but he was ruthless with Lorn."

"You weren't close to your father?"

Lavos shook his head. "Lorn had to beat him down and banish him when he stepped up for leadership. Dad and Decker were a lot alike."

"Damn. I'm so sorry. Are you two handling it okay? I can't imagine what I'd feel if my brother had to fight my father."

"He gave Lorn no choice. We expected that fight to happen eventually, and Lorn had my full support."

"Your mother?"

"She's always welcome to visit the clan but she left with him. He's her mate."

"Damn."

"It's been rough all around, but Lorn was the best choice to take over the clan. We sure as hell weren't going to allow Nabby to get control. We used to dub him Decker Junior. He acted just like him."

251

"A greedy prick?"

"Cruel, a bully, and he got off on the pain of others."

"Where is this Nabby?"

"Buried near a few of Decker's other most trusted that he left behind when he fled the wrath of Lord Aveoth. Nabby was the first to officially challenge Lorn."

"I was serious about offering to stick around for a bit. I've got nothing going on right now and everyone is invested in your brother holding this clan."

"Won't your clan miss you?"

"I travel a lot for Trayis. It's fine."

"Do you mind if I ask exactly what you do for your clan?"

"We've been buying up some land to expand our territory. Some of the surrounding human families left the area but still retain ownership. I track them down and see if they wish to sell to our clan. Some do. Some don't."

"Do you ever convince the latter?"

Wen shook his head. "Rarely. Their fathers and grandfathers, sometimes great-grandfathers, are the ones who busted their asses to stake claims to the land put up by the Homestead Act. They had to survive and thrive to keep it. It's an important part of their family history, and some even hold gatherings over the summer months every year. We'd never take that from them by messing with their minds."

Lavos definitely liked the guy.

"We also visit the pack formed by our relatives who left Alaska. They settled in Colorado."

"I've never been."

"It's damn pretty. I actually bought some land there." Wen grinned. "It's near the pack."

"The alpha doesn't mind?"

"He knows I have no interest in taking over his territory, and he's found it handy having a VampLycan around from time to time. I once dreamed of moving there but then my brother died. I'll eventually give the land to the pack, but for now, I just like being able to call it home from time to time."

"Sounds nice."

"It's close to the territory that some of *your* ancestors live in too. The Lycans left for Colorado together and split their territory among four different packs."

"We were forbidden to keep in contact with them."

"Yeah. It seems nobody from Decker's clan keeps in touch with their Lycan families. The other clans do, but not to the extent that Trayis encourages it with our people. Family is important. One of his brothers is the alpha of our lineage pack."

"How did that happen?"

"Trayis's mother was a Vampire victim, and after he took charge of the clan, she left with her Lycan parents. She mated a Lycan and had another child. Trayis and Arlis are actually half-brothers."

"They're close?"

"As close as two brothers can be, living so far apart, but yeah, they seem tight. It's another reason I'm welcome there. I'm one of Trayis's friends, as well as an enforcer. I'm trusted by the pack to never do them any harm. They have no fear of us."

"That's good."

"It is. Even a few of the GarLycans visit their family pack. You should go one day and meet them." Wen glanced around. "So you want me to stick around for a bit? I have to admit I'm curious as hell about this clan, and I would like to help you and your brother keep it." He held Lavos's gaze.

"We'd appreciate it. Thanks."

Chapter Sixteen

Jadee and Kira sat a few feet apart on a couch in a cozy living room. She'd met the father, Davis, who'd been nice, but he'd gone back outside to pull guard duty. It left them alone.

"I bet you have a million questions." Kira grinned. "You can relax. Dad can intimidate, but then again, all the men in the clan do."

"Everyone is so big and in shape. I feel tiny."

"Me too," Kira admitted. "I take after my mom. Short. They're also muscular because they shift into another form, and it's quite a workout. I used to envy how much food these people can put away and never gain an ounce of flab. I looked at a cake and could feel my stomach bloating."

Jadee glanced at Kira's body. "You don't seem to have that problem anymore."

"I can't full-on shift yet but I can grow claws. It speeds up the metabolism. I've noticed a difference since my attack."

"Lavos said you were mostly human, then a Vampire turned you, but now you're like the others here."

"Except for changing forms." Kira lifted her hand but then paused, staring at Jadee. "I was going to show you but I don't want you to be afraid of me. We're family now. I'm trying to put myself in your shoes. Are you completely wigged out? Lavos said he told you everything, but he's a man. They have a different idea of that than we do."

"I'm not exactly the run-of-the-mill person. I grew up listening to stories about people and things not human. I'd love to see what you can do. I was more worried about my throat."

"That I'd want to suck your blood?" Kira laughed. "It's just Lorn's neck that tempts me. You're safe. The bloodlust only kicks in when he's around, and I think it's only still happening because I associate it with sex." She winked. "Newly mated."

"Show me the claws, please?"

Kira straightened her hand and lifted it higher. Her fingernails began to grow longer, the tips curving a bit and growing sharper as Jadee watched.

"That's *so* cool."

"I know." Excitement laced Kira's voice. "I never thought I'd be able to do that. Lorn thinks I might be able to full-on shift one day but I'm not so sure. Of course, I'm worried what I'll look like if ever do transform." She dropped her hand, the claws sliding in. "Have you seen Lavos shifted?"

"Once."

"Scary shit, right? VampLycans don't look like wolves. They're too humanoid in shape. It's not so bad for a guy to look terrifying, but a girl?" Kira shook her head. "And what if not all of my body shifts? Like if my breasts remain human?"

Jadee wasn't sure what to say to that.

Kira leaned forward a little. "Sorry. This is new to me too, only I've known about VampLycans all my life, obviously. I was raised in this clan but I'm an expert on knowing how it feels to be an outsider. How are you handling the reality that humans aren't the only people on the planet?"

"I'm not a fan of Vampires."

256

"Me either." Kira twisted more in her seat, getting comfortable. "Even though I guess I owe one, even if he didn't mean to do me any favors."

"I understand. Lavos told me what happened to you. You're so lucky to be alive. I hate Vampires. They're pure evil."

"There's supposed to be a few good Vampires but I haven't met any. Most are assholes."

"I definitely met the asshole kind," Jadee admitted.

"Lavos is a good man. You can trust him. I had some human friends when I went to college, so I'm trying to imagine what you might be worried about. I felt like an outsider in the human world too, since I always had to keep my guard up and pretend I fit in way better than I actually did. You want the low-down on everything here?"

"That would be appreciated."

"First off, you won't have to worry about Lavos being a player or abusive. Mates don't cheat or beat on you. He's in this relationship with you one hundred percent, for life. His instincts are strong and he wants you protected from all harm. Period."

"That's great to know."

Kira nodded. "Now the clan... I mean, every race has their freaks and maniacs. I won't kid you. I've met a few fucked-up VampLycans, but most of them are solid. Lavos and Lorn, my dad, and the carefully chosen enforcers of our clan are amazing. You can trust them to never hurt you. But the rest of the people here?" Kira shook her head. "Never trust anyone, okay? Unless Lavos or I tell you they're good, don't let your guard down."

"I've been warned already. They don't like humans."

"Some of them hate them. Let's just say I didn't have any good friends besides Lorn. Some of them tolerated me when I was still mostly human, a few were kind, but I watched my ass so I didn't have a so-called *accident*. It was a real concern. It's going to take time for everyone to adjust to the new way this clan is being run by my mate, and to grow to trust you not to do them any harm."

That had Jadee snorting. "As if I could."

"Physically, to be blunt, you're about as scary as a baby bird to them. Not at all. They're way faster, stronger, and lethal in a fight. They'll mostly be worried that you're going to pull a stunt like film them when they aren't in human form and load it to the internet to expose them to the world. That makes you a serious threat, Jadee. Swear to me you'll never do that. It would start a war like you can't imagine."

"I would never." It hurt her feelings that Kira would even suggest it.

"I had to ask. Lorn told me your father and his team were myth busters or something along those lines. I watch shows about people going in search of Bigfoot and to prove the existence of aliens."

"That's true about my father but I wasn't a part of his team."

"Don't you feel you owe it to your father's memory to prove he didn't waste his life looking for the proof he sought?"

"It got him killed." Jadee tried not to take offense. Kira said she was trying to put herself in her shoes, so she did the same. "Let me tell you a little about my childhood. I spent three weeks in Scotland while my father and his friends were hunting for the Loch Ness monster. I get sick on boats, and guess what we did every day and night? Yeah. Out on a boat, looking for a sighting. It was miserable.

"Then I was stuck for two weeks in some Brazilian jungle because someone reported cat-shifter people. The only thing we caught was some mysterious fever from infected bug bites and days of puking, with the worst case of the runs to go along with it. We were lucky it wasn't some deadly disease.

"Don't even get me started on the time I nearly froze to death on some mountain over a snow beast rumor. That's how I spent Christmas one year. Forget about Santa bringing me a new doll. I was praying I wouldn't be buried alive under an avalanche. Four people died in a camp less than a mile from us on day two, after part of a snow bank came down on them. I was six, Kira. I had no business being there."

Sympathy softened Kira's features. "It sounds rough."

"I was fed up with that life by the time I hit my teens and begged my dad to let me live with my grandma. He fought me at first, but finally gave in. I didn't care about whatever my dad was hunting. I just wanted a stable home, a normal life, and to not be a part of that. Kids didn't think it was cool that I'd traveled all over the world. They teased and tormented me when they found out what my father did for a living and why he wasn't around. My grandma raised me during my teens.

"Those creatures and things he was looking for? I grew to resent them—because they were more important to him than I could ever be. He missed my high school graduation to go to England. He blew me off for a fucking *ghost*. He justified missing that important event in my life because he got some grainy video footage that he thought might actually prove *his* life had meaning. I'm glad his did in the end...but I suffered for it."

Kira took Jadee's hand and squeezed. "You're breaking my heart."

"I don't mean to. I'm mostly over it because you can't change the past. You can only learn from it. The point is, you never have to worry about me being anything like my father. His obsession got him killed and caused me a lot of emotional pain. I just want to enjoy life and never be in the spotlight. Clear enough?"

"Yes."

Jadee studied Kira closely. "I'd never do anything to hurt Lavos, and I understand that it would put a target on my back too. I give you my word, for what it's worth to you, that I will never tell another person about what I've learned."

"That's good enough for me." She let Jadee go. "I will admit, I'm so glad Lavos found you. We're family. I'd always hated being an only child. I'm hoping we become as close as real sisters."

"That would be great."

"It would." Kira grinned. "So, back to VampLycan 101. What do you want to know? You can ask me anything."

She thought about it. "Will it bother Lavos that I can't shift?"

"It doesn't bother Lorn that I can't. It's not an important factor. I wouldn't worry about it. Very few couples shift to have sex in the other form. I've come across it while I was patrolling." She grimaced. "So not sexy. Do you think Lavos is hot shifted? I love Lorn but it doesn't do it for me."

"Lavos looks terrifying."

"Exactly. The women look like that too. I honestly can't tell the sexes apart unless I'm familiar enough with them to identify their eyes or markings while they're shifted. They get a little furry between the legs, so it's not like you can spot girl or boy parts with ease unless the view is right.

260

I wouldn't worry about Lavos wishing you could shift. Most prefer sex in skin."

"That makes me feel better. I'll admit, I feel a little insecure. I saw some woman hitting on him earlier today. She was gorgeous, and a VampLycan like him."

"He mated and wants *you*. Be honest with him, Jadee. He'll always tell you the truth. Mates don't play games or lie to each other. They don't cheat either. You can talk to him about anything or ask him any question. You're his other half. I think that's the most important thing I can tell you. You didn't marry a human. You merged your very life and body with a VampLycan. He's a part of you now, and you're a part of him. Two become one. It's emotional and physical. Do you understand?"

She let the words sink in. "You mean that, don't you?"

"Yes. A lot of mates die if they lose their other half. They just don't want to live. The ones who survive were either not mated long or have small children. They know they're needed so they manage to hang on. I worry about one particular woman in our clan because she lost her mate and her kids are almost mature. I don't know if Perri will keep living once her children leave her home." Kira sighed. "Welcome to the world of VampLycans. Promise to heed my warnings about being careful of who you trust. You're not just risking your own ass anymore. Lavos's life is on the line too."

It gave Jadee a lot to think about. "Okay. Thank you for telling me all this. I have one more question."

"Ask away."

"I don't want to be rude, but...your dad looks *so* young."

261

Kira laughed. "Most VampLycans age like a human until we hit about twenty. Then it slows down big time. My dad looks to be in his early thirties, at most, but he's way older."

Jadee wanted to ask when he was born but she didn't. "So VampLycans live a long time, huh?"

"The first generations are around two hundred years old. Let's just say that they look like my dad does. Early to mid-thirties."

"Shit!"

"Did Lavos tell you drinking his blood is going to do a number on your body? You won't age in human years anymore, Jadee. Accept his blood during sex. It will make you stronger too. Forget catching a cold, and you'll heal faster over time."

"This is a lot to take in, but it doesn't suck."

Kira smiled.

* * * * *

Lavos finished his meal and laughed at the easy flow of conversation around the table. He liked the other clan enforcers, especially Wen. The guy was laid-back with a good sense of humor. He kept feeling glares directed his way and stayed alert, paying close attention to who seemed to hate him. One of those was Mya.

He got up from the table, along with everyone else, to mingle. It didn't take the woman long to come after him. She stepped in his path, her eyes turning near black and her nostrils flaring.

"You mated a human!" she spat. "I'm insulted."

"It had nothing to do with you. Instincts won't be denied."

262

"So you just...what? Left for a few hours, ran into a human, and decided to fuck her while you were on duty?" Her claws grew. "You wouldn't test a mating with me, but you did *her*?"

Lavos stepped back, not wanting to have to fight her or cause a scene. "She was working for our clan. Not that she knew what we were," he added. "I'd met her before and was strongly drawn to her. Today just happened, but I don't regret it. She's my mate."

"You bastard! I'm better than some human." Her fangs extended and she took a threatening step forward.

Trayis, leader of one of the clans, was suddenly there. He gripped Mya by the back of the neck and she froze, her eyes widening. Trayis winked at Lavos, then leaned in, putting his mouth close to her ear.

"What have I told you before, Mya? Don't be a pushy bitch. Some men aren't impressed with your aggressive behavior. You snuck over here without my permission but I let it go. I know you want to leave my clan since I keep a close eye on you, but I just had dinner with Lorn. He wouldn't take your shit either. Go home. That's an order." He released her. "Now." His voice deepened.

Mya fled.

Trayis smiled and held out his hand. "Sorry about her. Every clan has a few problems. You just met one of mine."

Lavos shook his hand. "Thank you. I didn't want to have to get into it with a woman but she looked ready to fight."

"That's Mya. She cleans up nice in a dress but she's no lady." Trayis released him. "She's been coming on to me for ten years so I know how she can be when she's after a man."

"You ever test a mating with her?"

"Hell no. She's beautiful, but a lot of our women are. I don't fuck the ones in my clan. I learned a long time ago that no good comes of it, and none are my mate, if strong attraction is any indication. I don't feel that way about any of them."

"What lesson did you learn? May I ask?"

"I was sleeping with a woman like Mya once. She kind of unofficially started acting like she was my mate and it caused problems. I put a stop to it as soon as I found out she was using her lover status to bully some of my clan. It's a good thing you took a mate so fast. Otherwise, that's likely a lesson you'd have learned as Lorn's lead enforcer. Some women come after you for the power, and even if you're just their lover, they'll try to take advantage of your position to bolster theirs."

"My mate is human."

"I know. Congrats."

"Thank you."

"I'm actually glad it happened. Not the Mya thing, but you taking a mate while we were here. It proves your brother is nothing like Decker. He'd have killed you both. You for breaking his law, and her just because of her bloodline."

"Decker had no tolerance." Lavos sighed. "And not all of our clan will be happy about my mate. Decker poisoned them against humans. We actually have another clan member who recently claimed a human mate. Lorn accepted her, as well. He's nothing like Decker."

"Decker thought everyone was out to fuck him over—and he was right. You can't do that much bad without making a hell of a lot of enemies. You reap what you sow."

"Agreed."

Trayis glanced around. "I've been watching the faces of your clan. Most seem okay, but that group in the far corner is trouble."

Lavos knew the ones he spoke of. "They're elders who were loyal to Decker."

"Ah. Watch them."

"We are. Especially since we expect a few of them to raise hell over my mate."

"They should come live in my clan. That would cure them of being race snobs."

That interested Lavos. "Why?"

Trayis seemed to consider his words before he spoke. "We joke that it must be something in the water, but we've had a higher rate of mated pairs birthing sons in our clan for the past forty years. It's not as drastic as the Gargoyles. Their daughter birthrate is extremely low. But the men in my clan have learned to appreciate women, no matter what their bloodlines are."

"Is that why you so easily accept your clan mating humans and full Lycans?"

"Partially. You've unfortunately met Mya. Some of our younger unmated women abuse the power they wield over the single men in my clan. I can't tell you how many times I've had to break up fights when they use the lure of possible sex to pit horny men against each other. It's like a twisted game for them to see how much trouble they can cause, even if it's brother against brother." His tone deepened, anger showing through. "It pisses me off, so I encourage our men to seek out women from anywhere they can. I send the unmated to visit Lycan packs often. If they come across a human mate while they're traveling, so be it. Every man who finds a mate is one less for Mya and her group of friends to mind fuck."

Lavos considered everything Trayis had said, filling in the blanks. Mya had been aggressive and wanted to start a fight when she didn't get her way. He was glad Trayis had stepped in or it might have turned into a scene. "I don't blame you."

Trayis smiled, his good mood back. "Elders can be assholes. I might be one, but at least I'm open to change. I want my clan to be happy and don't give a shit about them all being pure VampLycans." He jerked his head in the direction of the corner. "Ones like those are toxic to our long-term survival. They didn't learn a damn thing from the Gargoyles."

"You mean how picky Lord Aveoth and his clan are about not mating with VampLycans?"

"I've made friends in other parts of the world. The GarLycan clan in the cliffs is the only one I've ever heard of. Lord Aveoth's clan is thriving. Not so much for pure Gargoyle clans. They're dying out. They don't breed with Lycans."

"I wasn't aware."

"They mostly only steal human women to be their breeding vessels. The Gargoyles make the pregnant women drink their blood so the kid comes out all Gargoyle. From what I've learned, it's why so many of them are born male. All the human traits are also overpowered during breeding.

266

Lycan genetics could pass through, but Gargoyle bloodlines still dominate." Trayis shrugged. "They wouldn't relish having children who could possibly get traits they hate. We VampLycans get mostly Lycan traits, but I can't say we got screwed out of the good Vampire powers." His eyes began to glow. "It comes in handy."

Lavos grinned. "Yes, it does. Though my mate is immune to mind control," he admitted.

Trayis allowed his eyes to dim to normal. "Share your blood with her often. It will make her stronger. And especially when she's carrying your young in her belly. Otherwise you risk having a child unable to shift."

Kira came to mind. She'd been born too human, despite having a VampLycan father. "So you're saying…"

"It makes your children stronger in the womb. The down side is lots of boy births. Though, I've asked some of my mated couples to try something."

"What?" Lavos was curious.

"To cut back on sharing blood while they try to get pregnant, wait until the pregnancy takes, then feed the female blood after. That way the sex of the child is already determined. We had four girls born after I asked. It looks promising."

"Good to know."

"Unless you want sons. Then feed her blood all the time." Trayis grinned. "The experiment might be wishful thinking on my part, since I'd welcome more girls being born into our clan, but it's a learning curve, right? It's not like we have thousands of years of history to learn this shit from by studying the past."

"True."

"I'll leave you to it and mingle. It was good talking to you."

"You too," Lavos admitted. He watched the clan leader walk away and smiled at Lorn when he caught his brother watching him, assuring him everything was fine.

His mind returned to Jadee. He wanted to get back to her but he had a few hours to go. Being social sucked.

Chapter Seventeen

Jadee kept quiet as Lavos walked her home. She'd been worried about seeing Lavos's older brother again, but there had been no need. Lorn had given her a hug, welcomed her to the family, and had gone out of his way to be friendly.

"What are you thinking about? Did Kira say something that upset you?"

"No," she stated honestly. "I was thinking about your brother. He was so unfriendly the first time we met. I'm so glad he seemed happy we're together."

"Lorn was stressed that day. He also worried you posed a danger to us, and I was being an idiot by not allowing him to attempt to remove your memories. It's his job to protect his clan first and foremost. He's genuinely happy that I found my mate."

"Even if I'm human?"

He squeezed her hand. "Yes."

"Kira explained about how I could be dangerous if I told anyone that your people exist. She gave me VampLycan 101. It was great. I learned a lot."

"Uh-oh. What did she tell you about us?" He opened the front door and ushered her in first, flipping on the lights.

She turned and faced him. "It was all good stuff."

He closed and locked the door, pulling her into his arms. He kissed her forehead and smiled down at her when he backed up a little. "I'm glad to hear that. Did you two get along?"

"Yes. She was an only child too growing up. We hope to become as close as sisters. I'm looking forward to that. I really like her."

"Good. Lorn and I are very close, best friends. It would be wonderful if our mates are too."

"I'm so happy I came here, Lavos."

"I am too."

"How did the dinner at the lodge go?"

"Better than expected. It looks as if the other clans truly support us. I hope they'll worry less, now that they've spent more time with Lorn and I. We're not like Decker. One of the enforcers from another clan is even going to stick around for a bit."

"To watch you guys? Kind of play spy?"

"No. Wen offered to help us. It's possible some of our people will challenge my brother for leadership. In other clans, that wouldn't be a problem. Unfortunately, Decker didn't exactly encourage our clan to behave honorably."

Jadee frowned.

"The right way to challenge for leadership is for one member to approach Lorn and fight him. In this clan, they might group together and attack my brother to make the odds unfair. He's tough, but it would be hard for him to win against, say, five VampLycans who ambush him."

"So what should be a one-on-one fight can turn into a brawl?"

He chuckled. "Yes."

"That sounds shitty and underhanded."

"It is. We're still weeding out who's accepting Lorn and the ones who are plotting to kill him. But enough about that. It's a grim subject. Are you hungry?"

"No. Kira and I had grilled ham and cheese sandwiches. She eats a lot. I'm shocked she's so thin."

He laughed. "Welcome to this world. We all put away a lot of food at meals. She's becoming more VampLycan every day, according to my brother."

The thing foremost on her mind popped out. "Does it bother you that I'm human?"

"No." He answered without hesitation. "Not at all. I worry about you because you're frail. I won't lie about that, but you being mated with me will make you stronger."

"That's what Kira said. Does it bother you that I'll never shift?"

He pulled her tighter against him, hugging her. "Never."

"I was worried about that."

"Don't be. That's silly." He smiled to soften his words. "I think you're incredibly sexy just as you are. I'm not so sure I could honestly say that if you were hairy."

She laughed. "You kind of scare me when you change."

"I'd never hurt you."

"I trust that. It's just the whole looking like a hell beast and your eyes going dark."

"Hell beast?"

"Kind of similar to a devil dog, if you want the truth. Like you should be sitting at the feet of Satan himself."

"I didn't realize I looked *that* bad."

"I'm sure you're very handsome for a shifted VampLycan, but considering I'm not used to seeing them, you're scary." She worried she might have hurt his feelings. "Please don't be offended."

"I'm not. You accept me, and that's all that matters, sweetheart."

"How did it go with that woman?"

"What woman?" He arched his eyebrows.

"Don't try to look all innocent. You know who I'm talking about."

A teasing glint showed in his eyes. "You're the only woman I notice."

"Cute."

He hugged her tighter. "Still jealous? There's no need. You're it for me, Jadee."

"Can I get a straight answer?" She rubbed her hands along his shirt, lightly massaging him.

"Fine." He sobered. "Your scent is all over me and everyone could smell that I'd mated. Tha—"

"How can they tell? I mean, couldn't you have just hugged me as a friend?"

He took long seconds before he spoke, seeming to think over his answer. "It's more than the scent I carry on my clothes from coming into physical contact with you. It's kind of tough to explain, but Lycans put off pheromones. When one is horny and single, that scent can attract the opposite sex." He winked. "When one is mated, we put off different pheromones. The I'm-mated-and-not-interested-in-anyone-else kind. They're particularly strong right now because…"

"You're going through Lycan PMS?"

He threw back his head and laughed, then stared down at her. "Yes. We also just exchanged blood, so there's no missing that you're a part of me. The fact that I wanted your scent all over my clothes as well is a bold statement of how proud I am to be mated to you."

"How did that woman react?"

"Mya was angry, but her clan leader stepped in and ordered her to leave our territory. She's a troublemaker for Trayis, and was seeking to find a mate in our clan. She targeted me because I'm second-in-command. I found her annoying when we first met today, I had no interest in sleeping with her to test a mating, and all I could think about was you. Any more questions, mate?"

She smiled. "Just one."

"What is it?"

"Why are we still dressed? I missed you."

He lifted her off her feet, walking them both to the couch, then eased her back onto her feet in front of it. He let go, backed off a little, and pulled his shirt over his head. "Get naked with me."

Jadee had a feeling she was going to love being mated to Lavos. "Race you."

Lavos's cell phone rang and a vicious snarl tore from his throat. "I have to get this."

She stilled, watching him jerk his phone from his pocket, accept the call, and put it to his ear. "What's wrong?"

He listened, his face twisting in anger. "I'll be right there. Can you send Davis to watch my home?" He paused, listening. "Tell him thank you." He ended the call and shoved his phone back into his pocket. "Velder called an emergency meeting. I have to go back to the lodge. I'm so sorry. It's important."

She watched him bend, snatch up the shirt he'd just discarded, and put it back on. Disappointment struck. "Are you taking me back to Kira's?"

"No. Stay inside with the doors locked. Davis was busy, so Bran offered to patrol around our house to keep you safe. Don't be alarmed if you see a black-haired man outside. He won't try to come in."

"Who is Bran?"

"He's the father of a friend of mine who also mated a human. Veso refused to join the meeting because he's still on his honeymoon. I don't have that option. I need to go."

"Because you're lead enforcer."

"Exactly. I won't be long." He leaned in and planted a kiss on her lips. "Lock the door after me. You're safe."

He left and she followed him to the door, twisting the bolts with a deep sigh. She hoped this wasn't her future, them being interrupted often and him having to leave.

"Damn." She turned, studying the living room. "At least I have time to get acquainted with my new home."

* * * * *

Lavos entered Lorn's office. He'd hung around outside his home until Bran had actually arrived to patrol. He wasn't willing to take a chance that someone would attack Jadee. He glanced around the large space, surprised to see not only all four clan leaders, but at least three of each of their enforcers present too. Kar and Garson were standing behind Lorn's desk, where is brother sat. He crossed the room, getting close to his brother. Tension hung in the silent room, so thick it almost had a scent.

Velder sat in a chair in front of the desk, the two other clan leaders next to him. It seemed they'd been waiting for Lavos to arrive, because Maku, Velder's man, closed the door.

"What's going on?" Lorn stared directly at Velder.

"I've just received a call from my son Kraven's mate."

"Problem?" Lorn tensed.

"Kind of. Bat and Kraven made friends with the nest master of Los Angeles. Bat talks to Michael at least once a week. She told him about the Vampire attack on your clan."

Lavos sighed. "Did we piss this Michael off by killing those bastards who came after us and now he wants war?"

Velder shook his head. "Michael has been a friend to the VampLycans. He helped Kraven protect Bat when they were in his territory. Fucking Decker had the Vampire Council and the local Lycan packs searching for her."

Lavos had heard something about that. "Decker wanted to give her to Lord Aveoth, right?"

Velder glanced at the two clan leaders in the chairs on each side of him. "You'll want to hear this too, Trayis and Crocker. That's why I insisted you be here."

Trayis was the one to speak. "What's wrong?"

"I've told you about Michael."

"The master of L.A.?"

Velder nodded at Trayis. "Yes. He's got one of the largest nests in the United States. The reason for it is that he takes in strays."

That confused Lavos. "Strays?"

Velder shrugged. "From what Bat and Kraven have said, he actually has a heart and morals. They like him a lot. You know how humans go to L.A. to become movie stars? Well, it seems Vamps go there seeking sanctuary from harsh, abusive masters. Michael accepts Vamps with his same beliefs."

"Which are?" Lavos asked.

"He likes to keep the peace between races, values human life, and even allows Lycan packs to exist in his territory. Most masters use their nests as slaves. Not Michael. They're allowed to work and have somewhat normal lives for Vamps. He doesn't take their money or force them to sleep in only one place. From what I've gathered, he only demands they have to follow his rules to stay in his territory."

"What are his rules?" Crocker looked interested.

"Don't kill humans. Don't use them like cattle. Don't cause a war. No selling or distributing drugs to make money or to control humans. No blood stealing or turning a human into a Vamp without permission. Shit like that,"

Velder answered. "I did my own checking on him since I knew Bat and Kraven were fond of him. I only heard good things."

"Rare for a master," Crocker muttered.

Velder nodded. "That's why Kraven likes him. Michael kept his humanity. Bat told Michael about the Vampires that attacked Lorn's clan and gave him all the details. He sent out a mass email to his nest, asking for information on a master who called himself a king to see if anyone knew Charles Borrow. As I said, Michael takes in strays. A female Vamp responded. She used to be part of Borrow's nest before she fled to Los Angeles."

"Borrow is dead," Lavos pointed out.

Velder held his gaze and smiled. It was cold. "Michael called the female, and learned that Charles Borrow always kept three Vamps very close to him. He referred to them as his court. They were his most trusted. He never traveled without them by his side. I remembered the details of the attack on that nest. Vlad played the part of assistant and caretaker to Borrow. Veso killed this Vlad during his initial escape from that mine with his mate. Denny sounded like the one that was found hiding under the pile of bodies. It was his job to play jailer to their human victims and make certain the master always had live food. That's the one you killed, Lavos."

The implications sank in, and Lavos understood. "We can only account for three full Vampires dying—*including* Charles. There should have been four. One *did* get away."

"What about the four that died the night they kidnapped Veso and attacked Kira? Maybe one of them was the last of Borrow's supposed court." Lorn glanced at his brother.

Velder caught Lavos's gaze. "No. Listen to what else I have to say. The Vampire Council probably sent a few of their own with Charles Borrow. The missing one is named Horton. It was his job to bring in new Vamps to the nest when they wanted to increase their numbers and defend it. The Vamp woman who spoke to Michael said Horton made soldiers sometimes to terrorize anyone in the nest who pissed off him or Borrow. He's supposed to be a real sick bastard, and she believes he'll do anything to seek vengeance for the loss of his master. He worshipped Borrow to an almost godlike degree." He paused. "He also fits the description given by that soldier who made others."

"Goddamn," Lorn growled. "This Horton made Mitch."

Velder gave a sharp nod. "Michael did more than get us that information. He called other masters he's made secret alliances with. Not every nest is comfortable with the power the Vampire Council wields. The good news is, he got a lead on Horton's location. It's not exact, but there were enough rumors to pinpoint a city neighborhood. Horton destroyed the nest he came from. Word was, they were too happy to see Borrow gone and liked the taste of freedom. They wouldn't bow down to Horton and follow him."

"Less assholes in the world," Lavos said. "They had to be nuts to have a master like Borrow."

"It's not all good news though." Velder hesitated. "Horton slaughtered them and has hooked up with rogues. They've been spotted in Washington State. Vampires *and* Lycans are taking orders from him. He's reached out to some nests and packs, spreading lies about us."

"What kind?" Crocker's eyes darkened, going black. He was obviously angry.

Velder took his time to answer, glancing at different faces in the room, finally staring at Lorn. "Michael used his contacts to reach out to those same packs and nests. Horton told them that a team of VampLycans attacked his nest, took Borrow and his court captive, and brought them here to torture and gain information."

"That's bullshit," Lorn snarled, rising to his feet.

Lavos put his hand on his brother's shoulder, instantly on alert. He glanced around, worried that the other clans might attack. "That's something Decker might have done, but not us. It's a lie," he growled. "They attacked us, invaded our territory, and kidnapped Veso."

"They turned my Kira into a Vampire," Lorn yelled. "She almost died!"

"Easy," Velder soothed. "I said Horton was telling lies. I don't believe them."

"I don't either." Trayis actually smiled. "Sit down, Lorn. You're amongst friends. We all know Decker sent those bastards here to kidnap one of your clan. Borrow wanted a VampLycan to breed with his human relative, and Decker sure as hell wouldn't give up one of his enforcers right now. They're all he has to keep his ass alive. None of us would have attended the dinner today if we didn't have total faith that you're honorable."

Lorn sat. Lavos released his shoulder and breathed easier.

"What kind of shit is Decker trying to start now?" Crocker's eyes were still near black and hair had grown along his face, his Lycan side showing through. One glance at his hands revealed that his claws had come out.

"Easy, my friend." Velder reached over and placed his hand on his arm. "We all hate Decker and knew he wouldn't go quietly. He's been a pain in our asses since the beginning, but I don't think he's responsible for what Horton is doing right now."

"Bullshit! He killed my mate. He needs to die!"

That bit of information shocked Lavos. He could tell his brother also hadn't known when Lorn sharply sucked air into his lungs. *Decker killed Crocker's mate? When? How?* He didn't ask though, not wanting to upset Crocker again.

"Decker *does* need to die—and Lord Aveoth is hunting him," Velder quietly stated. "This is a different problem though. One started by Decker but now it's our mess, yet again."

Crocker closed his eyes, and when he opened them, they were much lighter and some of the hair had receded from his face. "I'm listening. Go on."

"My guess is that Horton blames us *and* Decker for Borrow's death. He's spreading that lie to nests, packs, and rogues to fan the old fears that we'll one day wipe them all out to be at the top of the food chain. According to Michael, he's told them we've spent all these years breeding an army. That they were kidnapped by us to gain numbers and locations of other nests and packs in the lower forty-eight, since we stick to Alaska."

"That doesn't even make sense," Garson spat. "I mean, we hate the Vampires who attacked our Lycan ancestors, but we leave Vamps alone unless they're going after Lycan women to repeat the past. We sure as hell wouldn't go after any packs, since we protect them."

Lavos shot his friend a warning look to keep his mouth sealed. Garson had a tendency to blurt things out when he was upset. Now wasn't the time.

Garson gave him a nod and leaned back against the wall, glowering.

"Lycans fear us," Trayis reminded them. "My half-brother tells me that other packs question his sanity when they hear that he's in contact with me. They believe I'll one day challenge him and slaughter his pack because I must see them as weak. Of course I don't, and it's not true. Still, that's the first thing they think."

"I think Horton is trying to convince nests and packs to join forces and come after us before we slaughter them," Velder said. "We need to kill this miserable son of a bitch before it's more than just a band of rogues listening to his bullshit."

"We'll send teams after him." Crocker sat up straighter in his chair.

Wen made his way forward, drawing attention. He cleared his throat. "May I speak?"

Lorn nodded. Trayis turned his head to peer at his enforcer. "What is it, Wen?"

"I think that would be a mistake. This Horton is claiming we've already sent out a team to kidnap members of his nest. It would only add credibility to his story and possibly spread panic in the city he's in. And there's no way for a team of us to enter any territory without it drawing notice. I'm sent on missions often for my clan, and I visit different cities. I've always let the masters and alphas know if I need to be in their territories for a few days. They're wary, but one VampLycan isn't seen as a dire threat. I think you

281

should just send me. I won't raise any alarms, and if they call around, they'll hear I do this often."

"We've been adding to our territory. Wen's the one who tracks down landowners to see if they'll sell to us. He's right. One VampLycan doesn't freak them out much but a team of us would," Trayis agreed.

"Michael doesn't know the exact number of the rogues Horton is leading." Velder seemed to study Wen. "You look fierce, and I know Trayis must have a lot of faith in you, but it would be a suicide mission to go in alone. The nests and packs could also attack you."

Wen smirked. "Tell him, Trayis."

Everyone stared at the clan leader. He grinned back at Wen. "If anyone could do it, it's him. Not only is Wen one of my best fighters, but he's a genius when it comes to figuring out how to make friends with other races. What's your plan?"

Wen's expression became all business. "Horton is gathering rogues, trying to build alliances to take us on—so what's more tempting than a rogue VampLycan who can help him win his war? He'll want the exact numbers of each clan, their locations, and to learn our weaknesses."

Lavos had to give the enforcer credit for having balls. "You want him to capture and torture you? Because that's what he'll probably do."

"I'll convince him I'm on his side. We'll have VampLycans wanting both of us dead as our common bond."

"He'll never buy it. He sounds crazy but not outright stupid."

Wen held Lavos's gaze and smiled again. "He's lost his beloved master, slaughtered his own nest after they rejected him, and broken the rules set by his own council. Do you know what they'd do to him if they learned he let loose a soldier that slaughtered a human town?"

"They'd order his death," Lavos answered.

"Exactly. He's desperate enough to want to believe I could help him. He might hold me prisoner at first, but I'll get him to let his guard down. It will be the last thing he ever does. Dead men don't tell more lies or cause problems."

After a bit more discussion, it was decided that Wen would be given a chance to take Horton out alone. Thoughts of Jadee distracted Lavos for the rest of the meeting. She currently might be in danger from a few disgruntled clan members loyal to Decker, but it would be another story if Vampires and Lycans started an outright war with them. He'd have to stash her inside his den to keep her safe.

Chapter Eighteen

Jadee rushed to the door when someone pounded on it. She stared out the window and then opened the door. Lavos smiled at her, entering the house.

"Sorry. I don't carry keys. I forgot about that when I told you to lock up after I left."

"Is everything okay?"

He pulled her into his arms and kicked the door closed behind him. "The clan leaders and enforcers had to hold an emergency meeting."

She clung to him. "Was this about me?"

"No. They got a lead on the Vampire who created Mitch."

Anger and pain hit. She'd lost her dad because he'd been turned into a soldier by that freak. "Are they going after this son of a bitch? Are *you*?" She made an instant decision. "I want to go with you if you are."

He gripped her arms and forced her to put a little space between them, staring into her eyes. "No. Neither of us are going after that bastard. Someone else is though. I won't have you in danger."

"But—"

"No." He shook his head. "Let's not make this our first fight as mates. I'd rather we argue about silly things, such as who gets to be on top when we go to bed and make love." He eased his hold on her arms and ran them down to her hands, threading his fingers through hers. "An enforcer will take out that Vamp. You and I will stay here to bond."

She bit her lip, part of her wanting to protest, but then she remembered everything she'd gone through. Did she really want to come face to face with another Vampire?

The answer was simple. *No.*

"Okay."

His eyebrows rose.

"I'm not stupid. As long as that son of a bitch dies, I don't care who gets to take off his head. I just want him to pay for all the deaths he caused."

"He will." Lavos tugged on her hand. "Follow me."

Jadee walked behind Lavos as he went upstairs and entered his bedroom. He walked over to the dresser, got something out of the top drawer, and turned. "Have I told you how much you mean to me?"

"I know. You mated me."

He slowly approached her with a smile. "You're my everything. When I was sixteen, I hated my life. My dad really is a dick. He was rough on Lorn and I growing up. You've heard about Decker. I had hit this stage in my life when I wondered why I was on this Earth. Everything was just so miserable. My brother saw what was happening to me, the depression I felt, so he planned a trip for us. We told everyone we were going hunting but instead we borrowed a car from a human, drove to the airport, and went to meet my mother's mother for the very first time. To this day, no one knows. Mom had told us stories while we were growing up about how wonderful Grandma was."

Jadee smiled back at him. "It sounds like an adventure."

"It was. Grandma is really funny. She hugged us a lot, kissed us; she's very affectionate. We never really had that growing up. My dad yelled at

285

our mom if she coddled us too much. The Lycan pack is the opposite of how this clan used to be. They are super friendly, everyone is close, and the alpha's a good guy. The night before we had to return home, my grandma pulled me aside and asked me why I seemed so sad. I didn't want to leave, but I knew I had no choice. Lorn had lied to get me away and he would have been punished if he'd returned without me. Decker also would have sent enforcers after me. No one was allowed to leave this clan alive."

Jadee reached out and put her hand on his chest. "What happened?"

"My grandmother told me to have faith that things would get better, and that one day I'd find happiness. She took off her ring and placed it in my hand, telling me to keep it with me at all times as a reminder. It was a symbol of hope for the wonderful future she promised me I'd have one day."

Tears filled Lavos's eyes and he slowly lowered to his knees in front of Jadee. Her heart pounded and she had to swallow hard. Her own eyes watered.

He opened his hand and the silver ring he usually kept on a chain was in his palm. "You're my happiness, and my wonderful future that I've been waiting for. I want you to wear this ring now as a symbol of my love and a promise that we're going to be happy forever."

Her hand shook as she offered him her left one. He used his index finger and thumb to gently push it on her ring finger. It fit as if it had been made for her.

Lavos grinned. "See? You're perfect for me."

Jadee threw her arms around his neck, sinking to her knees and clinging to him. "You're perfect for me too. I love you, Lavos."

286

"I love you too, baby." He cupped her face. "Remember how I said next time we'll take it slow when I'm making love to you?"

She grinned. "*Next* next time?"

"*Next* next time," he agreed.

He maneuvered until he was at her back and wrapped his arms around her waist. She peered at him over her shoulder, eyebrows arching as he shoved her pants down.

"In a hurry?"

"Always."

His hand delved between her thighs, rubbing her clit with his thumb.

She closed her eyes, moaning. "You're so bad."

"In the best ways."

The way his voice deepened, taking on that sexy gruffness, turned her on more. She reached back, fumbling to get his pants open. He used his free hand to help until his cock was free. She wrapped her fingers around it, stroking his rigid shaft as he continued to massage her clit. She was getting soaking wet, aching to have him inside her.

"Bend and brace," he demanded. "I need you now."

She let him go and lowered her upper body, spreading her hands apart on his floor, locking her elbows straight. She resisted making a crack about doing it doggy style but she thought it. Lavos entered her slowly, his thick cock breaching her pussy. She moaned his name.

"Say you're mine. I need to hear the words."

"I'm yours," she got out.

Lavos drove into her deep and groaned. "I'm yours too. All of me." He gripped her hips with both hands and slowly withdrew, then slammed in deep again.

"Yes!"

"No control," he warned, right before he started hammering her hard and fast. He leaned forward, reached around her, pressing his hand against her clit and curving his body around her back. The other arm he used to hold himself up by placing it next to one of hers.

Jadee wondered if she could die from pleasure. The climax burst through her and she would have collapsed if it wasn't for Lavos holding on to her so tight. He snarled her name and she felt him come inside her. He slid his hand from her pussy to her stomach, cupping it.

Jadee caught her breath and grinned.

It seemed he was still suffering from his version of Lycan PMS, and she wondered how long it would last.

It didn't matter. Whatever the future held, she had faith they'd see it together.